The Elvis Bird

A Benjamin Miles Mystery

D. E. Woolbright

The Elvis Bird is a work of fiction. Names, characters, places, and incidents are the products of the author's imagination or used fictitiously. Any resemblance to actual events, locales, or persons, living or dead, is entirely coincidental.

2022 Punctilious Press

First Edition

Copyright © 2022 By David E. Woolbright

All rights reserved.

ISBN 979-8-986-42070-7

For Benjamin "Sam" Pate, a great teacher and naturalist.

1. Dead and Gone

The Ivory-billed Woodpecker confines its rambles to a comparatively very small portion of the United States, it never having been observed in the Middle States within the memory of any person now living there.

-James Audubon, *The Birds of America*

The disturbance on the recording – so obviously out of place – immediately piqued Miles' attention, teasing him away from the repetitive monotony of the work. What started as a low, distant hum, transformed over the next several minutes into the recognizable purr of an approaching boat – *putter-putter-chump, putter-putter-chump*. The volume see-sawed hypnotically, growing ever louder as the craft navigated the difficult waterway. When the boat was virtually on top of the automatic recording unit, the engine stopped abruptly. The silence that followed was broken by a dull thud as the craft ran aground. The entire swamp suddenly paused to listen.

The lights scattered across the lengthy console in the dark audio lab glowed red and green and yellow as Miles waited expectantly. Recessed lights in the ceiling provided the only other ambient light, brightening the corners of the tiny room. He leaned forward and stared expectantly at the monitor. The usually complex spectrogram had been reduced to a single, straight line.

"Get out now," said a man's voice impatiently. The line exploded colorfully with each spoken syllable. Conversations were rarely captured in the expedition's recordings. Miles pressed the headset tighter against his ears.

"Where?" It sounded like a young man's voice.

"There."

"It doesn't look stable."

"It's fine, get out."

Someone crawled out of the boat with a clatter.

"Now what?"

The person had moved further away from the ARU and the voice sounded fainter. Suddenly, the sound of a gunshot ripped through the swamp, leaving secondary echoes of the blast suspended in the air like the ashes of a spent firework. There was a splash. And then silence.

Miles stared at the spectrogram. The bright red image, which was the gunshot, drifted lazily across the screen and then disappeared altogether. Slowly, the sounds of cicadas and tree frogs began to return, and the display was repopulated with abstract patterns of light. In just moments, the stygian serenity of the swamp had been restored, another of its watery secrets had been hidden.

Miles gripped the chair's armrests and waited for a resolution that would neatly explain what he had heard, but the disturbance had been swallowed up in the tea-colored waters of the Okefenokee. Mystery and the sounds of the native wildlife were all that remained.

Someone cranked the boat. It sputtered away from the ARU in alternating volume – *putter-putter-chump, putter-putter-chump* – just as it had arrived. The engine's noise grew fainter over the next several minutes and then disappeared altogether. The recording ended abruptly with the usual click, and Miles reached forward and pushed a button to prevent the automatic queuing of the next selection.

What the hell?

The recording had been made weeks ago by his colleagues in the Okefenokee National Wildlife Refuge. Miles had designed the computer algorithm which selected the recording from a database of others. It was supposed to target the two distinctive sounds made by Ivory-billed Woodpeckers.

Why had the algorithm selected this particular recording? To Miles' ear, it didn't contain *any* evidence of Ivory-bill activity. He reached for a control knob and repositioned the recording back to the moment when he had heard the first voice. Over the next half hour, Miles replayed the event multiple times, trying to recognize the voices. He couldn't. The audio quality was clear enough, but the conversation was just too brief.

They might be team members servicing an ARU. The units were often moved from location to location in the swamp. Each unit contained a battery that required periodic replacement, and the disks needed to be downloaded every few days.

Why had there been a rifle shot? It didn't make any sense. Field teams sometimes carried rifles for protection, but they were rarely fired. Miles had grown up on the outskirts of the Okefenokee, and he knew it well. Alligators were mostly indifferent to the comings and goings of boats. They preferred to lie in wait for easy prey along the muddy banks, or to simply sleep in the muck. Cottonmouth water moccasins were an aggressive species of snakes that would sometimes crawl into a boat if threatened. But biologists seldom discharged their weapons, even for snakes or alligators. Biologists preferred living animals to dead ones.

Miles noted the location of the ARU displayed on the screen and copied it onto a flash drive. He popped the drive into the computer underneath the console and clicked *Save*.

What were these people doing in the swamp? Servicing an ARU would take much longer than the brief incident on the recording. Miles wiped his brow, and suddenly the room felt stifling. He had worked all evening, and now it was after midnight. He got up and walked out of the cramped lab leaving the equipment running and the door open. Back in the darkness of his office, he slumped down at his desk, exhausted.

The Cornell Lab of Ornithology's modernist building sat perched on the edge of a pond on the outskirts of Ithaca, New York, amid a two-hundred-acre wildlife preserve. Through his office window, Miles strained to see the surrounding wetland in the dim moonlight. All he could see on this evening was a shadowy thicket of trees outlining the distant shore.

Perhaps it wasn't a rifle shot?

Miles knew better. He couldn't erase the gunshot from his thoughts, nor could he forget the eerie silence that had followed the splash. He didn't like guns. He never owned a gun. This was unusual for someone growing up in the South where gun ownership was a God-given right, even an expectation for young men.

Miles looked down at the thumb drive in his hand. The location he had written on it might help. Still, no one on the field team had been reported missing in the past few weeks. Everything was normal, right?

He reached for his cell phone and began to search the contacts list before pressing select. The phone rang and rang before his colleague, Jim Hopkins, finally answered.

"Miles? What the hell? Do you know what time it is?"

"Sorry. I was doing some work in the lab."

"Why are you in the office at this hour?"

Miles pictured Hopkins – the womanizer. He was never around after five. The guy had a weakness for women and had paid for it over and over. Miles' ex-wife had despised him from the start of their friendship, but despite Hopkins' obvious character flaws, he had always been a generous friend.

"Is everyone all right?" Miles asked tentatively.

"Of course, we're all right. What's happened, buddy?"

THE ELVIS BIRD

Miles walked over to the window. He leaned his head against it and stared out across the pond. The glass felt cool against his forehead – reassuring.

"I heard something alarming on one of the recordings."

"What was it?"

"A gunshot."

"So?"

"It was a gunshot!"

"Down here, I hear gunshots all the time. Everybody has a gun and a pickup truck. They issue them at birth. It's illegal to hunt in the Okefenokee, but they do it anyway."

"I know but ..."

Hopkins interrupted and recounted how they'd made hundreds of recordings – thousands of hours of material. "I'm surprised you haven't heard lots of gunshots already. We're bound to have recorded a few rednecks out for some fun."

"Fun? I think someone was murdered, Hoppy. I'm calling to make sure everyone in our group is *alive*."

"You're kidding, right? If someone were dead, don't you think you would already know about it?"

But Miles knew what he had heard. "Someone was murdered."

"You're working too hard," Hopkins said, "We're all just copacetic down here. One big happy family. Now can I get back to what I was doing?"

Miles turned away from the window. "It just doesn't make sense. Why would the search algorithm select a gunshot recording? There wasn't anything on that recording related to birds."

"How can I put this delicately? Oh yeah - your search algorithm isn't worth a damn, Miles. And we can't find a bird that has been extinct for seventy years. There's a shocker. This expedition was a mistake from the beginning. Ivory-bills are dead and gone. Haven't you figured that out by now?"

"Don't say that."

"Where was the recording made, Miles?"

He looked down at the disk. "Sector A9."

"When?"

"Four weeks ago."

"Hold on."

Miles could hear Hopkins shuffling papers in the background. He picked up the phone after a few minutes.

"We haven't done any fieldwork in that area lately, so it must have been some local hunters on the recording. No one has been near that ARU for weeks."

"So, all of the students are fine?"

"The students left weeks ago, Miles. The only people left in camp are a few research associates and technicians. We'll be finished in a couple more weeks. The search is over. We lost. Go home. Have a drink and forget it. Hell, if I were you, I'd have two drinks."

"Don't say that, Hoppy. We still have time to find that bird."

THE ELVIS BIRD

"At this hour, you'd be better off looking for a different kind of bird." In the background, Miles could hear the muffled sound of a woman's laugh.

"Hey, buddy," said Hopkins.

"Yeah?"

"If I were single like you, I wouldn't be alone in the office tonight. Know what I mean?"

###

Miles settled back in his chair. Perhaps Hopkins was right. If he had given up the search sooner, paid attention to his marriage, gone home at five each evening, things might be different – he might still have a partner. He reached for some binoculars beside his desk and maneuvered his chair to have an unobstructed view of the pond outside. He scanned the shoreline for a particular tree he had been observing over the past few weeks, but the clouds had shifted across the moon during his conversation with Hopkins, darkening the landscape and obscuring his view.

Somewhere across the pond, a woodpecker huddled inside a tree with its mate. Three or four small eggs would be hatching soon. The bonded pair were working together – the female incubating the eggs and the male gathering food. The hatchlings would become independent in a few weeks.

It seemed straightforward now. Keep searching or just give up. The recording was disturbing, no matter what Hopkins said. A scandal could sink the remainder of this expedition. Miles lowered the binoculars and placed them on the floor beside the desk. Regret and fatigue covered him like a blanket, and he closed his eyes to think.

2. Birdman Extraordinaire

I have always imagined that in the plumage of the beautiful Ivory-billed Woodpecker, there is something very closely allied to the style of colouring of the great VANDYKE.
-James Audubon, *The Birds of America*

An attractive brunette was standing in the doorway, and Miles squinted to get a better look.

It had taken a moment for him to gather himself after she had knocked on the door. Instinctively, he had pushed away from the desk and swiveled the chair to face the interruption. Did she notice he had been asleep? She had dark eyes and a short, smart-looking haircut. Her tailored suit was charcoal gray. Silver bracelets dangled on her arm. Her knee-length skirt revealed long, athletic legs and high-heels. She must be lost – a visitor to the lab who had wandered down the wrong hallway. He was about to get rid of her when she preempted him.

"Do you always sleep in your office?"

He mugged a smile. "Only when I'm not awake."

The brunette looked at him as if she had expected a better answer. He felt compelled to add, "I worked late last night – I fell asleep at the desk."

A BENJAMIN MILES MYSTERY

"What does your wife think about that?"

This was no visitor. Miles debated how to respond. "I'm no longer married."

The brunette stepped inside and tapped the hand-made sign on his door with a manicured nail. Someone had written in bold, red letters: "Birdman Extraordinaire."

"So that's you – the extraordinary Birdman?"

Miles waved the idea away with one hand, "Ignore that." He stood up, walked over to where she was standing, and extended his hand. "Just some students having fun at my expense. I don't believe we've met. I'm Benjamin Miles – but don't call me Benjamin. Only my mother calls me that. All my friends call me Miles."

"*Miles,* it is. I'm Susan – Susan Swail – *everyone* calls me that – even my mother." She took his hand and looked past him to his desk, covered in papers and books. "By the looks of things, I've caught you at a bad time."

"Not really." Miles turned to see what had captured her attention. "This is pretty much how my office always looks."

"Now that is extraordinary! How do you find anything in here?" She scanned the room, surveying the clutter.

"I have a system. I just put everything that's important on top of the desk. Whatever I need is under it somewhere."

She gave him a discerning smile and waited. Miles noticed that he was still holding her hand and released it.

"Sorry. Would you like some coffee?" He casually brushed the hair off his forehead with his now unoccupied hand. "I can't function without coffee."

"That would be lovely. Black, no sugar."

He turned and walked back to the desk, trying to press out the wrinkles in his tee-shirt, but quickly abandoned the task as hopeless and began to give the desk a once-over. "Let me see now, where's that extra cup?"

She walked past him as he continued to rummage around. "All in all, nice digs, Miles, even if it is a bit messy. I love the panoramic view. Is my office anything like this one?"

"So, you're an ornithologist?" he said, looking back over his shoulder.

"Me? A birdman?"

She didn't dress like an ornithologist.

"Birdwoman?" he offered.

"Mathematician."

Fully awake now, the synapses were starting to fire. "You must be the new visiting professor,"

For the past six months, Miles had skipped most of the search committee meetings for the visiting position – it had dragged on and on as most university committees do. In fact, he had been ducking his departmental responsibilities for months to devote all his time to the Ivory-bill expedition. The department had advertised for an algorithm designer with audio experience – someone with computer savvy and expertise in searching big data. The brunette – Susan Swail – must have fit the bill.

"Dr. Fitzsimmons emailed to say that you would be my faculty liaison for the day. It appears that I'm completely in your hands today, Miles."

He was still leaning over the desk, and he paused to consider what she had just said.

She continued, "Perhaps you can start by showing me to my office?"

Bill Fitzsimmons was well-known in the birding community as the influential director of the Cornell Lab of Ornithology. His attention to detail in running the daily affairs of the lab was legendary. Miles had been ignoring the director's emails for weeks.

"Fitz assigned you to me?"

There was a long pause.

"You didn't read his email, did you?"

Miles turned around to face the medicine.

"Not exactly."

"*Not exactly* as in *No, I didn't read it*?"

He raised his finger as if to hold off further comment.

"No harm done. I'll just check with Fitz right now." Miles looked at his watch. There was a pause. "I'll have to check later. It's a bit too early to call him, you see. We're probably the only ones in the department at the moment." He turned back to the desk and continued to search.

"I thought you bird-watchers got up at the crack of dawn?" she said.

"Only the early-bird watchers," he offered, sheepishly, "I'm more of a late-bird watcher. Today is an exception."

THE ELVIS BIRD

"I could see that when I knocked on your door."

"Ha! Here's the cup!" said Miles. He held it up in triumph. "I'll be right back. The coffee pot is just down the hall. Black, no sugar, right? Make yourself at home."

When he returned with the coffee, Susan was standing at the window, holding the binoculars he had placed beside his desk the night before.

"Are you a birder?" He balanced her cup carefully on a stack of student papers sitting on top of the desk. She shook her head and waited to see if the cup was stable.

"Then, you'll need to learn a few rudimentary things about birds for this job."

"I'm all ears, Birdman."

Was she being impertinent? He wasn't sure.

"We could start with the bird sanctuary," he said, directing her attention out the window. The sun had risen minutes earlier, and the mist that floated over the lily-covered pond was beginning to dissolve. The distant trees on the opposite shore were visible now.

"See if you can spot a bird across the pond," he suggested.

She turned and raised the binoculars to eye level and began to scan left and right.

"What kind of bird?"

"Do you mind?" He indicated that he wanted to help.

"Please do."

Miles stepped behind her and gently turned her shoulders until she faced the tree with the roost cavity.

"Look for a woodpecker." He pointed out the general direction with his finger. "You'll need to learn to recognize this bird on sight."

She raised the binoculars. After a minute of searching, she said, "I don't see anything." Miles repositioned her shoulders slightly and raised the binoculars gently with his palm.

"Birds usually live in trees," he said.

She lowered the binoculars and gave him a look.

"Funny boy."

He shrugged. "Try again. Look for the tallest tree — there's a bird that makes a home in it. You should see a cavity in the tree about twenty feet off the ground."

She raised the binoculars again.

"Got it."

"Now, don't turn away. Keep watching the nest."

She studied the tree for several more minutes.

"How long do I have to keep this up, Birdman?"

The nickname again. Odd. He was beginning to like the sound of it.

"Patience," said Miles, "Ornithology requires patience."

At last, a bird appeared and crawled out of the hole.

"What kind of bird *is* that?" she asked.

"You really *don't* know much about birds, do you?" said Miles.

She lowered the binoculars. "Your department advertised for an algorithm designer, remember? Numbers, patterns, procedures. Knowledge of birds was optional."

THE ELVIS BIRD

Miles took the binoculars from her and put them on the floor beside the desk.

"It's a Pileated woodpecker. Dryocopus pileatus."

"And what's so important about Dryocopus pileatus?"

He ignored her question. "How about an Ivory-bill? Ever heard of an Ivory-billed Woodpecker?"

"Isn't that the extinct bird that made headlines a few years ago?"

"That's the one. Pileateds are often mistaken for Ivory-bills. The field marks are quite similar, but the Ivory-bill is even larger. It's one of the largest in the world."

"You said *is*. I thought Ivory-billed Woodpeckers were extinct."

"Maybe…"

Susan turned back to the window to look for the bird. Miles stepped closer and caught a whiff of flowers and lemon.

As they were standing shoulder-to-shoulder, each turned to look at the other, face-to-face, inches apart. In the morning sunlight, Susan Swail looked radiant. Miles couldn't look away. He hadn't thought about a woman since his divorce, certainly not a colleague. What was he doing?

"…maybe not," he said finally, catching his breath.

"Interesting."

Was she reading his mind?

"I love a mystery, Birdman. Tell me more about this bird, since I don't have anywhere to go at the moment – not having an office." Did he detect the faintest of smiles at his expense? She stepped away from the window.

Miles recovered and pushed a chair up close to his desk, and she sat down. He joined her. She reached for the coffee cup and carefully raised it in a mock toast. "Your class awaits."

He started tentatively. "I'll give you the Ornithology 101 version." He leaned back in the chair. "Ivory-bills once populated hardwood forests throughout the South, but over time, timber companies logged most of those forests out of existence. The birds were dependent on the hardwoods and slowly disappeared with the trees. The last confirmed sighting of an Ivory-bill in the U.S. was back in the 1940s."

"You're from the South, aren't you? You have an accent."

"Well … yes."

"Sorry. Go on," she prompted. She blew on the coffee and stared at him over the cup.

He began again. "Everyone assumed Ivory-bills were extinct until Gene Sparling, an expert birder, spotted one in the swamps of Arkansas – this was 2004. Then another birder, David Luneau, looked into it and managed to capture a few seconds of an Ivory-bill on video. Cornell investigated both of these claims, and after several other sightings by the university, announced that the bird wasn't extinct after all."

"It's just that your accent isn't very pronounced. It's quite subtle."

"Look, if you're not interested…"

THE ELVIS BIRD

"No, I'm very interested. I remember hearing about this story on NPR. They called it the Lord God bird. Why was that?"

"Because when people see it for the first time, they usually say 'Lord God, what is that bird?'"

Why was he so taken by her? This is how Hopkins would respond.

"Continue," she prompted, "Go on."

He shifted in his chair. "The story also made the New York Times. The idea that this bird had somehow managed to survive the destruction of its habitat captured the public's imagination. Congress got interested and wanted to establish a protected reserve just for the bird."

Was she listening to anything he was saying? She was about to take another sip of coffee. Instead, she lowered the cup. "So, what happened next?"

He took a breath. "Well, the bird simply disappeared. We kept searching the Big Woods of Arkansas for several more years without another sighting."

"You lost it? How do you lose a bird?"

"You have to understand," said Miles, "A single Ivory-bill requires several square miles of habitat. It lives in lowlands and swamps – places where searching is extremely difficult – impossible at times."

"But you already had proof of the bird's existence on the Luneau video, right?"

She was listening.

A BENJAMIN MILES MYSTERY

A note of regret entered his voice. "Scientists began to question that the bird on the video was indeed an Ivory-bill. They thought it was probably a Pileated Woodpecker instead."

"*Dryocopus pileatus.*"

"Yes."

"But not you."

"I *know* the bird on the tape was an Ivory-bill."

"How can you be sure?"

"Because I've seen an Ivory-bill with my own eyes."

"Really?"

Miles started to launch into the story of his own experience when there was another knock at the door. It was Mrs. Sanderson, the lab director's secretary.

"Thank goodness! I've been looking for you everywhere, Professor Swail." Mrs. Sanderson stepped inside. She looked at Miles. "Pardon the interruption, but Dr. Fitzsimmons insisted I get Professor Swail settled into her office. He said you might forget, Dr. Miles."

Mrs. Sanderson turned back to Susan. "Dr. Fitzsimmons was delayed at a breakfast meeting with the university president and sends his apologies, Dr. Swail."

Susan rebalanced the coffee cup on the stack of papers and placed a hand on Miles' shoulder. "Can we continue this later?"

Miles nodded. "Call me when you're free," said Miles. He stood up to walk them to the door.

THE ELVIS BIRD

When the women had left, Miles began to sort through the stacks of papers on his desk. He stopped when he uncovered a manila folder with Susan Swail's name printed on the tab. Hopkins had sent it to him months earlier, and he had simply tossed it on the pile unread, along with dozens of other applications the search committee had considered. Now he wanted to know what it contained.

He opened the folder and slowly flipped through the pages: Ph.D. in Combinatorial Mathematics, tenured associate professor at Stanford, glowing recommendations from mathematicians at several prestigious schools, an extensive list of publications in top-drawer journals. A list of papers that she had recently published caught his eye. They all dealt with audio search algorithms. Interesting. That seemed like an odd detour for a Combinatorial mathematician. When he finished reading, he tossed the folder on top of the pile.

Why would someone on such a fast track want to take a visiting position out-of-field, even at Cornell? It was something he could consider later. At the moment, he wanted to listen to the tape again in the cold light of morning.

3. Double Knock

Descending the Ohio, we meet with this splendid bird for the first time near the confluence of that beautiful river and the Mississippi; after which, following the windings of the latter, either downwards toward the sea, or upwards in the direction of the Missouri, we frequently observe it.
-James Audubon, *The Birds of America*

"Where did you learn to use the audio equipment?" asked Miles.
It was later that afternoon. He had cued up the Elvis cover of the old Arthur Crudup tune *My Baby Left Me*, and the sound of a twangy fifties-reverb guitar was giving Miles' tiny audio lab a retro vibe. Susan was sitting beside him with her arms extended over the console, tapping her foot in time to the music. The tangle of bracelets on her arm jangled along as she manipulated the complex array of sliders and dials that stretched out in front of them.

She lowered the volume and sat back in her chair. "UC Berkeley runs a center for new music and audio technology. A friend called me for some help with a research problem. The solution involved searching a large audio database for specific patterns. I was a bit skeptical at first, but I looked at it – as a favor - and it seemed like an interesting mathematical problem that I could solve. Eventually, I did some lab work on-site. That's when I tackled all the practical stuff. How about you? How did you get involved with all this?"

"It's a long story. I grew up in Georgia – on the edge of the Okefenokee."

"I already knew that."

"You did?"

She held up her cell phone. "Five minutes on Google, Birdman. Privacy is dead."

Had she taken the time to look him up?

Miles smiled and nodded agreement as she replaced the phone on top of the console.

"It's a long way from that swamp to Ithaca, New York," she said, "How did you wind up *here*?"

Miles swiveled his chair toward hers. Their knees were almost touching.

"I've always loved birds."

"So, you started life as a birdboy? Is that your story?"

Miles chuckled.

"I've been chasing them since I was a kid. The search eventually led me here."

"Well, here we are, Miles, ready to work." She smiled. "What skills do I need for this job?"

Miles swiveled back to the console. "Our best chance of finding an Ivory-billed Woodpecker in the dense vegetation of the Okefenokee is simply to hear it. The expedition is organized around that idea."

A BENJAMIN MILES MYSTERY

He pointed to a sign on the wall: *All the Ivory-bills that I have ever seen I located first by hearing them call and then going to them. — James Tanner.*

"Who is that?" asked Susan.

"Tanner was a Cornell graduate student who laid out the path we're following. He recorded Ivory-bills back in the nineteen-thirties."

"That's a long time ago," said Susan.

"We should start by reviewing the sounds of an Ivory-billed Woodpecker," said Miles. He typed out commands rapidly as he continued talking. "This recording we're about to hear was made by Arthur Allen, the scientist who started this lab." Abruptly, Elvis stopped crooning, and the display screen was filled with a waveform and a spectrogram.

"That's an Ivory-billed Woodpecker's call," said Miles pointing at the spectrogram on the lower part of the screen. It consisted of a repeating collection of vertical, white lines in a sea of black.

He pushed a button, and the recording began to play as a vertical green line marched across the screen. "Ennnk! Ennnk! Ennnk! Ennnk!"

"Is that a bird?" asked Susan.

"Some people refer to it as a *kent* call. Audubon described it as a *pait*."

"Play it again."

Miles reset the recording. "Ennnk! Ennnk! Ennnk! Ennnk!"

"It sounds like a clarinet player with a fat lip."

THE ELVIS BIRD

Miles played it once more.

"Ennnk! Ennnk! Ennnk! Ennnk!"

"It's the only definitive recording of a pair of Ivory-bills that exists," said Miles, "Professor Allen recorded it on the Singer tract of Louisiana back in the nineteen-thirties."

"Singer?"

Miles nodded.

"The sewing machine company. Even back then, it was obvious that the bird was disappearing. Companies like Singer were busy logging southern hardwood forests out of existence. The company needed wood to make sewing machine cases. Professor Allen tried to purchase the land to preserve the bird's habitat, but Singer wouldn't agree to sell it."

"Play it again, Miles." She inched forward in the chair and stared at the spectrogram closely.

"Ennnk! Ennnk! Ennnk! Ennnk!"

She looked at him directly. "The last notes of a dying species. It's a call for help, isn't it?" she said.

Miles turned back to the screen.

"I suppose in a way, it was. The recording was made at close range, virtually underneath the birds' nest. We don't know what an Ivory-bill would sound like at a distance. That's one of the problems with our current search algorithms."

"Is this all we have to go on? It's not much to work with."

"There is one other thing."

"What's that?"

"When the bird is foraging for food, or communicating with other birds, it makes a distinctive double-knock. Like this." He tapped his finger twice on the console.

Susan reached over and tried to repeat the tap sequence.

"The first knock is more pronounced," said Miles. "Emphasize that." He tapped on the console again to demonstrate.

She repeated the tap sequence, this time emphasizing the first tap. "Ta-tap."

"That's it," he said.

"Ta-tap," she repeated.

"Can you play an Ivory-bill double-knock sequence for me?" she asked.

"We don't have a recording of that. What we have are hundreds of double-knock recordings of Pileated woodpeckers."

"Like the bird across the pond, right?"

"Right. They sound similar. That's the best we can do. You'll have to use those."

"How large is the database?"

"We have thousands of hours of material made in the Okefenokee, and more data is transmitted to us each day. The expedition will continue recording for a few more weeks before wrapping up. The team deploys fifteen autonomous recording units – ARUs – each unit records eight hours a day, four hours each morning, four each night."

"So, my job is to find this "Annnk! Annnk!" in your database?"

"Kent calls sound higher than that."

"Like this? Innnk! Innnk!"

"Do you mind?" He reached over and gently pinched her nose. "Try it again."

"Ennnk! Ennnk!"

"That's it!"

Pinching her nose and pleased with herself, she continued.

"Ennnk! Ennnk!"

A passing secretary stopped to look in at the commotion.

"I think she's got it!" Miles offered. The secretary shuffled off, shaking her head.

"So, can you find these two sounds in our database?" asked Miles. "We don't expect perfect identifications, but the current algorithm needs to be improved. We don't want to miss any potential candidate sounds. If a recording might contain Ivory-bill activity, we want to select it. In the end, it takes a human ear to make the final judgments. After your algorithm identifies the best fits, we'll have experts make the final decisions."

"Like yourself?"

"Yes, I'll probably be the one making the final determinations."

"Over the last year, I've done a lot of work with filtering algorithms. The technical term is *combinatorial hashed time-*

frequency constellation analysis. We can use that technique to target the bird's double-knock and kent call. And by using artificial intelligence software, we can train the computer to recognize potential Ivory-bill activity accurately."

"I'm running out of time, Susan," said Miles. "I need to find this bird immediately. We only have a few weeks."

"I'm also working on an audio fingerprinting algorithm. It's a new technique we can use to search a database for specific patterns quickly, but I'll need to do an in-depth analysis of your database."

"When can you start?" asked Miles.

"Right away. Just give me access to the data. If your bird makes a peep on those recordings, I'll find it."

"There's one other thing," said Miles. "Before you agree to join the Ivory-bill project, I think you should know what you're getting into." Miles typed another command on the keyboard, and a different spectrogram appeared on his display. "We recorded this in the Okefenokee just a few weeks ago. I first heard it last night. I'll warn you, it's disturbing."

Miles started the recording and sat back in his chair.

The sing-song cadence of the approaching boat filled the room and sounded more ominous now that Miles knew what was about to happen. He tried to gauge Susan's reactions without looking at her directly. At the sound of the gunshot, she turned her head and closed her eyes, straining to hear. She was motionless throughout the rest of the recording, and it was difficult to read her thoughts.

THE ELVIS BIRD

"What do you think?" asked Miles, when it was over.

"Play it, Sam," she said. "Play it once, for old time's sake."

"Great movie," said Miles. "I'm an old movie buff, too – I prefer oldies to most of the new ones."

"Then we have that in common, Miles."

He started to re-cue the recording, but Susan reached forward and touched his hand. "Do you mind?" she asked, pointing at the control board.

"Be my guest."

She made several modifications with the sliders, and then Miles restarted the recording. When it had finished playing, she asked, "Who are these people?"

"I'm not sure. I don't recognize their voices. I've been debating what to do about this, if anything. I called Jim Hopkins last night and we discussed it. He's a colleague of mine."

"James Hopkins?"

"Yes. How do you know Jim?"

"He chaired the search committee that hired me. When I interviewed for the job, he took me to dinner."

"I'll *bet* he did."

She ignored the comment. "Why did you call Hopkins?"

"He's running the Ivory-bill expedition in the Okefenokee."

She nodded recognition. "I can clean up the recording," she said. "Filter it a bit. Maybe enhance the voices. Perhaps you'll be able to recognize them when I'm done."

"You're the expert. Have at it."

Susan angled her chair toward Miles. "What did Hopkins make of it?"

"Hoppy? He told me to drop it. He never worries about anything. The thing is, he's probably right – it isn't anything. Hunting is illegal in the Okefenokee, but people do it anyway. The sound of gunfire on a recording is not that unusual. But this just seems different."

Susan put a hand on his shoulder. "He's wrong. You should report it to the authorities in Georgia – immediately. Tell them you have a recording of a suspicious gunshot that occurred in the Okefenokee. Someone needs to investigate."

"That could derail the whole expedition," said Miles. "What's on that recording could be anything … or nothing … even a prank."

She let him sit with that idea for a moment. "We both think it was something else."

Miles didn't want to say the word he was thinking: Murder. What effect would a murder investigation have on the search? Fitzsimmons might cancel the project immediately. What would happen to the birds if Cornell abandoned the search at this point? Susan seemed confident in her belief that he should report it.

"You're right," he said, finally. Miles reached for his phone, and Susan leaned in closer as he searched for a number to call.

"Folkston?" she asked, looking down at his phone as he was typing.

THE ELVIS BIRD

"Gateway to the Okefenokee."

He tapped the number and waited.

The voice on the other end was deep and resonant. "Folkston Police department. Sergeant Booker speaking."

Miles was comfortable with the vowel-inflected accent of a fellow southerner. He introduced himself, explained the nature of the recording, described in detail where and how it had been made, and why he wanted the police to review it.

When Miles had finished, Booker responded, "Let me make sure I've got this, Pro-fessor. You're an ornithologist with Cornell University. Is that right?"

"That's right, Sergeant."

"You wouldn't be related to Miss Doris Miles, would you? *Miles* is sort of an unusual name around these parts. Miss Doris lives here in Folkston. I think her son went off and became a scientist somewhere up North."

"Doris is my mother."

"Well, damn, it's a small world. Ain't that something! Now, you say you have a recording of someone being murdered, and this recording was made in the Okefenokee just a few weeks ago?"

"That's right. I don't know if anyone has been murdered or not, Sergeant. It's just suspicious. I'd like you to check it out. Decide for yourself."

"We can do that. Sure can."

"Has anyone in the Folkston area been reported missing over the last couple of weeks?"

"No, sir. No missing person reports here Pro-fessor, but tell you what, you send me a copy of that tape, and I'll give it a listen. The captain's gonna wanna hear about this for sure."

"It's not on tape. Everything's digital. I can email it to you – today."

"I'll get right on it then. And I'll let the captain know, too. Anything else we need to do for you?"

"No, I just want you to listen to this recording, that's it."

"I'm on it then. I'll be looking for your email."

Miles was about to hang up, but Booker kept chatting. "You know, Pro-fessor, this is off topic, but I don't think we've ever played you in football."

"How's that?"

"Georgia. I don't think we've ever played Cornell in football. I'd remember a thing like that."

"I'm sure you would, Sergeant."

"We'd probably whup your ass if we ever did play you, that's for damn sure." Booker started to chuckle.

When the Sergeant recovered, Miles thanked him and put the phone aside. It took a few minutes to edit the recording down to the relevant parts, type out an email to the Folkston police, and attach the audio file. Miles hesitated before hitting *Send*. Instead, he reached for the phone again and called the director.

He glanced at Susan while the phone was ringing. "I'll just double check with Fitz."

Fitzsimmons answered directly. Miles took a few minutes to describe the details of the recording but omitted his

THE ELVIS BIRD

conversation with Booker. The director listened closely, interrupting with only an occasional question.

When Miles had finished his explanation, Fitzsimmons weighed in, "I suppose we have no choice but to notify the police, but I want to hear the recording before you send it. Damn it all. Let's hope this doesn't get out in the media. You're showing Professor Swail around today, right? She's with you?"

"We're in my lab right now," said Miles.

"Good. Why don't the two of you come by my office this afternoon? Let's say at three o'clock. Send me that recording as soon as possible. We'll need to minimize the damage." Fitzsimmons rang off without waiting for a response. Miles tapped the *Send* key and turned to Susan with his palms up, shaking his head.

"You did the right thing, Birdman. Now, let's go hunt Ivory-bills."

Miles appreciated her enthusiasm – his was waning. Perhaps Susan could help after all. After their afternoon talk with Fitzsimmons, he would get her up to speed on the Okefenokee database.

Miles was about to pocket his phone when it began to chirp out loud– it was a bird ringtone his ex–wife had downloaded for him. The birds were finches, and they always sounded insistent – like his ex-wife. Fitz must have forgotten something. He glanced at the phone but was surprised to see the caller's name: George. His brother never called his cell.

A BENJAMIN MILES MYSTERY

"Sorry – I need to take this," he said to Susan. He put the phone to his ear. "George? Hang on, will ya, Georgie?" Miles slipped easily into southern-speak. He covered the phone with his hand and was about to excuse himself when he realized that Susan was already standing at the door.

"Where are you going?" he asked.

"See you later, Miles," she said. "You know how to find me, don't you? Just put your lips together and "Ennnk! Ennnk!" With that, she was gone.

Miles was still smiling when he remembered that his brother was waiting on the phone.

4. Nice Suit

On the Atlantic coast, North Carolina may be taken as the limit of its distribution, although now and then an individual of the species may be accidentally seen in Maryland.
            -James Audubon, *The Birds of America*

The phone call from his brother was bad news. His mother was hospitalized with a possible stroke. Taken to the Mayo Clinic, Jacksonville. No, he couldn't talk with her just yet. George would call him back after her tests were finished and he had consulted with her doctors. Nothing he could do at the moment. Hang tight.

Miles had never given much thought to losing his mother. Doris was the parent who had been the steady, ever-present caregiver of his childhood. His father was an FBI field agent, a heroic figure to a young boy, and later his trusted advisor. But the bureau job had required him to travel widely and often, and when Miles recalled his childhood, his father was often missing in his recollections.

While his father's professional exploits filled the family stories, it was Doris who occupied his earliest memories, and it was Doris, his stubborn, independent mother, who had shaped him. She encouraged his early interest in birds and fueled his love of reading. She insisted that Miles made A's in school and disapproved of anything short of his best effort. Doris was delighted when he decided to pursue an advanced degree in biology at the University of Georgia, and later she helped finance his Ph.D. at U.C. Davis. She had been less than enthusiastic about his marriage, and when he announced that he and his wife were divorcing, he was shocked by her initial reaction: "What took you so long?"

"It wasn't all my wife's fault," he'd protested.

"She promised to support you, no matter what. That's what wives do."

It was certainly what Doris had done. He wanted to confess that his dogged pursuit of the Ivory-bill had eroded their marriage, ended it, if he was honest, but she wouldn't have listened. Her son could do no wrong, and wives were supposed to support their husbands no matter what. Her confidence in him was unconditional and unexamined. Doris had remarkable inner strength and grit, and now he had trouble imagining her sidelined in a Florida hospital room. Before his brother's phone call, he had never considered that she might die – Doris was too stubborn to allow it.

"Enough," he said out loud to no one, dismissing the idea with a word. He stirred out of his office chair. A glance at his watch revealed he was late for the meeting with Susan and Fitzsimmons. He found Susan waiting for him outside the director's office. When he walked into the departmental suite, she was sitting on a sofa with her legs crossed. The red soles of her shoes caught his eye.

THE ELVIS BIRD

"Glad you could join us, Birdman. I thought you had taken the afternoon off."

"Sorry. Family emergency."

Susan's expression turned to one of concern. Before Miles could explain, Mrs. Sanderson, who was sitting at her desk across the room, stood up and announced, "Dr. Fitzsimmons can see you now." She crossed the room and ushered them into the inner sanctum. "Follow me."

Miles was always impressed by Fitz's enormous office. Unlike his own, it was spacious and neat, appointed with antiques, and the director's panoramic window provided a commanding view of the entire pond, not just a portion of it. The room was designed to impress each monied visitor with the school's stature in the academic community, the weighty importance of the director, and by association, all the faculty and staff who did the good work of the lab.

Miles crossed the room, bowed, and genuflected grandly as Fitzsimmons approached.

"Cut the crap, Miles," said Fitzsimmons. "Pay him no attention, Dr. Swail, he's incorrigible."

The director was a likable, impressive man with impeccable academic credentials, a national reputation for helping birds, and a remarkable record of raising money for the lab. His head was crowned with fine, white hair and his rimless glasses gave him a slightly boyish look. He had the air of a man who portions his time and energy like a chef measuring out the ingredients of a complicated recipe. Miles admired him but would never tell him so. The director also had impeccable taste in expensive clothes. It was a bit unusual for a scientist who needed to observe birds and spoke to the demands of running the a prestigious school. On this day he was resplendent in a bespoke blue suit, a red bow tie, and tan Meccariellos. Miles always felt underdressed in his presence.

"Nice suit, Fitz!" said Miles shaking the director's hand, "That's new, isn't it? Looks Italian. Did you give yourself another raise?"

"Do you like it, Miles? I can put you in touch with my tailor," he gave Miles' tee-shirt a casual glance and then smiled at Susan, "He's a creature of habit, Dr. Swail – bad habits. Is he taking good care of you today?"

"Host extraordinaire," she said, giving Miles a private wink.

"I would ask you two to sit down and chat, but I have to catch a flight in a couple of hours, so I need to make this brief." The director turned to Susan. "Miles shared a recording with you this morning – it contained a gunshot that occurred in the Okefenokee during our expedition there."

"I think it was more than a gunshot," said Susan. "I think someone was murdered. Miles thought it might influence my decision to work on the project. He asked my opinion about what to do with the recording."

"So that's when Miles called me?"

Susan nodded.

THE ELVIS BIRD

"I hope it hasn't discouraged you from working on this project. The team will complete the fieldwork soon, but it will take months to review all the data. We could use your help. Does this sound like a project that would interest you? We do have others."

"I'm interested. But I'm also curious why I wasn't told about the project when I interviewed for the job."

"That's a fair question." The director was standing directly in front of his desk, and he leaned back against the edge of it. "The whole project is very hush-hush. If the public knew we were looking for Ivory-bills, the Okefenokee would be flooded with tourists and curiosity seekers. We can't let that to happen. The only people who know about this project are all employed by the lab and sworn to secrecy."

"I see."

"So, the recording didn't change your mind?"

"No."

"Good. I've listened to it here in the office. I'm sure there is a simple explanation for what we've all heard, but we do need to know for sure." Fitzsimmons turned to Miles. "I assume sent the recording to the police in Georgia, right?"

"Yes. The Folkston police department."

"It's important we keep this out of the media until we know more. Publicity would only hurt the expedition, and there's no point in letting that occur if the police can explain what we've heard on the recording. Do you agree?"

Miles nodded.

"Good. I happen to know the governor of Georgia. We've worked together on some environmental legislation. I'll make some private inquiries. Perhaps all this can be quickly resolved."

"So, carry on as usual?" asked Miles.

"Carry on. How's the search going, by the way?"

"Not very well."

"Perhaps Professor Swail can change our luck?" Fitzsimmons turned a hopeful glance on Susan and stood up from the desk.

"I think she can," said Miles.

The director placed his hand on Miles' shoulder and turned him gently toward the door.

"I don't want to sound discouraging, Miles. We have enough money to finish the expedition, but if we don't turn up some definitive evidence in the data soon, we'll have to move on to something more promising. I'm thinking long-range here. A different project altogether. We can discuss the direction of your future work when I get back from this trip."

"You know this bird exists, Fitz," said Miles.

"I know it does. You don't have to convince me. I'd like to prove this bird survived as much as anyone. That's why I funded this project."

"But you plan to cancel any further work if we can't find evidence of the bird soon."

"I have to balance all the resources of the lab, Miles." Fitzsimmons turned to Susan. "No matter what happens,

Dr. Swail, we need you here at the lab, and we're delighted you decided to join us."

Miles turned to face Fitzsimmons at the door. "Is there anything else we need to discuss?"

"No, I can't think of anything," said the director, "Just don't send that recording to anyone else. We don't want someone leaking it to the press."

"It's safely in my lab."

"Good. Keep it there until we hear from the police."

Mrs. Sanderson appeared as if on cue to usher them outside. When they were in the hallway, Susan grasped Mile's arm, "Tell me more about your family emergency."

Miles debated how much to reveal. "My mother is in the hospital. Possible stroke. I'm waiting for my brother to call me back."

"Sorry, Birdman."

"She's a tough lady – my mother."

"I'm sure she is. Still, you shouldn't have to wait alone."

"It's fine," said Miles. "I'll be fine." Miles nodded and smiled uneasily.

Susan looked him over. "I'm famished. I know it's early, but how about taking me out for dinner? You'd be doing me a favor."

It sounded like an excellent idea.

5. I Know Your Name

To the westward of the Mississippi, it is found in all the dense forests bordering the streams which empty their waters into that majestic river, from the very declivities of the Rocky Mountains.
            -James Audubon, *The Birds of America*

Miles looked down at the flashing cell phone that was lying beside the empty wine glass. The apprehension that had disappeared after finishing his first glass of a serviceable Merlot returned the moment the phone lit up.

"It's my brother," he said to Susan as he continued to stare at the phone.

"You should take it," she said from across the table.

Miles reached for the phone. The birds continued to chirp happily until he gave it a quick swipe.

"What's the news, Georgie?" asked Miles.

"They think she's had a TIA."

The tenor of his brother's voice had an urgency that competed with the conversations of other couples sitting nearby in the tiny restaurant. Miles pressed the phone tightly against one ear and covered the other with his free hand.

"What does that mean?"

"Transient Ischemia Attack. It's like a stroke, but the doctor said it doesn't usually cause as much damage. They took a CAT-scan. They don't think there was much permanent damage – *this* time. Evidently, she's had others in the past. Did you know about those?"

"No, she never mentioned anything to me."

"That figures, neither did I. The doctor wants to keep her at the hospital overnight for evaluation. She started some blood pressure medication, and she has to begin taking an aspirin every day."

"I can book a reservation tonight. I can fly down tomorrow."

"I don't think you need to come right now, Benny."

Only George and his mother called him Benny. The name evoked another place and time. Another life.

"She's ok for the moment. But we need to talk about moving her into a home. We need to find a place that can look after her full-time."

"She's not going to agree to that."

"Maybe not, but she *is* getting older. And this isn't the first time she's fallen."

"She fell?"

"Yep. She was standing on a step-stool in the kitchen, putting away some dishes."

"Did she break anything?"

"Nope – she landed on her ass. Probably bruised her pride, but then I'm no doctor."

"That's not funny, Georgie."

"Yes, it is. It's pretty *damned* funny if you think about it. Thank God, Miss Mildred stopped by and found her. She called an ambulance, and then phoned me."

"Are you at the hospital now? It sounds like you're in a car."

"She kicked me out of the hospital. Can you believe that? She made the doctor write it on her orders: No Visitors. The doctor walked me out of the room himself– the little twit."

Miles had to smile.

"Anyway, I tucked tail and left. Now I'm in the car on the way home. Did I tell you I bought a new Mercedes?"

"No, you didn't tell me – I never hear from you."

"I installed the horn from my old Buick Park Avenue on it. The damn thing sounds like a train. It plays four notes at one time – an augmented fifth chord, I think. It'll scare the bejesus out of you. Give a listen."

"What?" asked Miles. He glanced at the next table – a couple was chatting animatedly. On the phone, he could hear George blowing the horn in the background. It did sound like a train. He waited for the noise to stop.

"I'll book the airline reservation and get back with you, Georgie."

"Give it some thought first. If you do come down, we'll need to make a plan before confronting her. Maybe together we can convince her to find a nice place on the beach – somewhere I can drop in and check on her – a home with some graduated nursing assistance, you know? She might listen to both of us if we gang up on her."

"She never listens to anyone," Miles pointed out.

"I admit this won't be easy. She's one hard-headed old bird – bless her heart."

Susan set her wine glass on the table and looked at Miles with concern.

"I'll get back to you, Georgie," said Miles, smiling nervously at Susan. "Call me if anything changes."

A waiter appeared at the table as Miles was getting off the phone and apologized for the delay in service. Miles took the opportunity to order a second bottle of wine.

"How's your mother?" asked Susan when the waiter left. She leaned across the table and placed her hand on top of his.

It was a simple, affectionate gesture – something his ex-wife would have done in these circumstances. A sense of helplessness came over Miles, and he couldn't speak for a moment– unhinged by the touch of another person. He took a moment to recover, but he was emotionally triangulated by concern for his mother, his unexamined feelings of grief over his failed marriage, and a sense of hopelessness at ever finding the damned bird. Reaching for his glass, he poured out the last of the wine, and started to gulp it down.

"It's my Mom," he said between swallows.

"I'm sorry, Miles."

"No, she's ok," he said.

A BENJAMIN MILES MYSTERY

He unfolded his napkin, placed the silverware on the table, and wiped his eyes. "She's in the hospital in Jacksonville – for observation." Miles couldn't stop his tears. "I'm sorry … I'm never like this …I don't know what's come over me." He took another swallow of wine.

The phone rang again. It was his mother.

He put his glass down abruptly and lifted the phone. "Mom?"

"This is your mother – Doris."

"I know your name, Mom."

Susan stared at him, puzzled – Miles shrugged.

"I'm glad *you* can remember it because I forgot it for a while this morning. But I'm feeling much better now. I'm in Jacksonville. They put me in the hospital, and they won't let me go home."

"I know, I just talked to Georgie."

"Don't mention that boy's name! I want you to fly down and get me out of this place."

"Georgie said the doctors need to look you over."

"I'm perfectly fine now, so come get me out. When you get here, you can see for yourself. I can't sleep in this place – the bed is too hard and I want to go home."

Miles imagined his mother sitting up in bed, ramrod-straight, indignant at being clad in a standard hospital gown that revealed areas that ladies should not display. She wouldn't like that. Nor would she abide the other indignities that hospitals routinely visit on patients.

THE ELVIS BIRD

"You'll have to stay the night, Mom. They're still running tests. Why are you so angry with my brother?"

"George wants to sell my house and put me in an old folks' home on Jacksonville beach."

"He just wants to take care of you."

"Can you see me in an old folks' home, Benny? I'd rather die. Besides, I hate beaches!"

Miles pointed out that George only wanted her to be safe and happy, but Doris wasn't buying it.

"If you don't come soon, I'll die, and George will bury me in the nearest sand dune. Benny, you don't want to visit your dead mother in a sand dune, do you?"

"No, Mom. I don't."

"Then, if you love me, you'll hurry on down. See you soon, kiddo. Oh, and tell George I'm not going to an old folks' home."

The phone went dead before Miles could respond.

6. Immovable Object

The lower parts of the Carolinas, Georgia, Alabama, Louisiana, and Mississippi, are, however, the most favourite resorts of this bird, and in those States it constantly resides, breeds, and passes a life of peaceful enjoyment, finding a profusion of food in all the deep, dark, and gloomy swamps dispersed throughout them.
-James Audubon, *The Birds of America*

After reaching maximum altitude, the plane leveled off, and Miles settled back in his seat, releasing his grip on the armrests. The seat belt indicator switched off, but he decided to leave his seat belt fastened anyway. Better safe than sorry. He was not a happy flyer.

Everyone around him seemed perfectly at ease: the stylishly dressed young mother playing with her child in the adjoining seats, the elderly woman watching a movie in the row ahead, the heavyset businessman across the aisle, lazily dividing his time between the newspaper in his left hand and the scotch and soda in his right. He envied the ease with which they all traveled, oblivious to the impending explosion and the mid-air collision that Miles alternately imagined.

Over Washington, he raised the plastic window that shielded his view and turned the circular dial on the overhead eyeball to wide open, directing the air conditioning onto his face. He pressed his cheek against the cold plastic window and watched the city scroll past at 30,000 feet. The cold air and the window's view eased his anxiety.

He usually avoided plane trips, but this was an emergency – and Doris had summoned him. He thought of his mother and how independent she had become – even before his father had died ten years ago. A *stubborn cuss* was how his father had described her, but he always said it with a wry smile on his face, or in a tone of voice that revealed his true feelings of admiration mixed with amusement. His parents had been happy and content. It seemed they didn't require anything but each other to make life worth living. As a couple, they presented a united front to the world and their children. They never argued publicly.

After his father died, Doris seemed to develop an even harder edge. She could be ornery even. Convincing her to move to the beach would be difficult if not impossible. Perhaps George had the wrong end of the stick. Maybe they shouldn't try to move her out of her home? Why was he even considering it?

"Would you like a drink?" The practiced attention of the smiling stewardess interrupted his thoughts.

"Coffee," he said. He watched the stewardess – a brunette like Susan – pour a cup of coffee and extend it to him on a plastic tray. He made a mental note to call Susan as soon as he was off the plane. Good idea. He would ask her to begin searching the audio database for other human voices found on the recordings. That might turn up some new evidence or throw some light on the whole matter. If there was a simple explanation for the gunshot, he could forget the whole ugly episode and concentrate on Ivory-bills. He had staked his professional reputation on the existence of these birds, and he damned well wanted to give them his full attention.

The coffee was tepid. Miles lowered the tray on the seat ahead and sat the cup on it. Why had he been so emotional in the restaurant the night before? Susan had insisted on driving him home after drinks. Tipsy after three glasses of wine! Still, she didn't seem to mind giving him a ride home. In the future, he would limit himself to two glasses of wine with dinner.

Miles' stomach told him that the plane's equilibrium had suddenly changed, and they were descending – they must be nearing Jacksonville. He looked across the aisle to the window of his fellow travelers. The cloudless blue sky extended clear to the horizon, and he realized they were flying parallel to the Atlantic. The pilot's voice – barely audible – interrupted with an announcement that they would be landing in twenty … minutes … no delay. Finish your … beverages. Please turn off … all electronic equipment.

Miles cinched his seatbelt tighter. The child in the next seat was resting her head in her mother's lap. The heavyset businessman had finished his drink and was standing in the aisle, retrieving his bag from the overhead bin. The elderly woman in the seat ahead had fallen asleep during the movie.

THE ELVIS BIRD

Miles re-gripped the armrests and closed his eyes. He leaned back and braced for landing. Landing an airplane was the worst part of the flight. He hated the plane's circling and maneuvering as it got into its final position for the approach. Most accidents occurred during landing and take-off, right?

He turned his face into position against the cold window, and then he saw it: the Okefenokee. From the air, it was wondrous, extending as far as he could see – grassy marshes, treeless plains, islands of hardwoods, black rivulets of streams, and a canal. The great primordial swamp inched past his window at two-hundred miles per hour. Perhaps somewhere in that expanse, he would, at last, find the bird. But where? It would be like looking for a penny lost in a lake. And what about the damned recording? What exactly had occurred on that boat ride? Had someone been murdered, or was it something that could be easily explained? Too soon, the swamp receded, and the view began to change – the terrain transmogrified into concrete highways and condos and shopping malls.

An hour later, he was traveling south on Florida's Interstate 95, his stomach still uneasy from the flight. He put the windows down on the rented blue Lexus and opened the sunroof to take in the tropical smell and to clear his head. The balmy salt breeze tossed his hair as the car easily out-maneuvered the other traffic whenever he pressed hard on the accelerator. A disembodied female voice on the GPS suggested that he exit to the right in the next one hundred yards. He would be at the Mayo Clinic in twenty minutes.

A BENJAMIN MILES MYSTERY

Spindly palm trees and short, bushy saw palmettos surrounded the hospital's parking lot. There was an adjoining hotel on the hospital grounds, and he pulled into a space facing its entrance. He could see the hospital from his parking space. He turned off the engine and paused to enjoy the warmth of the morning sun and to steel himself for his reunion with Doris.

Within minutes he was sweaty from the Florida sun. He locked the car, crossed the parking lot, and entered the hospital foyer to ask for directions to her room. His mother was on the fourth floor. He located her room, and as he approached the door, he heard a commotion within. He stopped and peeked in. The sturdy black nurse at his mother's bedside would not be deterred.

"Now look, Miss Miles, you know you have to take your medicine if you want to get better."

Miles waited in anticipation. This might prove interesting – the immovable object and the irresistible force. He looked in again. The nurse was blocking his mother's view of the door, but Miles could see her leaning forward in the bed, her arms gripped tightly around her knees.

"I feel fine, nurse, and I don't like taking medicine that I don't need. Please, call my doctor."

The nurse didn't budge.

"Miss Miles, we don't need to bother your poor doctor – he has his own problems without you adding to them. This pill is for your blood pressure, and yours is high. Until we get that down, we're going to keep you right here in that bed.

THE ELVIS BIRD

Now, why don't you make my day, and take your medication?"

"My blood pressure is fine."

"Take the medicine, Mom." Miles had stepped into the room.

The nurse moved aside so Doris could see who was standing at the door.

"Oh, gimme the damn medicine," said Doris. She extended her open hand, and the nurse handed it over with a cup of water. Doris tossed it back with a swallow and handed the cup back to the nurse.

"Why does it take an emergency for you to come to visit me? Don't you love your mother?"

"Bless you," said the nurse, winking at Miles as he approached the bed. "The lips of the righteous nourish many." Turning back to Doris, she added, "But fools die for lack of judgment. That's in the bible, Miss Miles."

Doris was ready. "And a wise son brings joy to his father, but a foolish son grief to his mother." Chuckling, the nurse made a swift exit.

Miles walked over to his mother and hugged her. "Cut me some slack, Mom; I live in New York. It's not easy to get down here."

Miles held her close and then at arms' length to judge the effects of the stroke. Her color looked good, and her eyes were clear, but he still had doubts. Was this woman, this rock, permanently fractured in some hidden way? She gripped his arm firmly—a good sign.

A BENJAMIN MILES MYSTERY

"Get me out of here, Benjamin. The sooner, the better."

7. You Don't Need Feathers

Would that I could describe the extent of those deep morasses, overshadowed by millions of gigantic dark cypresses, spreading their sturdy moss-covered branches, as if to admonish intruding man to pause and reflect on the many difficulties which he must encounter should he persist in venturing farther into their almost inaccessible recesses, ...

-James Audubon, *The Birds of America*

Miles got out of bed before the sun had risen and changed into running shorts and a white tee shirt that was emblazoned *Cornell* over a big red bear emblem. He wanted some exercise before facing his mother again. It had been a struggle the previous evening convincing Doris to stay overnight, but in the end, he had appealed to her frugality, explaining that she had already paid for another night, and she might as well take advantage of it. Besides, it was too late to drive her back to Folkston.

Outside the hotel, he located the Lexus and decided to head east with the idea of taking his jog along the beach. It had been years since he had visited Jacksonville, and he was curious about the changes that had occurred. He soon discovered that the beachfront was dominated by homes, hotels, and condos that sprawled lazily along US-1, monopolizing the available space and reminding visitors that the beaches were private. Stay out. He drove for miles down the coast before giving up and parking the car in a strip mall. The sun was already peeking over the treetops when he got out of the vehicle. The initial coolness of the morning had vanished, replaced with a creeping heat and humidity that would soon dominate the day. He locked the car and set out.

It didn't take long to work up a sweat. The highway reminded him of the summer vacations his family had taken to Miami, packed together in a '57 Buick Special. US-1 was the highway of old Florida: serpentariums, Burma Shave signs, Johnny Walker billboards, alligator farms, and Seminole Indian outposts. All of it sadly supplanted now by the endless monotony of an interstate running from Jacksonville to Miami.

He slowed his pace to admire the stunted oak trees that huddled tightly together along the highway like grizzled old men, providing an impenetrable canopy barrier between the sea and the land. After another quarter-mile, he found an unpaved side street leading to the ocean, and he took it. Soon he was breathing in the heady aroma of the sea. The dirt road abruptly petered out. He crossed the dunes and jogged down to the shoreline. Herring gulls were patrolling the coast in groups of three and four, lazily riding the air currents, and periodically diving into the water for a meal. Ornithologically, they were interesting birds. Each year their plumage turned whiter as they aged, and he was reminded that *his* plumage was beginning to show the first traces of gray.

He stopped to remove his shirt, drawing it over his head and using it to shield his face from the sun as he lay back in the sand – a pleasant fatigue crept over him as he gave in to the eternal rhythms of the waves crashing onto the shore. The cell phone, which he had placed on his chest began to vibrate and awakened him. He held up the phone and took a glance: "Cornell Ornithology." Damn.

"Hello?"

"Professor Miles?" He recognized the voice of Mrs. Sanderson.

"Peggy?"

"We've been trying to reach you," she said, "There's been an accident in the lab. A fire."

Miles sat up straight. "Is everyone alright?"

"Dr. Swail was injured. She's in the hospital. Dr. Fitzsimmons asked me to call and let you know."

Miles felt it in his stomach as fear and dread gripped him suddenly.

"How is she?" he asked tentatively.

He stood up and wiped the sand from his arms and legs with his free hand, and then he turned away from the ocean and pressed the phone tight against his ear.

"No word on her condition yet. It only happened hours ago."

"Let me talk to Fitz."

"He's not here. He's at the hospital with Dr. Swail. Cayuga Medical. He said he'd get in touch with you when he knows more."

Miles' thoughts were racing.

"Call me back as soon as you hear anything, Peggy," he said finally.

Miles pocketed the phone and started to run back to the car. The deep, loose sand slowed his pace, and by the time he reached the main highway, he was completely winded. As cars whizzed past, he bent over with his hands on his knees to catch his breath. Why was he running? What could he possibly do to make things better? Regaining his composure, Miles pulled out the phone and searched for the number for Cayuga Medical Center. After two calls and an operator transfer, the phone in Susan's hospital room was ringing.

The connection was poor.

"Susan?"

"Is that you, Miles?"

"Yes. Thank God, I got through. How are you?"

"My head hurts a little."

"You were injured?" Miles turned and walked a few steps away from the highway.

"I'm fine now. You sound worried, Birdman."

"I am worried!"

"I thought the only thing that attracted your attention was feathers."

"You're kidding, right?"

THE ELVIS BIRD

"You're a bit obsessed with birds, Miles, didn't your ex-wife mention that?"

"I'm not obsessed."

"Single-minded then. Absorbed. Call it pre-occupied."

"I'm passionate about birds if that's what you mean."

"Except for your mother, the only thing you talked about at the restaurant was finding the Ivory-billed Woodpecker."

This wasn't going as he had imagined. The sinking feeling in his stomach suddenly returned. Perhaps he had misinterpreted her initial interest. It wouldn't be the first time he had misread signals. Was he really better with birds than women?

"What happened in the lab last night?"

"It's all very fuzzy. I was working late on the Okefenokee data, testing some search algorithms. That's all I remember. When I woke up, I was on the floor, and the overhead sprinklers were running. The room was on fire. Dr. Fitzsimmons suddenly appeared and dragged me out of the lab by my feet. He saved my life."

"Good on Fitz. I'll have to buy him a tie."

"I was using your lab, Miles. The fire destroyed your lab equipment."

Miles imagined the burnt-out lab. It would take months to rebuild. The Okefenokee database was housed there as well. Would it have been backed up? Doubtful. Parts of it, maybe most of it, could be reconstructed from computers at the campsite. What about the gunshot recording? He had sent a shorter, edited version to the police – he could retrieve that from his own email.

"The important thing is that you escaped unharmed.".

"So, how's your mom?" she asked, changing topics.

"They're letting her go this morning. I promised to take her back home today."

Miles could hear a commotion in the background.

"My nurse is waiting," said Susan, "I have to go. Talk with you later?"

"Ok. Bye then."

"Chiao, Birdman," she said and quickly clicked off.

Bye then? Very lame. What was he thinking?

He tried calling Fitzsimmons' number. No answer.

8. Gateway

The broad extent of its dark glossy body and tail, the large and well-defined white markings of its wings, neck, and bill, relieved by the rich carmine of the pendent crest of the male, and the brilliant yellow of its eye, have never failed to remind me of some of the boldest and noblest productions of that inimitable artist's (VanDyke) pencil.
-James Audubon, *The Birds of America*

"This place is wasting my time," announced Doris. Miles was sitting in an uncomfortable hospital chair he had dragged closer to her bed.

"Don't be difficult."

"Bad coffee, too." She held up her cup to make the point and forced a smile as she gazed expectantly at her son.

She did seem healthy enough. Her complexion was suitably pink, and she had combed and arranged her white hair and fixed it in place with several hairpins. Her hospital gown had been replaced by a fresh, better-fitting one that made her seem less crazed than the night before. She quickly finished her breakfast, and afterward, the nurse from the previous evening stopped by to take her vital signs.

"You're going home today, Miss Miles. I saw it on your chart. The doctor is making his rounds and he should be here soon. You take care, now. I don't want to see you back here anytime soon."

Doris replied, "You can bet your paycheck that I won't be back."

As the nurse was leaving, Doris called to her, "Thank you for your help, Christine!"

Four hours later, the doctor had still not arrived to examine and release her. Miles had fallen asleep in the chair, his head resting at an odd angle. He slept fitfully, and he woke intermittently whenever his head slumped forward. Doris had tuned the TV to CNN, and in his groggy state, Miles had a sense of being tortured slowly by the doleful tones of Wolf Blitzer. He awoke to a story on the imbalance of US trade with China. It was time to get out of the room and find some coffee.

Miles returned with two cups of Starbucks regular blend, and a newspaper stuck under his arm. Doris was waiting beside the bed dressed in her street clothes, combing her hair.

"The doctor said I could go home," she said cheerily.

"He's already come and gone? I wanted to speak with him," he said incredulously.

"You just missed him," she said, amused.

"I was only gone for a few minutes. You sent him away on purpose, didn't you?"

"The doctor is a very busy man, Benjamin. He didn't have time to wait for my wayward son to return. If you

THE ELVIS BIRD

wanted to talk with him, you shouldn't have left the room. Oh, good! You brought coffee."

Miles handed her a cup.

"I'm beginning to remember why I left home so many years ago," said Miles. "You're impossible. You know that, right? What did he say about your condition?"

"He said I'm fine."

"That's it? We waited four hours for that diagnosis? You're fine."

"No. He also wanted me to stay on my medication, and he said I could leave immediately. Now get me out of here."

Miles stared at the old woman. She was like a thick oak limb that someone had cut, shaped, and polished for a particular purpose – a walking stick, perhaps. He had certainly leaned on her enough over the years. This stick of a woman had served faithfully – unbroken and unbending for years. But now?

The blue Lexus gave a good ride. His mother seemed happy to be out of the hospital again. As for himself, Miles was relieved to be taking her back to his childhood home. Folkston was the *Gateway to the Okefenokee* - the place that had fueled his early fascination with birds. He would live at home for a few weeks to make sure his mother could care of herself, and spend some time in the field with the Cornell team who were camping in the Okefenokee. There was still the disturbing business of the recording to deal with, and he would take that up with Hopkins when he visited the camp tomorrow. And what about Susan? Something about her made his heart feel lighter.

After they crossed the Georgia line, Miles telephoned his brother, George, who sounded relieved that Benjamin was handling his difficult mother for a change. Good. Watch her close. Call me if you need anything.

On a whim, Miles decided to phone Hopkins and have some fun. Hopkins answered on the first ring.

"Miles?" Another poor connection.

"It's me. Look, Hoppy, I'd like to fly down and visit the camp. Just give the word. I could be there tomorrow. The lab can afford it, and I want to get in on some of the fun."

"No way. We talked about this weeks ago, Miles. Stay at Cornell and coordinate the search. Besides, the lab can't afford it, and nothing is happening here anyway. Be a good boy and stay put."

"That's a mistake, buddy. You need me there. Last chance to change your mind."

"Bye, Miles."

Miles tossed the phone into the car's console, amused at the thought that he would see Hopkins the next day. He pressed harder on the accelerator, and the speedometer edged up to eighty as the car hugged the arrow-straight highway. The road to Folkston was paralleled by endless miles of railroad tracks and pine trees. As the car sped along, he glanced across the seat at his sleeping passenger. A blissful smile revealed Doris' dreamy thoughts: Soon, they would be home.

9. Grail Bird

Would that I could represent to you the dangerous nature of the ground, its oozing, spongy, and miry disposition, although covered with a beautiful but treacherous carpeting, composed of the richest mosses, flags, and water-lilies, no sooner receiving the pressure of the foot than it yields and endangers the very life of the adventurer, ...
- James Audubon, *The Birds of America*

Jim Hopkins looked puzzled as the blue sedan eased off the old, unpaved logging road and into the campsite. Miles parked the Lexus next to a white university van, where it seemed out of place among the Jeeps and pickup trucks parked in a row near the Cornell-red tents. It was early morning, and the still-dark sky was beginning to lighten on the eastern horizon.

Hopkins was a tall, tan, wiry man who looked at home outdoors – one of those hard-edged guys with a ready complaint. He was a difficult colleague, but Miles had found him generous in their personal dealings. It was Hopkins who offered Miles a place to stay during his divorce. They had formed an unlikely friendship, partly because Miles admired the man's pluck, and partly because Miles felt that Hopkins always paid dearly for his sins.

THE ELVIS BIRD

This morning, Hopkins wore a rakish Aussie hat that covered his shaved head, and a khaki shirt paired with baggy cammo shorts. His well-worn Moab boots were stained dark brown by the tannic swamp water of the Okefenokee. He kept staring at the car, and Miles could see that he wasn't happy. The ruse had worked.

"What the hell are you doing here?" Jim asked as Miles stepped out of the car.

"I grew up in Folkston. This is my backyard, Hoppy."

Hopkins gave him a look of disbelief.

"So, you were just pulling my chain when you called me yesterday?"

"Who better to do it than your old buddy?"

Hopkins started to laugh. The two men shook hands and headed off toward the center of the camp. Inside the main tent, Miles greeted a handful of colleagues who had gathered around a coffee maker. Hopkins filled two cups and handed one to Miles. They sat down at an empty table, and Miles proceeded to describe his mother's health situation. He would be staying at her home nearby. No cost to the lab. He had ample time to kill. And he wanted to spend some of it in the field like a real ornithologist – looking for Ivory-billed Woodpeckers. He omitted mentioning that he also wanted to investigate the gunshot recording – no reason to poke the bear prematurely. Besides, there was nothing new to report. His inquiries to the police were still going unanswered.

Hopkins listened patiently and then grunted a response, "I don't need you here." He gestured with his coffee cup as he continued talking, "Fitzsimmons wants you in Ithaca, sorting out the data. We need you *there* to do the heavy lifting for us *here*. Got it? Did you even tell him you were coming down?"

"Haven't you heard? There was a fire in my lab."

"I heard. I heard. Fitzsimmons phones me every night to check on the progress we're making – which is none, by the way. You know he micromanages everything about this expedition."

"Then you know that the audio lab is a mess, and it won't be usable for a couple of months."

"Then move to another lab. There's nothing for you to do here. You'll just be in my way."

Hopkins stood up and commandeered the coffee pot and then topped-off Miles' cup.

"Does Fitzsimmons even know you're here?"

"He knows."

Hopkins sat down without bothering to return the pot. He poured another cup for himself, took a sip of the coffee, and spat it on the ground. "Who made this swill?" He looked around the tent for the villain, but everyone had left.

His attention returned to Miles. "It's lucky for Swail that Fitz was working late when the fire broke out. How's she doing, anyway?" said Hopkins, "I hear she's working for you now."

"I called Susan again last night. She should be out of the hospital by now – a minor head injury."

THE ELVIS BIRD

"So, you called *Susan* again last night, did you? I didn't think you had it in you." He patted Miles on the back. "If I were in Ithaca, I'd be after that too. Nice work, buddy!"

Miles raised his arm quickly and tossed Hopkins' hand away.

"It's not like that, Hoppy."

"It's exactly like that, and about time, too. I'm happy to see that you finally developed some cojones. You should never have let your ex-wife take yours in the divorce settlement."

Were his feelings for Susan that transparent? Or was Hopkins just needling him on instinct? "Don't bring my ex-wife into this. Do you want my help here or not?"

Hopkins stood up abruptly and with a quick flick of the wrist, emptied his cup on the ground.

"No. I don't. But, I can't stop you, so I guess you can stay. But only because your lab isn't functional, and you're already down here. The grad students left camp a couple of weeks ago, so I suppose I can generate enough low-level grunt work for someone with your highly-developed skills."

"Good."

"It's just you and me and the field staff now – as long as Fitzsimmons doesn't drop in to make trouble."

"When can I start?"

"It's your lucky day, pal. I'm going out to move some ARUs this morning. Bring your new cojones."

A BENJAMIN MILES MYSTERY

###

The Cornell campsite was perched on a riverbank on the western side of the Okefenokee in a forest of pine, bay, and oak trees. It was an area of dense shrubs and generally fewer trees than the eastern regions of the reserve. Hopkin's white Carolina skiff sat anchored at a dock next to several similar-looking skiffs in the still, tea-colored water – all the boats had been towed down from Ithaca for the expedition.

Hopkins climbed in first. The skiff was a flat-bottom fishing boat, with a narrow design and shallow draft for easy maneuvering in tight channels. It was large enough to hold seven or eight passengers comfortably, along with some equipment and room for storage.

Hopkins moved mid-section to the wheel, which was protected by an overhead cover. Miles took a seat directly in front of the wheel facing the bow. With Miles settled in, Hopkins cranked the engine and eased the boat away from the dock. It had been years since Miles had visited the Okefenokee, but over the next half-hour, as they moved deeper into the primordial swamp, the landscape changed with each turn in the river, and Miles watched the sights and felt strangely at home. He soon grew tired and leaned his head against the support structure that held the wheel and began to recall the events of the past year.

The original idea for the expedition – searching for Ivory-billed Woodpeckers in the Okefenokee – had come to

THE ELVIS BIRD

Miles unexpectedly after receiving an extraordinary phone call from Perry Fielder, a childhood friend who operated a tour guide business out of Folkston.

"I saw the Grail bird today, Miles."

The two friends hadn't spoken for several years, but Miles recognized the distinctive accent of his old friend immediately,

"Was he living with Big Foot?"

"I'm serious."

Miles was unsure how to respond. "Don't kid me about this, Admiral."

"I'm not kidding. I saw the Lord God Bird himself."

Perry Fielder was an expert birder and an experienced guide. Miles sat back in his chair and took a deep breath. "And just where did you see God Almighty?" he asked skeptically.

"Here in the Okefenokee. Near Minnie's Island."

As boys, Miles and Perry had played together in the immense swamp, but that was decades ago and years after the bird had been declared extinct. Given the changes over the last century, the Okefenokee was an unlikely place to find an Ivory-billed Woodpecker. Still, the bird had once lived there - as late as the nineteen-forties. There were even claims of a few sightings in the fifties and sixties. Over time, the Okefenokee had become a place where old-growth forests had made a significant recovery. Could the swamp still support a few hardy Ivory-bills?

A BENJAMIN MILES MYSTERY

Miles had heard rumors of scientists from other universities searching for Ivory-bills further west on the Georgia-Alabama border.

"When did you see it?"

"This week. Two sightings. Each time in the late afternoon. I haven't found its roost cavity yet – but give me time."

Miles had taken the call in his office. He maneuvered his office chair away from the desk with his feet and stared across the pond, trying to calculate probabilities. He often heard from amateur birders claiming to have seen an extinct bird in their back yard. Too many people confused Ivory-bills with the smaller, similar-looking Pileated woodpecker – a dead ringer to an untrained eye. Miles routinely dismissed calls like this one and placed as little credence in them as Elvis sightings. Perry *was* an expert birder in his own right, a trusted spotter. But even experts are sometimes fooled. Still, what if he were right?

"Can you describe it?"

"He was wearing a name badge that said, 'Hi, I'm Campephilus Principalis.' Miles, you know I would recognize that bird."

He trusted Perry's judgment about birds implicitly, but after years of frustrating searches and false leads, Miles still maintained a scientist's healthy skepticism.

"And you're sure it wasn't a Pileated woodpecker," Miles suggested.

"Too damn big."

THE ELVIS BIRD

"Did you see it fly?"

"Yes. It took my breath away. White underwing on the back, not the front. It flew in a straight line, like a duck. It was completely different from a Pileated's flight – I'm telling you, it was an Ivory-bill."

Miles got up and shut his office door.

"What about knocking? Did it knock?"

"Two distinct knocks. That's how I spotted it. The first was more pronounced. Just like Audubon described."

Miles' excitement was palpable.

"Any vocalizations?"

"None. Not a peep."

"We need those, too."

"I'll keep trying."

If Perry was right, it was a discovery that would shake the ornithological world. In the end, Miles decided to believe him. Convincing Fitzsimmons hadn't been so easy.

"Have you lost your mind, Miles?" said Fitzsimmons when Miles requested funds to investigate Perry's claim. "This man, Fielder, runs tour boats for a living."

"He's an experienced birder. I trust him."

"We're not chasing Ivory-bills again. We already did that in Arkansas, remember?"

"We have to go investigate this. Tanner would go if he were here today – you know that. Allen, too. Like it or not, when anyone mentions Ivory-billed Woodpeckers, they think of Cornell. Are you going to let someone else, some other university, find this bird?"

Fitzsimmons looked like a man in pain.

"Do you know what would happen if the media discovered that Cornell was looking for Ivory-bills in the Okefenokee?" said Fitzsimmons. "Let me make it plain for you. We would be publicly ridiculed. I would be ridiculed! And you might be looking for a new job."

"We can keep it a secret, Fitz. No one has to know. We'll announce to anyone interested that the lab is there to conduct an inventory – and that will be true. We can go count birds – a small research expedition with a few graduate students. If we happen to spot an Ivory-bill while we're there, we can make history."

Fitzsimmons had eventually caved to Miles' request and agreed to finance a small group of faculty and graduate students for a few months. It was only later that Miles learned he wouldn't be leading the field team for the investigation. He wouldn't be going to the Okefenokee at all.

"I need you here in the acoustics lab," said Fitzsimmons. You're familiar with the Okefenokee. You can work virtually. Coordinate the fieldwork from here, based on the data we get from the ARUs. I need your ears in Ithaca."

Miles couldn't believe what he was hearing.

"Fitz, when I was a kid, my grandfather described seeing Ivory-bills in the Okefenokee," said Miles. "It was something he remembered all his life. It was transformative. If anyone should go to the Okefenokee, it should be me. This is my project. It was my idea."

THE ELVIS BIRD

But Fitzsimmons was unmoved. "If we find anything down there, you can be on the next plane."

"So, if it's not me that's going, who's going to be the on-site coordinator?"

"Jim Hopkins."

"Hopkins? He's never directed a single on-site project. Why are you sending him? We wouldn't be going at all without my contacts."

"He needs it more than you do."

"What does that mean?"

Fitzsimmons stepped closer and placed a hand on Miles' shoulder.

"This is just between you and me, but you're both up for promotion soon. *You* have a strong research record – I'm not worried about you – your pal Hopkins could use a few more lines on his vitae if you get my meaning." The director patted Miles on the back and added, "And if anyone asks, I didn't just say that."

###

"Earth to Miles," said Hopkins. He was calling from the wheel.

"I heard you. Keep your eyes on the river," said Miles.

"Bullshit. You fell asleep."

The skiff was moving out of the scrublands and into the open expanse of Floyd's prairie. The enormous, flooded field supported a variety of grasses that grew out of the dark tanic water. The wind blew strongly in the exposed plain, bending the grasses and gently moving the floating vegetation back and forth. An occasional distant island, crowned with shrubs and small trees, broke the plain's monotony and gave the illusion of solidity. In truth, the islands were floating barges of organic peat that would quiver under the weight of a human foot. The prairie was a place of otherworldly beauty and danger – a place where dark, unmoving logs with sleepy, unconcerned eyes floated along the edges of the watery pathways: Alligator mississippiensis. The Creek Indians, who once populated the swamp, called the area *O-ke-fin-o-cau*. Land of the Trembling Earth.

The two men spent most of the day moving around from site to site, replacing batteries in the school-bus-yellow autonomous recording units that were strapped to tree trunks scattered across the swamp. Each ARU contained a microphone, an amplifier, a frequency filter, a programmable computer, and a hard disk drive. After downloading the data stored on each unit, the men changed the batteries and moved the units to more promising locations based on a schedule that Miles constructed weekly from the comfort of the Cornell acoustics lab.

After servicing the last ARU of the day, Hopkins crawled back into the boat and pronounced, "This has been a complete waste of time – you know that, right? Not just today, but the whole expedition. We haven't seen a trace of your buddy's bird, Miles. Not once in six months."

THE ELVIS BIRD

"The search isn't over yet," Miles offered optimistically. But Hopkins looked like a man in need of a drink.

"It's over," said Hopkins. "We're just going through the motions. This swamp has two hundred and thirty-five different bird species, and not a damned one of them is an Ivory-billed Woodpecker. Your man Fielder doesn't know his ass from an Auklet. And there aren't any damn Auklets in this swamp either, just in case you're wondering." Hopkins looked at his watch. "It's late, let's get back to camp."

Miles grabbed his arm.

"First, I want you to take me to the place where Fielder spotted the bird," said Miles. "It can't be far from here."

Hopkins gave it some thought. "Twenty … thirty minutes."

"Well? Let's go."

Hopkins hesitated, but then relented and walked back to the wheel to start the engine. At first, he worked the skiff deliberately through the narrow rivulets, but after reaching a larger channel, he applied the throttle generously. The skiff bucked and then settled back into the water. The river turned in a northerly direction. Soon, the terrain and waterways seemed familiar to Miles, and he recognized the general area as a place he had visited as a child. Hopkins guided the boat into one of the narrow trails leading to Minnie's island. On approach, he angled the skiff toward the island's only landing site. As they approached the rickety wooden dock, Miles noticed several alligators sleeping in the mud underneath it.

"This is it," said Hopkins as they edged up to the dock. "This is where Fielder spotted Elvis – or claims he did." Hopkins shut off the engine, stepped onto the dock, and tied off the skiff. "Follow me, friend – bring the binoculars." He jumped from the dock to the shore and called back, "Watch your step, Miles. It's always dinnertime around here." He began to chuckle over his little joke.

Miles grabbed the binoculars that Hopkins had left near the wheel and hurried to catch up.

"Where are we heading, Hoppy?"

Hopkins was already striding away. Without bothering to look back, he shouted, "We're going to see something no other living soul has seen."

"What is it?" called Miles.

"Just be quiet and keep up."

The two men followed a narrow, meandering path around the island's edge through a thicket of cypress and bay trees. The trail soon petered out and was replaced by saw palmetto, pepperbush, and other shrubs. They had traveled several hundred yards through the overgrowth when Hopkins suddenly held up both hands, signaling for Miles to stop. He whispered over his shoulder. "Ivory-bill roost. Halfway up the tree." He pointed to the most massive hardwood in the area.

Miles fumbled for his binoculars in anticipation. He quickly sighted the oblong-shaped cavity about fifty feet off the ground.

"It's the right shape and size," said Miles.

THE ELVIS BIRD

"Damn right. Fielder may have found the bird, but I found the roost."

Could it be? The almighty throne of the Lord-God bird? Were they looking at the first Ivory-bill cavity discovered in over sixty years?

"If you think this is an Ivory-bill roost, then why are you so discouraged about the search?" asked Miles.

"I come here every few days. The bird that built that roost abandoned it months ago. If that bird *was* here, it's long gone. And a hole in a tree is just a hole – even if the Lord God himself made it."

"I'm not leaving," said Miles.

"Look, we installed an ARU out here months ago. If the bird comes back, we will record it."

"I don't care. I'm not leaving." Miles removed a rectangular canvas from his backpack and spread it on the ground for protection against the damp sod. He sat down.

Hopkins looked at his colleague and smiled. "I had the same initial reaction, buddy."

He reached for a metal flask in his back pocket, unscrewed the cap, and handed the flask to Miles, who took a swig and gave it back. Hopkins joined him on the canvas. The two men sat like supplicants at Holy Communion – not saying a word – each hoping the bird would suddenly appear – each taking alternate turns with the flask.

"Elvis is more likely to make an appearance than that bird," whispered Hopkins after half an hour. He grinned broadly at Miles and took another swig. They continued passing the flask back and forth until it was empty. In the west, the sky had turned ominously black, and in the late afternoon, the men heard the first low-pitched rumbles of an approaching thunderstorm. Storms were becoming more frequent as the weather turned warmer. A flash of light appeared, filling the sky with lightning and briefly illuminating the towering late-spring clouds. Hopkins stood up and stretched.

"Time to go. We can't get caught in this swamp during a storm."

Miles looked up at the cavity and thought of all the years he had invested in searching for the Ivory-billed Woodpecker, and the circuitous route that had led him to this particular tree. He wanted to stay and wait it out, despite the approaching storm. Ivory-billed Woodpeckers were known to return to their roosts at sundown. There was still some daylight left. The bird might appear at any minute. Miles could even spend the night.

"I know what you are thinking. But, let's come back when we're better prepared," said Hopkins.

Another flash of light filled the sky. Miles counted the seconds before the thunder.

Hopkins leaned over and offered a hand up. Reluctantly, Miles took it and then picked up the canvas and folded it into a square and stowed it in his backpack. The two men arrived back in camp just ahead of the storm.

10. TIA

...whilst here and there, as he approaches an opening, that proves merely a lake of black muddy water, his ear is assailed by the dismal croaking of innumerable frogs, the hissing of serpents, or the bellowing of alligators!

-James Audubon, *The Birds of America*

Doris was sitting patiently in the swing on the porch of her turn-of-the-century farmhouse as Miles pulled off the highway and parked the Lexus in the front yard, following his adventure with Hopkins in the swamp. The tin-roofed house was a wooden square, quartered into four spacious rooms, and bisected by a wide hallway that encouraged the breeze to enter and linger like a welcome visitor. All the rooms had high ceilings, with correspondingly high windows containing their original glass panes. The antique panes transmitted light imperfectly and had made Miles' childhood view of the outside world a wavy blur. As an afterthought, his family had grafted a small modern kitchen and bathroom onto the structure's backside. All in all, it was a plain, functional design. For as long as Miles could remember, his family had lived in the same house.

A BENJAMIN MILES MYSTERY

"I'm starved," he said, as he walked up the broad porch steps and hugged his mother.

"You had a call from the police," said Doris. She reached into her pocket, pulled out a slip of paper, and eyed it closely. "Sergeant Booker. That must be Fred Booker's boy. He left his phone number." She held out the paper, and Miles took it.

"I'll be along in a minute, Mom. I need to make this call."

"What's this about, son?"

Miles hadn't mentioned the shotgun recording to Doris.

"We can discuss it over dinner. Let me return his call first."

"You're not in trouble, are you, boy?"

Miles shook his head and smiled.

Doris stepped inside, and Miles took a seat on the porch swing. It creaked under his weight as he dialed the number.

"Folkston Police department. Sergeant Booker speaking." The familiar deep voice.

"This is Benjamin Miles, returning your call, Sergeant."

"Pro-fessor!"

"That's right. It's Professor Miles."

"I finally have something to report to you, Pro-fessor," said Booker.

Miles stopped the movement of the swing with his foot. "What's that?"

"The captain decided to send the recording to the state crime lab. I sent it myself just today."

THE ELVIS BIRD

Several days had passed since he had first called Booker. Miles decided not to voice his disappointment.

"When can we expect to hear something?"

"I wouldn't hold my breath. That could take weeks. Months, even."

"Someone was murdered, Sergeant. Can't you speed things along?"

"It's like I told you when you first called, nobody has been reported missing. It would be different if we had a body, but at this point, we don't even have a name to investigate."

"Will you call me when you hear something?"

"You'll be the first person on my call list, Pro-fessor."

###

Doris had prepared a large meal. Miles ate his dinner ravenously and sipped his coffee at the same wooden table where he had sat as a child. In Ithaca, after his wife had left him, he would usually pick up a take-out meal on the way home from the lab. It occurred to him now that it was a pleasure being cooked for by another soul – the transformative gift of a simple meal – a gift he had taken for granted when he was married.

When they finished dinner, Doris picked up his plate and silverware, along with her own, and was taking them to the sink when she stopped in mid-stride. Suddenly, she dropped the dishes on the floor, where they shattered. The silverware clattered and bounced into the corners of the room.

"Oh!" she said.

"What's wrong, Mom?"

Miles stood up from the table and reached for her hand, and put an arm around her. He led her back to a chair.

"I'm fine," she said after a few minutes.

"What happened?" he asked.

"Sinking spell. The doctor said I might experience some dizziness. It's nothing."

"What else did the doctor tell you that you're not telling me?"

She took his head into her hands, pulled him closer, and kissed his forehead.

"I've already told you, Kiddo. He said to take my medicine and go home."

Miles stared into her eyes. She had lovely blue eyes. Her wry smile suggested that if she *were* keeping a secret, she planned to keep it to herself. He considered pressuring her for more information, but in the end, he decided that trusting her was a better path. The incident passed without further mention.

After Doris had gone to bed that evening, Miles opened his laptop and waded into the e-mail that had accumulated in his inbox and deleted most of it on sight. He quickly found the object of his search:

THE ELVIS BIRD

Birdman,

I'm back home and feeling much better now. The fire destroyed the file containing the gunshot recording. No backup here.

You sent it to the police, right? So, you must have another copy? Has Elvis made an appearance, or are you still searching? More importantly, how's your mom?
Susan

Miles quickly typed:

Susan,

Mom's health has me worried, but she's much happier at home than in the hospital.

We can't find Elvis anywhere, but Hoppy did show me his home in the swamp. If you were here, I'd enjoy taking you out into the Okefenokee and spending some evenings together there. The Okefenokee has an otherworldly beauty that is quite lovely.
Miles

After reading it over, he highlighted the entire message and pressed *Delete* before starting over:

A BENJAMIN MILES MYSTERY

Susan,

Mom has me worried, but she's much happier here than in the hospital. I have a copy of the shorter, edited recording that I sent the police – it's in my email. Concerning the bird: Elvis has left the building (Not sure he was ever here).
Miles

When he had finished, he tapped the mouse, sending the message on its way. Then he crawled into bed, plumped up his pillow, and placed the computer on his chest. He tilted his head back and squinted as he typed *Transient ischemic attack*. There were 938,057 hits on Google. He selected the first one:

TIA's are early warning signs of stroke and have many possible causes. Treatment might include aspirin or anticoagulants. Blood pressure medication might also be indicated.

Prognosis: Unclear. Many strokes can be prevented with proper treatment.

After closing the laptop, he slid it under the bed, readjusted his pillow, and turned off the bedside lamp. He debated sending Susan a second e-mail, but in the end, he resisted. What else would he say? Tomorrow he would question Hopkins about the recording.

It was a fitful night's sleep.

11. Bird Glue

Would that I could give you an idea of the sultry pestiferous atmosphere that nearly suffocates the intruder during the meridian heat of our dogdays, in those gloomy and horrible swamps!
                    -James Audubon, *The Birds of America*

Early the next morning, Miles rose expectantly for a quick breakfast with Doris before driving straight to the campsite. He parked the Lexus among the red and white university vehicles. As he set off for the main tent, he noticed that Hopkins' truck wasn't among them. He soon found the daily work schedule posted conveniently beside the coffee maker at the edge of the tent, and as he started to pour himself a cup, someone tapped him on the shoulder.

"You're with me today."

He turned to find Bert Williams standing there, hand extended. Williams was a blond, heavyset man with a broad smile and a ready laugh. He was a mid-westerner, an engineer who had stumbled into ornithology by accident. After completing an EE degree at the University of Illinois, Williams had taken a job at a California electronics company that built GPS systems for cars. Miles had recruited him to work on the lab's avian migration projects.

Miles took his hand. "Where's Hopkins?" he asked.

"He posted the schedule and announced he was taking the day off. He said he'll be back tomorrow."

"Where did he go?"

"Didn't say."

Odd.

"I didn't know you were assigned to this project," said Miles.

"Fitz sent me down last week." Williams proudly held up a miniature device between his fingers like a kid showing off a prized marble. "We're testing these." He was holding a plastic box full of the tiny components in his other hand. "It's my latest GPS transmitter. Light enough for a canary. I'm itching to try them out, and I need help gluing some birds this afternoon. Hopkins appointed you."

"I'm your glue man?"

"I could use you. All the graduate students returned home weeks ago."

Miles had wanted to question Hopkins about the recording today. He also needed to make an inventory of the audio material that was available on the expedition's computers. With luck, they could reconstruct the database that had been housed in his now defunct lab. With Hopkins absent, that would have to wait. At least the congenial Williams would be a pleasant companion for the day.

"Where are we going?" asked Miles.

"Pine Island – it's on the western edge of the reserve. Yesterday, I set up some mesh traps there."

THE ELVIS BIRD

After selecting an available skiff, the men loaded Williams' electronic equipment – computers, transmitters, receivers, antennae, and a drone – into the stern of the boat along with several kit bags stacked on top of the pile. The equipment filled the stern with just enough room left for one person to sit and work. Miles offered to pilot the skiff so Bert could test out each transmitter one last time, before deploying them in the field.

The route to Pine Island was challenging and required Miles to maneuver through a collection of narrow passages and runs. The main canals in the Okefenokee are ten-feet deep and filled with peat – up to fifteen-feet in places – the result of plant decay over the past six thousand years. But smaller passages are often shallow and filled with cypress knees – the remnants of ancient logging operations. During one leg of the trip, Miles carelessly let the skiff drift too near the edge of a deep channel. When he turned sharply to avoid hitting the bank, an encroaching tree limb drifted across the stern. Bert began to yell, and Miles turned to see what the commotion was.

A limb had snagged Bert's compression bag, and now it sat perched on the gunwale, partly supported by the branch. The bag teetered precariously as the boat rocked gently in the water. Bert lunged for the bag, but clumsily moved the limb, and the bag fell into the water. It quickly sank to the bottom.

"What was in the bag?" asked Miles.

"Some clothes," said Bert. "And my lunch," he added as an afterthought.

They spent the next half hour trying to recover the bag with a long wooden pole used to maneuver the skiff in tight spots before giving up..

"This swamp keeps its secrets, Bert. Back in the fifties, a navy bomber crashed in the swamp and they never found a trace of it. It simply disappeared."

"But, I just bought a new rain coat," said Bert, staring sadly into the murky depths.

They arrived at Pine Island mid-morning, and Bert began to move some of his equipment into the bow. When Miles had finished tying off the boat, Bert walked back to the stern and offered him a handful of transmitters. "Put these tags in your pocket," said Bert, "And bring the glue. It's in there." He pointed to a red box beside Miles' foot. "My grad students sometimes forget the glue."

Miles leaned over, opened the box, and began to poke around as Bert watched.

"I'm curious," said Miles. "Why were your graduate students sent home early? Didn't you need their help? I thought you had an on-going research project with several of them."

"I did – and it was a damned inconvenient time for them to leave. Right in the middle of the week, too – kind of strange."

Miles spotted the bottle of glue, put it in his pocket.
"When was that?"

THE ELVIS BIRD

"Must have been three weeks ago. I complained to Hopkins, but he said he didn't have a choice - Fitz made the decision. When I pressed him on it, he said Fitz had given up hope of ever finding Elvis, and that he needed to cut costs."

"How much does it cost to fund a few graduate students for a few extra weeks?"

Bert shook his head and shrugged.

They spent the rest of the afternoon tagging a few Prothonotary Warblers and Eastern Meadowlarks that had become entangled in Bert's mist nets the night before. The yellow warblers looked brilliant against the dark green foliage of the swamp. Each bird called out plaintively as Bert removed it from the net – *wheat, wheat, wheat, wheat, wheat.* After extracting a bird, he held it gently in both hands, exposing its scapular region, and Miles glued one of the transmitters on with the epoxy.

Each transmitter weighed less than three grams and generated information describing the bird's position and activity to a receiver back in the boat. After a few hours without movement, the transmitter would boost its signal until it lost power. Depending on the bird's location, the signals could be detected by a hand-held antenna or a remotely controlled drone. The transmitters were too light to affect the bird's flight and were designed to fall off after a few months.

After releasing all the birds, the two men returned to the boat. In the bow, Bert opened the arms of an antenna, and mounted it on the hull. He switched a receiver on and opened his computer.

"Let's follow the warblers," he called out to Miles. He turned the laptop around so that Miles could see the red and yellow pixels that populated his computer screen.

"The warblers are in yellow," he said, pointing at the screen. "If we lose sight of them, I'll send up the drone."

Several hours later, the two men had tracked a contingent of warblers into the edges of the Chesser Prairie. It was a watery expanse of green lilies and grasses with stands of pine and shrubs defining its distant boundaries. Upon entering the plain, a pair of Florida Sand Hill Cranes began an eerie trumpet call.

"Garoo-a-a-a! Garoo-a-a-a!"

Bert spotted the pair dancing in a grassy area nearby. The four-foot-tall birds were hopping and flapping their wings. The naturally grayish birds appeared rust-colored – stained by the dark swampy water – their bald heads crowned in red. The agitated birds eyed the skiff warily.

"Garoo-a-a-a! Garoo-a-a-a!"

The two men stood transfixed by the calls as they floated past. Suddenly, each bird took flight, one after the other, heading straight for the boat. They flew directly overhead—so close the men could hear the sound of air flowing over their outstretched wings. They turned and watched as the pair disappeared over a distant line of trees. Miles slapped Bert on the back, and they both began to laugh at their good fortune.

THE ELVIS BIRD

It was late afternoon before they left the prairie, satisfied that Bert's devices were working successfully. The morning's weather report had mentioned a possible late evening shower, but conditions had worsened earlier than they had anticipated. It was Bert who first noticed the darkening sky.

"The wind's picking up," said Bert, who had taken the wheel. "Looks like another storm. It should blow over quickly, but you better check the radio."

The forecast was dicey, and the two men debated what to do. A storm had moved in from the west. They would need to head directly into it to get back to the western camp. Or, they could steer away from the storm and exit on the eastern side of the swamp. That would involve getting someone to drive sixty miles to pick them up. They finally decided to head back to the western camp ahead of the storm.

Miles took the wheel while Bert shouted directions using the computer's GPS. In a half-hour, the sky had darkened ominously, the storm had moved in, and it started to drizzle.

"Better grab your rain gear, Bert," suggested Miles.

Bert shook his head. "It was in my compression bag," he said, wistfully.

"Take mine," said Miles, feeling guilty about his part in losing Bert's bag. He started to unbutton his jacket.

Bert waved him off. "You keep it. I'm already soaked."

The drizzle quickly turned into a downpour. Everything in the boat was getting drenched as water began to collect on deck. Bert's laptop suddenly turned black as the computer failed in the driving rain.

The Okefenokee is a difficult place to navigate under benign conditions. It's a place where islands float and change position with the wind – a place where one wrong turn can send you in circles. Miles continued to steer into the storm, confident in his ability to navigate without a GPS. But when the waterway suddenly narrowed, hardly wider than the skiff, his confidence faded. They were quickly losing daylight, and the storm was growing nastier. He shut off the engine completely when it became apparent that they were lost. The boat drifted into a thicket of dense shrubs, where it stopped suddenly against the bank with a harsh thud.

Miles restarted the engine to pull away from the bank, but the skiff was stuck in the mud. Bert grabbed the wooden pole they had used earlier with the bag and walked forward. Standing in the bow, he began to push, trying to break the boat free from its entanglements, but the boat wouldn't budge.

"It's shallow enough here, I'll get out and disentangle the limbs," Bert declared, "Tell me if this has any effect." He stripped down to his shorts and looked cautiously around the entire boat before jumping into the waist-deep, black water. He was holding a machete. He waded along the edge of the boat, hacking through the limbs as he went. When he was directly in front of the bow, he announced, "It's stuck on a stump." He began to push the bow up and down, grunting as he strained. Gradually, the boat shifted position.

THE ELVIS BIRD

"I think it's working," shouted Miles.

Miles restarted the engine and applied the throttle, and the skiff broke free. It had moved backward a couple of yards in the channel when Bert began to yell. Miles killed the engine and ran forward.

"What's wrong?" he asked.

The big man was standing in a tangle of limbs. He held up his hand. "A damn snake. It was wrapped around a limb. I think it was a Copperhead. Help me up." Bert waded closer and reached up with his good hand.

Miles leaned over the side and pulled him out of the water. Bert shimmied into the skiff, rolling over the gunwale and onto the deck.

"It bit me on the finger. Right there." Bert pointed at the wound indignantly. "Damn, that hurts." Miles could see two tiny red punctures on Bert's index finger.

"Are you sure it was a Copperhead?"

"I didn't wait around for identification."

The two men debated what to do. Tourniquet? No tourniquet? Which was it? They couldn't remember.

"Just get me back to camp. It's not a very deep wound." Bert spoke calmly, but the finger had already started to swell, and Miles could tell he was in pain.

Miles eased the skiff backward down the narrow waterway. He was finally able to turn the boat around when the passage widened suddenly. After backtracking for half a mile, they turned onto a larger channel and spotted the lights of a distant boat. It turned out to be a dual-engine speedboat. When they drew alongside, a tall man wearing a wide-brimmed leather hat stood up in the bow. Miles idled the engine and strained to see the man's face in the shadows.

"You boys must be lost," the man suggested, stating the obvious. "That run you just came from is a dead-end."

"We need your help," said Miles, sounding slightly panicked. "My friend was bitten by a snake."

"Let's have a look see."

The man in the hat was wearing a rain slicker and produced a flashlight from the pocket. He aimed it at Bert, who was sitting on the deck in the stern. Bert held up his swollen hand.

"What kind of snake was it?" the man asked.

"Copperhead," said Bert.

"You'll live," the man said laconically.

"Can you give us directions out of here?" asked Miles. As he spoke, he could hear the desperation in his voice, and he tried hard to moderate it.

The man turned the flashlight on the equipment stacked in piles beside Bert. A look of realization came over him.

"I know who you people are," said the man. "You're with that university bunch. You're looking for that hoo-doo bird, aren't you?"

"That's right," said Miles, "We're with Cornell."

"Well, you've wandered out of the reserve. You're on my land now. Did you know that?"

"No. I told you, we're lost. Just give us directions back to our campsite and we'll leave."

THE ELVIS BIRD

"It's a damn waste of time and money is what that is," said the man in the hat. "That bird you're looking for disappeared fifty years ago. I've lived here all my life, and I've never seen one. I wish you people would just leave. You're bringing in tourists – causing trouble. It ain't right."

Miles stepped closer. "Just point us in the right direction, and we'll leave, Mister. Believe me. My friend needs medical attention." Miles was unashamed to plead now. There was an awkward silence as the man continued to look them over.

He finally nodded a direction. "Keep going straight up this creek. Follow your nose about a half-mile and look for a narrow stream off to the left. It'll take you back home. Just don't come back out here. Stay off my property."

Miles stepped back to the wheel. "What's your name, anyway?" asked Miles. He gave the engine some gas.

"Luther," the man shouted over the noise. "Luther Preston."

Miles shouted back, "I'm Benjamin Miles." The boat started to inch away.

A look of recognition came over Luther.

"I knew your daddy! Clayton Miles. He was an FBI man, right?"

Miles didn't wait to respond. He revved the engine, and the boat surged off downstream.

Bert took a seat beside the wheel as they were pulling away. "I've seen that guy before – at the camp. He came out one evening to talk with Hopkins. He was accompanied by a second guy – a young man, and they were both pretty angry.

I stuck around because I thought they were going to whip Hopkin's ass."

"Did they?"

"No. Lotta yelling, though. They eventually left."

"He's from an old Folkston family," said Miles, "Years ago they were bootleggers. Probably still are."

There was a sharp bend ahead in the stream, and Miles slowed the skiff and turned his head to take one last look back at Preston. A second, shorter silhouette had appeared beside him in the boat. In the rainy darkness, Miles couldn't recognize the second man.

The downpour settled into a steady drizzle by the time the two men found their way out of the swamp. The field staff had gathered together on the dock, nervously awaiting their return, and they began to clap and cheer when the skiff suddenly appeared in the distance.

To his discomfort, Miles spotted Doris standing in front of the entire group with her arms crossed over her chest. Hopkins had returned from his trip and was standing beside her, holding an umbrella over her head. Miles could see by the grin on his face that he was enjoying this. When the skiff was tied off, Hopkins handed the umbrella to Doris and jumped into the boat.

"I thought you two were going to be spending the night with the alligators," he said, just out of range of Doris' hearing. "Is this the kind of fieldwork you had in mind, buddy? No? Yo momma was worried."

"Don't make me kick your ass," said Miles.

Hopkins started chuckling.

"Where have you been?" asked Miles.

"None of your damn business."

"Why did you bring her out here?" Miles nodded at Doris.

"She insisted, and I never refuse a lady's request."

Miles shook his head.

Within minutes, someone had bandaged Bert's hand and was hurrying him away in a university van. Miles finished unloading Bert's equipment and stepped onto the dock where Doris was waiting patiently. He sidled up to her for a hug and recognized a long-forgotten parental look that made him feel twelve years old.

On the way home, her only comment was, "I like it much better when you work in the lab."

She was letting him off easy.

Miles checked his e-mail before turning in for the night:

Birdman,
 I made some progress on the voice algorithm today. Send me the Okefenokee data, if you have it, and I will search the recording for other voices. How's Doris?
Susan

12. Dead-end

The flight of this bird is graceful in the extreme, although seldom prolonged to more than a few hundred yards at a time, unless when it has to cross a large river, which it does in deep undulations, opening its wings at first to their full extent, and nearly closing them to renew the propelling impulse.

-James Audubon, *The Birds of America*

The next morning, Miles rose before dawn with a plan to visit his old friend Perry Fielder, before continuing on to the camp and a day's work in the swamp. He owed Perry a visit. Without his friend's tip, he wouldn't be in the Okefenokee chasing Ivory-bills. If there was time, he would play the edited version of the recording for the Admiral – it was available in the email on his phone. Maybe Perry could throw some light on it?

The Admiral's business was located in a pine forest on the edge of town. *Okefenokee Outfitters* was an adventure business that occupied an old filling station and trading post. In its heyday before the interstates, the highway that ran through Folkston had been a major thoroughfare, and the store had been a tourist stop for vacationers heading south to Florida's beaches. The interstate had ended all that. Over the years, the filling station had been repurposed several times. When the Admiral bought it, he covered the exterior in gray cypress, added some brightly-colored awnings, and installed some vintage gas pumps out front. He invested in a couple of expensive-looking speed boats, a narrow tourist barge, and several rows of trailers stacked three-high with kayaks, canoes, and inner tubes. There was even a tour bus. The place had a trendy, outdoor feel. Miles found the owner standing in the rear of the store. Perry Fielder looked up from a US geographical map, removed his glasses, and tossed them on the counter.

"Dr. Audubon! You should have warned me you were coming in today. I would have prepared you some breakfast."

Fielder stepped around the counter, and the pair embraced, patting each other on the back like bears. Perry was tall and lean, with a mane of thick, black hair. He had the deep tan and tough hide of an outdoorsman, and a permanent look of bemusement on his face as if he had just heard a good joke. His clothes were a combination of Marlin Perkins and Ralph Lauren.

"I didn't expect to see you here today – given the news," said the Admiral.

"What are you talking about?" Miles didn't like the concerned expression on the Admiral's face. His friend seemed to hesitate, as if he were debating what to say next.

"Why don't you take a seat on the porch. I'll get us some coffee - and the paper." He pointed Miles to a door behind the counter and disappeared without further comment.

THE ELVIS BIRD

The wooden porch that stretched across the back of the building was shaded from the sun by a cloth awning that sheltered a couple of picnic tables. The porch overlooked a swampy clearing, and beyond that, a pine forest. A brackish creek meandered away from the building and disappeared in the distant marsh grass. The stream was hardly wide enough for a boat to turn around, but it provided the Admiral with convenient access to the swamp. On the far side of the creek, a small log floated among the reeds. The log occasionally opened its eyes and changed positions.

The Admiral finally appeared on the porch balancing the coffee on a tray which he placed on the table. There was a newspaper under his arm. He filled two cups from a darkly stained carafe before sitting down, and then unfolded the paper and laid it in front of Miles before taking his seat.

"There's a full-page article about Cornell ornithology in today's Atlanta Journal. It's all about Ivory-billed Woodpeckers in the Okefenokee," he said. "I'll warn you - I don't remember seeing your name in this piece."

Miles leaned forward to get a better look. He opened the paper and quickly flipped past the news and editorials, he stopped on the science section. At the top of the page, was a picture of Jim Hopkins standing in front of one of the university's skiffs - he was smiling proudly. The headline read *Cornell Scientist Rediscovers Extinct Bird*.

What the hell? Miles scanned the feature story which described Cornell's efforts to find the Ivory-billed Woodpecker in the Okefenokee Wildlife Refuge. The article announced the bird had been found. His anger grew as he continued to read.

Hopkins had betrayed him completely.

Miles was too livid to speak. The consequences of the report were chilling. The newspaper publicity would bring groups of curiosity seekers and amateur birders to the Okefenokee, making it even harder for the team to finish their work. Or was their work here already finished? Critics would begin to demand definitive evidence that Ivory-bills had managed to survive in the reserve. What had changed? And why was Hopkins taking all of the credit?

"You didn't know about this?" asked Perry, incredulously.

Miles shook his head.

"I'm sorry, Miles. I know this is a blow. I'm already getting calls from tour groups out of Atlanta that want to book Ivory-bill tours. This is going to send my business through the roof."

Miles continued reading - a side-bar described the Ivory-billed Woodpecker and recounted its unfortunate history. It explained how the loss of old-wood forests throughout the South in the twenties had driven the bird to near extinction. But it was the main article which had Miles reeling. He looked it over again, more closely this time. The detailed article recounted Cornell's research effort in the Okefenokee over the previous winter months. It described how Professor James Hopkins, the Cornell field director, had discovered the bird following a tip from Perry Fielder – a local tour group operator. There was even a blurry picture of a single Ivory-bill in flight. Miles had never seen the photograph. He examined it closely and had to admit it did resemble an Ivory-bill. To Hopkins' credit (or perhaps he thought Miles would throttle him), the article quoted Hopkins as saying that neither his sighting nor the photograph was definitive evidence of the bird's existence. "More research is needed," admonished Professor Hopkins, "Cornell isn't prepared to announce at this time that the bird has survived."

But the rest of the article sounded much more optimistic about the rediscovery of the Ivory-billed Woodpecker. There were even a few quotes from ornithologists at other prestigious schools who described the bird in the picture as an Ivory-bill.

"I can't believe Hopkins gave this interview," said Miles as he closed the paper. "He never mentioned a word of this to me – or the photograph." Why had Hopkins left him in the dark? And what about Fitzsimmons? What role did he play in this whole sordid mess?

"At least they spelled my name correctly," said the Admiral cheerily. "And they mentioned the business."

Miles picked up the paper. "Can I keep this?" he asked.

"Sure. I'm sorry they left you out of the article. Damn newspapers. I was hoping you and I were going to be the ones to find that bird."

Miles stuck the newspaper under his arm. "I'll need you take me out in the reserve later this week. I want you to show me exactly where you first spotted Elvis."

A BENJAMIN MILES MYSTERY

###

Miles sat in his car fuming for several minutes. He gripped the steering wheel tightly while the engine continued to idle, and he formulated a simple plan: He would confront Hopkins as soon as possible and demand answers – after punching him in the face. Suddenly, he took his foot off the brake, stepped hard on the accelerator, and jerked the steering wheel sharply to the right. The Lexus spun, leaving a doughnut-shaped impression in the dirt and kicking up gravel as he sped away.

When Miles arrived in the campsite, he found it deserted with only a few trucks parked near the university tents. He got out of the car and walked into the main tent. Bert Williams was sitting alone at a table, surrounded by boxes of tiny electronic components.

"Where's Hopkins?" asked Miles.

"He left."

"Where did he go?"

"Didn't say."

"You saw the news?" Miles held up the newspaper.

Bert nodded.

"Where is everyone?"

"Hopkins gave everyone the day off."

13. Eat Your Cake

The transit from one tree to another, even should the distance be as much as a hundred yards, is performed by a single sweep, and the bird appears as if merely swinging itself from the top of the one tree to that of the other, forming an elegantly curved line.
                                -James Audubon, *The Birds of America*

"Finish your dinner," said Doris.

Miles continued to stare over his plate at the computer resting on the kitchen table. The news on the internet was worse than he had anticipated. It seemed that every major newspaper in the country had picked up The *Atlanta Journal* article. The *New York Times* gave the story twice as many inches as the Journal and even featured an extensive interview with Jim Hopkins that described the methods the team had employed to track Ivory-bills. Adjacent to the Times' black and white photograph of the bird in flight was Hopkin's photo with a caption that described his thrill at making the discovery. The article related the long, sad history of the Ivory-bill. It featured some old images of Tanner and Allen from the thirties and forties on the expedition that documented the last Ivory-bills ever seen in Arkansas. There was even a quote from Georgia's senior senator calling for federal money to protect the newly discovered bird.

"I don't understand all the fuss," said Doris. She was standing at the kitchen counter. "You said yourself that everyone mistakes Ivory-bills for Pileated Woodpeckers – and there's still plenty of those birds everywhere you go."

"It's a survivor, Mom - like you. Everyone thought it was extinct. We destroyed its habitat, we harvested every tree it needed for survival, but somehow, in spite of our worst efforts, this bird made it through. It is inspiring, don't you think?"

"Don't compare your mother to a woodpecker, Benjamin."

"Hopkins had no business releasing this story to the papers," said Miles. "Even if he did find it."

Doris affected a Jewish-mother accent to respond. "So, it's in the papers, what difference does that make?" She slipped Miles a second wedge of chocolate cake onto a saucer next to his coffee. "Eat your cake," she said, continuing with the accent.

"These articles will bring curiosity-seekers," he said. He adjusted his plate and picked up his fork. "Thank goodness the expedition is almost over. It's a bad idea to have tourists and amateur birders flooding into the Okefenokee while you're tracking a bird."

"Sounds like you've already found it – if you can believe the newspapers."

THE ELVIS BIRD

"That's the point. *I* didn't find it," he said moodily. He cut the slice of cake into three equal parts and forked the first one into his mouth.

"Well, your group found it, Honey. And you're part of the group."

"It should've been me, Mom. I can't believe that bird was right here in my backyard all along. Now Hopkins is the one getting all the credit."

"It was your idea to come here, wasn't it?"

"The Admiral was the first to suggest it. He should get the credit."

"But you convinced Cornell to investigate, Honey. And you directed them where to search. Without you, they wouldn't be here, so there you go."

Miles gave up the argument.

Doris put her hand on top of Miles' head and gave it a vigorous rub.

"I'm not fifteen, Mom."

"Your Dad would have said, 'If your head is wax, don't walk in the sun.'"

"What does that have to do with anything?"

"Nothing, I suppose. He just liked saying it whenever something went wrong. It always made him laugh."

"That reminds me," said Miles, "the night Bert and I got lost in the swamp, we ran into Luther Preston. He said that he knew Dad years ago."

"Yes, they were acquainted."

Miles stabbed the second piece of cake.

"What can you tell me about Luther Preston?"

"I know that he helped you and Bert get out of the swamp safely, and I'm thankful for that."

"What else do you know?"

"He's an old-timer around here. His family has been here since the twenties. They made their money in lumber and running liquor into Jacksonville. Maybe they dabbled in some other, shadier things, too. That family always liked to live in the shadows."

Miles' phone birds began to chirp and the display began to flash. He glanced down at the name. "I'll take this outside, Mom.".

Doris raised her hands in the air, still using the Jewish mother accent. "What? Secrets from your mother?"

Miles ignored her and headed for the porch.

"How are you, Susan?" His voice modulated a bit as he tried to tamp down the southern drawl that had oozed back into his speech over the last few days.

"I have bad news, Miles. Fitzsimmons asked me to call you."

"I've already seen it," he said resignedly.

"You have?"

"It's in every paper. Hopkins must have given interviews to all comers."

"I'm not calling about Ivory-bills, Miles."

"Why are you calling then?"

"It's about one of our graduate students. Lionel Ames. The South African."

THE ELVIS BIRD

Miles suddenly understood. He needed to sit down and took a seat in a wooden rocking chair beside the swing.

"What about him?"

"His parents phoned the school to say that he's gone missing. They've been making inquiries. He never made it back to Johannesburg after the semester ended."

Miles could see the young man in his mind's eye: handsome, tall, ambitious, funny. The gravity of the news registered in Miles' gut. Lionel Ames had been one of the first graduate students to sign up for the Okefenokee expedition. And now, he was missing.

"He was supposed to return home a week ago," she continued.

"Oh, no," was all Miles could muster.

"Don't jump to conclusions. He may still turn up. I hope he will. His parents say he was an adventurous sort. Perhaps he's gone walkabout."

"Does Hopkins know about this?"

"Fitzsimmons called him earlier and gave him the news."

Why didn't Fitzsimmons call him as well?

"Miles?"

"Yes?"

"What should we do?"

How do you fix a murder?

"I'll contact the police on this end. Has Fitzsimmons notified the New York state police?"

"I don't know."

"Make sure he calls them. If Fitzsimmons has any questions, tell him to call me"

"I'll do it." She added, "Be safe."

Miles started to say "I miss you." But Susan had already clicked off.

He walked back inside and sat down at the kitchen table. Was that Lionel's voice he had heard in the lab? It must have been. Before he could speculate further, Doris reached across the table, snatched the last piece of cake, and popped it into her mouth.

"You've had enough," she mumbled.

14. Elvis Himself

It never utters any sound whilst on wing, unless during the love-season; but at all other times, no sooner has this bird alighted than its remarkable voice is heard, at almost every leap which it makes, whilst ascending against the upper parts of the trunk of a tree, or its highest branches.

-James Audubon, *The Birds of America*

"You say this student was working here with the university, and he left Folkston on April 5. Is that right?" Pete Booker's bulging arms filled the short, tan sleeves of his starched deputy sheriff's uniform. Miles fidgeted in the wooden chair and wondered why he felt vaguely guilty answering the officer's questions.

"That's right."

"And you say he was scheduled to return home to Johannesburg – that's South Africa – on the tenth?"

Miles nodded.

Booker typed out the words with two large fingers, hunt-and-peck style on the dated computer. The tip of his tongue was slightly visible as he worked the keys.

"Is that two n's in Johannesburg?"

Miles nodded patiently, and Booker tapped twice on the keyboard, pleased with himself.

A BENJAMIN MILES MYSTERY

The office's cinderblock walls shone egg-shell white. An army surplus desk occupied one wall and filled half of the tiny room. Three government-issue office chairs sat facing the desk, their gray metal armrests almost touching. After a tedious hour with Sergeant Booker, Miles was anxious to leave.

"Ok!" said Booker finally looking up at Miles, earnestly. "That's about it. I'll pass this on to the captain and he'll contact the GBI. For something this big we'll need their help."

Miles reached across the desk to shake the officer's hand and immediately regretted it. The vise grip of Booker's massive paw was difficult to ignore.

"Thanks for comin' in Pro-fessor. I'll be in touch."

Evidently, Booker was oblivious to irony.

It was mid-afternoon when Miles finally walked out of the station looking for a stiff drink to clear his head of the afternoon's sad business. He decided to scout out the town for a bar, and after walking a few blocks without spotting one, he turned onto Main Street. The street had started life as a wide, ambitious thoroughfare. It began at the courthouse and ran west for a few blocks, before running out of energy and reverting back to a simple two-lane state road.

The old buildings of his childhood were still standing, but the businesses that once defined the town had been re-invented years ago. A Thai take-out restaurant was now a fixture in the old feed store. A tattoo shop occupied the old

THE ELVIS BIRD

pharmacy. No one on the street was in a hurry. The town's citizens seemed to be waiting out the heat indoors, and the only place that seemed to be doing much business was a restaurant on the corner. Miles decided to give it a try.

The sign outside said *Okefenokee Restaurant* and featured a hand-painted alligator with an incongruous, happy grin. Miles shaded his eyes with one hand and peeked in the front window. The restaurant was open and serving a handful of customers. He chose a booth at the front. The air conditioning chilled his brow as he sat down and reached across the table for an acetate-covered menu. A bubbly waitress appeared with a pad and a pencil in hand.

"What-cha want, Honey?" She looked at him expectantly.

He guessed they were about the same age. "You remind me of someone," said Miles. "Someone in the movies."

"Well, I've heard that line a few times, Sweetie, but what the heck? I'll bite. Who do I remind you of?"

She had a sweet smile and tight curls. Miles didn't want to say that she reminded him of Harpo Marx.

"My mistake," he said, "Just bring me some sweet tea."

"What's your name?"

"Miles. Benjamin Miles."

He thought the restaurant had a familiar feel, and after examining the room more closely, he recalled his family dining there on Saturday nights when he was a kid. His father had commented on the cedar panels that had once lined the walls. The timbers were from trees hauled out of the Okefenokee in the nineteen-twenties. The boards had been cut and planed in Hebardsville, a sawmill city near Waycross that thrived briefly and then disappeared overnight with the sudden realization that all the hardwood had been hauled out of the swamp.

The waitress reappeared with his tea and sat it on the table. She leaned in close and put a hand on his shoulder. "Say, are you Doris Miles' son?"

"That's right," said Miles. He was surprised she had made the connection. He hadn't been home in years.

"I thought so. She's such a sweet lady. She eats lunch here every week. She often talks about you."

When did his mother have an opportunity to bring him up as a topic of conversation?

"What's your name?" asked Miles.

"Velvia," she said before disappearing back into the kitchen.

Miles sipped his tea. Living in Ithaca for years had changed his sense of taste. It was much too sweet.

Miles glanced around the room. What was he doing here? How had his personal trajectory brought him back to Folkston? If he hadn't grown up on the edge of a swamp, he probably wouldn't be an ornithologist today. If industrialists hadn't deforested the South at the turn of the last century, the Ivory-billed Woodpecker would never have vanished. He wouldn't be sipping overly sweet tea in a half-empty restaurant in a sleepy southern town. He wouldn't have suggested searching for an extinct bird in the Okefenokee. Most importantly, Lionel Ames would not be missing.

Miles reached for his phone. He tried calling Hopkin's cell, but there was no answer.

###

Early the next morning, Miles waited impatiently on the dock for Hopkins to make an appearance. His colleague was late arriving, and Miles grew more irritable as the minutes ticked by. The morning air was still cool, and the humidity hadn't begun to climb just yet – a brief respite before the day's heat. Miles watched impatiently as the university skiffs puttered away into the reserve for the day's work. The still, black water beneath the dock transformed the channel into a natural mirror that perfectly reflected the trees and the sky. The mirror image changed to a watery blur each time a boat left camp.

Hopkins' truck finally appeared in the distant field, and Miles waved to get his attention. Impatient, Miles leaped off the dock and headed over for the confrontation.

"I'm going to kick your ass," he called out as Hopkins stepped out of the truck. Hopkins instinctively grabbed a duffle bag from the flatbed and held it up for protection as Miles walked up.

"Calm down," said Hopkins. "What's your problem?"

"You said that no one in this camp was missing. You lied to me, and now Lionel Ames may be dead."

"I didn't lie, Miles. He left camp with all the other students."

"The kid never made it home."

"He's not a kid – he's an adult."

"It happened on your watch."

Hopkins tried to step around Miles, but Miles pushed him backward into the truck.

"What the hell? Don't touch me, Miles."

"It happened on your watch, Hoppy."

Hopkins seemed to be weighing his options.

"I'm going to get some coffee now. Why don't you come with me, and we can discuss this like two adults?" He stepped around Miles and headed for the main tent.

"That's all you have to say?" called Miles, following closely behind.

Hopkins stopped abruptly and turned to face him. "Look, all I know is that Lionel packed his bags with the rest of the students and left camp a couple of weeks ago. Maybe he decided to do some exploring before he left the country? Who knows? I'm sure he'll turn up."

Hopkins headed off again with Miles on his heels.

"We need to search the swamp," said Miles. "It was Lionel that we heard on that recording."

Hopkins stopped at the entrance to the tent. "You don't know that. Forget the damned recording, will you? I told you, Lionel left camp weeks ago. If he's missing, let the police find him."

"I'm going out today to look for that boy," Miles insisted.

"Suit yourself. There are six hundred square miles of swamp out there. Have at it. As for me, I'm going out to look for a bird. If you had any sense, you would, too. Or have you forgotten that our asses are in a sling? Now that the story has broken, we've got to deliver the goods."

Hopkins started to enter the tent, but Miles grabbed his shoulder and held on tight.

"That's the other thing we need to discuss," said Miles. "According to the *Atlanta Journal*, you've already discovered an Ivory-bill in this reserve. We all signed a contract to keep this project a secret. Just what the hell is going on with you?"

Hopkins held up his hands as if to stem the inevitable storm.

"Let's go sit down. Quit yelling at me. Let's talk like reasonable men."

Hopkins stepped inside the tent and Miles followed. They sat down at the nearest table.

"Look, I can explain," said Hopkins.

"Good. I want to hear this."

"Something happened a few weeks ago."

"Yes, it did – you photographed an Ivory-billed Woodpecker and forgot to tell any of your colleagues."

"That's not how it happened."

"I'm listening."

"One morning, I decided to do my daily check on that nest cavity – the one I showed you on Minnie's Island. I've been searching for the bird that made that roost hole for months. The thing is, I spotted an Ivory-bill – on the edge of the Sapling prairie. I couldn't believe it. I tried to take a photograph, but the bird flew away."

"I'm still waiting for an explanation."

Hopkins leaned forward in the chair. "It's been pretty depressing here lately, buddy. You must know that. We sent the students away weeks ago without finding anything substantial. Fitzsimmons made me do that. The entire project looked like a bust."

Miles looked on stoically.

"I went back to the Sapling prairie the next morning, and I spotted the bird again. It was flying straight as an arrow over the prairie. I tracked it for several days. It was *exactly* like Tanner described. Wild-looking yellow eyes, and a beautiful white bill – not a yellow one like the specimens back at the lab. I finally managed to take a picture of it. The one you saw in the newspaper."

"The one you published in the *Atlanta Journal* without consulting anyone."

"It wasn't like that, Miles."

"Then tell me how it was, Hoppy."

"After so much work, so many months, I didn't want to take any chances with the photo. So, I e-mailed it to myself. I used my Cornell address, and I sent another to my private address as well. The evidence was too important to risk losing."

"That doesn't explain why you didn't tell anyone about it – or why you went public with the story."

"I'm coming to that," he said, irritated. "The day after I e-mailed the photo, I got a call from a reporter – a stringer out of Atlanta. He said he had evidence that Cornell had discovered an Ivory-billed Woodpecker in the Okefenokee. He wanted the exclusive story. I denied it at first, but he threatened to publish the story immediately if I didn't talk to him. He had details, Miles. I agreed to meet with him, because I wasn't sure what other information the guy might have."

"You're telling me you met with a reporter who called you out of the blue? It didn't occur to you that he might be playing you?"

"I couldn't ignore him, Miles. When I met with him in Atlanta, he had a copy of the damn picture. I don't know how he got hold of it. Maybe I got hacked."

"This doesn't make any sense."

Hopkins wiped his mouth with the back of his hand.

"I tried to make a deal with him. I told him I'd give him an exclusive interview if he would just give us some time before publishing the story. I tried to delay him, Miles, but he insisted on conducting the interview immediately. He promised not to publish the story before the expedition was complete. I was just as surprised as you when the article appeared in the Atlanta Journal."

"I can't believe you met with a reporter."

"At least he quoted me accurately – he said the picture of the bird wasn't considered definitive evidence that the bird had survived. He said that Cornell wasn't announcing the bird's rediscovery until we had more proof. I was trying to keep things as quiet as possible."

"That's cold comfort," said Miles.

"We'll be able to prove the bird exists now. I've seen it. It exists, and we'll get better photographic evidence, you and I. No one will be able to question the bird's existence again."

"You knew this was a bombshell. Why didn't you tell anyone?"

"I did, Miles. I called Fitzsimmons before doing the interview. It was Fitz who approved the whole arrangement."

15. Punch in the Stomach

Its notes are clear, loud, and yet rather plaintive. They are heard at a considerable distance, perhaps half a mile, and resemble the false high note of a clarionet. They are usually repeated three times in succession, and may be represented by the monosyllable pait, pait, pait.
  -James Audubon, *The Birds of America*

That evening after meeting with Hopkins, Miles returned home to find a Folkston sheriff's car in his mother's driveway. His first thought was that she had she suffered another stroke. But as he walked up onto the front porch, he was relieved to find Sergeant Booker and Doris sitting together in the swing, drinking tea. The porch's supporting rafter creaked under the weight of the heavy man as he gently pushed the swing back and forth with his foot. Booker had a dessert plate balanced on his knee.

"Evening Pro-fessor!" said Booker. He forked a large piece of the cake into his mouth.

"Call him Benjamin, Pete!" Doris said happily. She patted Booker's huge arm.

Between bites, Booker said, "This is a professional call … Miss Doris … I better keep it formal."

A BENJAMIN MILES MYSTERY

Miles approached Booker and was about to shake his hand before he thought better of it. "Here let me take that," said Miles, reaching for Booker's empty plate. "Just call me Miles, Sergeant, like everyone else."

"All right, I'll do that Pro-fessor Miles. I came out here to talk with you this evening."

"What's on your mind, Sergeant?"

"I got a call today from an Ithaca police detective who's investigating the disappearance of Lionel Ames. He wanted me to ask you a couple of questions. Would you mind?"

Doris looked concerned. "Is Lionel Ames the missing student?"

"Yes, Ma'am," said Booker.

"Have you got a picture of him, Pete?" asked Doris. "Maybe I've seen him in town."

"No ma'am, but I can get you one."

Miles took a seat in a wooden rocking chair beside the swing.

"How can I help you, Sergeant?" asked Miles.

"This Ithaca detective did some investigating at the university – email, mostly, but he uncovered some unusual correspondence between Lionel Ames and another Cornell professor. He thought you might be able to shed some light on it."

"I'll try."

"Good. Good. Do you happen to know a professor Swail? A Dr. Susan Swail?"

What the hell? Miles' pulse quickened.

THE ELVIS BIRD

"Yes. I know Dr. Swail."

"And what's your relationship with Dr. Swail?"

Good question, thought Miles.

"She recently joined out department – she works directly with me."

"I see," said Booker. He nodded, letting that fact sink in before removing a small spiral pad and a pencil stub from his front pocket. He took a minute to jot down a note.

"And do you know if there's a romantic relationship between Susan Swail and Lionel Ames?".

Double hell.

"I don't think so. I mean, I really don't know." Miles wanted to add, "I hope not."

"You never saw Dr. Swail and Lionel Ames together at Cornell?"

"No. She just started working at the lab. She's on the faculty. Lionel is one of our students. He entered the graduate program last year and joined the Okefenokee expedition six months ago. Lionel was already working here on the expedition by the time Professor Swail arrived on campus. I don't see how they could be connected."

"I see."

Booker made a second note and put the notepad and pencil back in his pocket. The swing groaned when he stood up.

"Well, it's probably nothing," he said. "Most of these leads don't go anywhere. Thanks for your time Pro-fessor

Miles. And thank you, Miss Doris, for the cake. Ya'll folks have a good evening."

Miles helped his mother up from the swing. They stood side-by-side at the top of the steps and watched as Booker drove away in the cruiser. Doris put her arm around Miles' waist and pulled him closer.

"So, Benjamin, tell me more about this Susan Swail woman. It doesn't take a detective to see that you're interested."

16. Something Dead

The hole is, I believe, always made in the trunk of a live tree, generally an ash or a hagberry, and is at a great height.
-James Audubon, *The Birds of America*

The article in the *Atlanta Journal* had done its work. Over the next week, TV crews began showing up in Folkston, and CBS did an Ivory-bill segment on the Sunday Morning program. Even NPR's Morning Edition featured the story, playing the old Tanner tapes of the Ivory-bill's kent call and distinctive double-knock.

Overnight, opportunistic capitalists hauled in trailers and erected garish billboards out on the Okefenokee highway: *SEE THE MISSING BIRD! ELVIS BIRD LIVES!* and *IVORY-BILL SOUVENIRS*. Two-story billboards were erected around the trailers, making them appear as enormous buildings to passing motorists, and pulling in unsuspecting travelers with offers of free orange juice, cheap pecan rolls, and plush-toy birds that resembled crazed Woody Woodpeckers. Even Miles purchased one.

There were changes in town as well. Double-decker tour buses, filled with day-tourists from Atlanta, Savannah, and Jacksonville, began arriving in downtown Folkston. Hungry hordes of visitors descended on the Okefenokee Restaurant, filling it with patrons and running off the regular customers. Locals took their lunch business over to the Cluckin' Chicken in neighboring Andrews to avoid the crowds.

Just as he had predicted, the adventure business picked up considerably for Perry Fielder. Okefenokee Outfitters began operating seven days a week with five tour boats and a selection of half-day and full-day tours into the swamp.

The refuge was soon overrun with visitors, as tour boats taxied excited sightseers up and down the Suwannee Canal from early morning until sunset. The mirrored waterways became clogged with marine traffic. At the public entrances to the reserve, miles of cypress boardwalks were alive with the noise of gleeful, ignorant families hooting and pointing at every bird they spied as they trekked along together in a happy, familial, obliviousness.

Jim Hopkins began hosting press conferences each morning and evening under the main tent at the Cornell encampment. He held forth to a crowd of reporters from a podium emblazoned with the university seal that had been hurriedly shipped down from Ithaca.

Every few days, Miles consulted with Hopkins in person, and with Fitzsimmons by phone, about a strategy for using their remaining time in the field. Given the promising evidence of the single photograph that Hopkins had made, along with his eyewitness account, Fitzsimmons opted to extend the expedition three more weeks. Everyone was hopeful that staying longer would lead to success in finding

THE ELVIS BIRD

other Ivory-bills. But it was now late spring, and the swamp was greening up quickly in the warm afternoons. Miles knew that sighting the bird would soon become problematic in the dense foliage of a primordial swamp. Ivory-bill hunting is a sport best pursued when trees are bare.

Days passed quickly with no further sightings. The bird that Hopkins had tracked and photographed had simply disappeared. The team set up several more remote video cameras to watch the nest hole that Hoppy had discovered. They had it surrounded. All in vain. The bird never returned to the giant Bay tree. Still, the single photograph that Hopkins had made inspired them to keep searching. They continued making observations and diligently logged sightings of the birds they were spotting each day. But each evening, when all the reporters gathered together under the main tent to hear the latest news on the search, Hopkins would reluctantly report their failure to make any additional sightings of the bird. The initial excitement over the discovery quickly faded among the impatient, news-hungry reporters.

One evening, after another failed day of searching, Miles returned to the encampment to find that all the reporters were gone. The crews, the equipment, the trucks - everything had simply disappeared. Miles entered the central tent and found Hopkins sitting quietly beside the podium nursing a whiskey. The two men looked at each other in recognition, and Hopkins just shook his head. Miles walked out without saying a word and headed for his car. He needed a drink.

He decided to take the long route home past Okefenokee Outfitters. Perhaps he could catch the Admiral before he closed shop for the evening? It was already dark when he spotted the Admiral's place, but the lights inside were still on. Miles turned off the highway and pulled into the empty parking lot. The Admiral spotted him getting out of the car and waited on the porch as Miles got out and walked up the steps.

"What took you so long?" asked the Admiral, "I told Doris that you should call me as soon as possible."

"I haven't talked with Mom since this morning. I've been out in the field. I just stopped by to see you on a whim. I thought we could get a drink? It's been a rough day."

"Then you haven't heard?"

"Heard what?"

"Better come in and sit down, buddy. I'll get us that drink. You're going to need one."

There was a table at the rear of the store near the cash register, and Miles took a seat. The Admiral disappeared behind the counter and returned with two shot glasses and a bottle of Jack Daniels. He poured an inch of whiskey into each glass and pushed one of the glasses over to Miles before taking a seat.

"What's this about, Admiral?" said Miles, picking up the whiskey.

THE ELVIS BIRD

"It's bad news. I discovered a dead body today – out in the swamp. I thought you should know about it."

Miles took a sip of the whiskey and tried to compose himself.

"Who was it?"

"I don't know. But I'd bet money it's related to that recording you sent me."

"One of our graduate students is missing. A South African named Lionel Ames. He left the country weeks ago and never arrived home."

"That doesn't sound good."

"Tell me what you saw."

The Admiral downed his drink with a single gulp and set the glass on the table before launching into the story.

"I took a group of tourists into the swamp for a half-day trip. It was The Elvis Tour. The boat was at capacity – three families, including this one obnoxious kid. On the way out, the kid kept trying to untie my life preservers. I told him twice to cool it, but the kid just ignored me. His daddy was sitting there watching it all play out, but he wouldn't do a damn thing about it. The kid finally managed to untie one of the life preservers. I was about to go straighten him out when he ran up to the bow. He was going to toss the life preserver overboard, when he stopped suddenly, and shouted out, *Hey, mister, there's something dead out there!*"

The Admiral paused long enough to refill his glass.

"I figured the kid was just pranking me, but I switched the engine off and walked up to the bow. Then he dropped the life preserver and pointed at something in the canal. He started yelling, *Over there!* He wasn't kidding. There *was* something dead over there. At first, I thought it was a gator. I grabbed a pole to pull this thing in, and when I got it up next to the boat, I realized it was a person – or what was left of one. Kids shouldn't see that kind of thing. It wasn't something anyone should see. I called the police, and they came out to deal with it."

Miles was staring blankly at his glass.

"You don't look so good, buddy," said the Admiral. He reached out and put a hand on Miles' shoulder.

"I'm not. I'm not good at all."

"Then sit back. Have another consult with Dr. Jack." The Admiral poured Miles two fingers of whiskey and walked over behind the counter.

"I'll put on some music." He reached under the counter for a stack of 33's. "There's a song that's been going around my head all day long."

He flipped through the stack of vinyl, selected one, and queued the record up. The tune began to play on the overhead speakers, and Miles recognized it immediately. It was an Elvis cover of *Any Day Now.*

"That verse about the blue shadow falling all over town always gets me," said the Admiral. He watched the record spin through the entire second verse before looking up at Miles, who had joined him at the counter, drink in hand.

"Damn, that man could sing." said the Admiral when the record had finished playing.

THE ELVIS BIRD

"God help us," said Miles, holding up the shot glass to his lips and then tossing it back.

17. The Profane and the Holy

The birds pay great regard to the particular situation of the tree, and the inclination of its trunk; first, because they prefer retirement, and again, because they are anxious to secure the aperture against the access of water during beating rains.
                              -James Audubon, The Birds of America

The coroner's office was an efficient-looking brick building located a few blocks off Main Street in downtown Folkston. Charlton County had constructed it cheaply in the sixties and purposefully tucked it behind a stand of slash pines and Indian azaleas. The shrubs and trees kept the morgue out of sight and out of mind. The citizens liked it that way.

The coroner had summoned Miles and Hopkins to help identify the body of Lionel Ames, and anxious to assist, they had arrived before the office was open. When they finally entered the building, it was freezing inside. The air conditioning was running constantly, and the windowpanes in the front door were frosted over. Miles wished he had brought along a jacket.

The deputy sheriff who let them inside occupied a desk near the front entrance. He had them sign a logbook and directed them to a waiting room while he called for the coroner. Miles began to shiver after taking a seat. It wasn't long before a small, nervous man in an ill-fitting suit appeared from an inner office and hurried over to greet them.

"I'm Coroner Bennett," he said without offering to shake their hands.

He had a cigarette stub in his mouth despite the *No Smoking* sign on the wall. Miles noticed that the cigarette wasn't lit. The coroner's eyes darted between the two men as he launched into a description of what they were about to see. It sounded like a well-rehearsed speech.

When he finished, he warned them not to touch anything once they were inside the examination room. The men nodded and he ushered them down the hall. Their footsteps echoed in the cement-block corridor as they walked along. They were about to enter the exam room, when the coroner stopped in his tracks, put his hand on the metal entrance door, and turned to give them one final instruction.

"I don't want to shock you gentlemen, but I'm warning you, there's not much left of that boy. We were lucky that Perry Fielder found the body when he did. To put it bluntly, the alligators ate most of him, and the swamp did the rest of the damage. Another week out there, and there wouldn't have been anything left to find."

Bennett looked at them like he was having second thoughts about ushering them inside.

A BENJAMIN MILES MYSTERY

"If you boys can't identify him, or if you just aren't sure, all you have to do is say so, and that will be the end of it. We can't afford to make a mistake. No matter what you tell me, we're going to run the DNA and dental tests to find out if this really is Lionel Ames. On the other hand, if you *can* identify him, you'll be doing us a favor by speeding things along."

"Got it," said Hopkins.

"All right then, boys, let's go. If you feel sick, there's a trash can beside the door."

The coroner tossed his cigarette stub on the concrete floor and stamped on it with his toe out of habit, before opening the door and striding in. The examination room was even colder than the lobby. Miles had anticipated a big reveal, but the remains were already lying exposed on a metal table in the middle of the room – a white sheet was folded at the feet of the corpse. A bright, surgical-style lamp hung from the ceiling and illuminated the metal table in a circle of light, leaving the rest of the room in semi-darkness – a kind of deathly chiaroscuro. Miles and Hopkins followed the coroner to the table and gazed down at the mortal remains of Lionel Ames.

A glance was all that Hopkins needed. He shook his head and turned to leave, but the coroner grabbed him by the arm. The two men looked eye-to-eye.

"Is this Lionel Ames?" asked Bennett.

THE ELVIS BIRD

"I can't tell," said Hopkins. He pulled away from the coroner's grip and walked out. His exit was punctuated by the sound of the metal door slamming shut behind him.

The coroner seemed unfazed. "Looks like it's up to you. Is this Lionel Ames, professor?"

Miles looked down at the table and took a deep breath. The two men stared at the body for a minute without comment. Under that clinical, white light, the horror of what had happened seemed mysteriously transformed for Miles. The longer he stood there, the calmer he felt. The profane became holy, and sacrilege turned to sacrament. His initial dread of making an identification was replaced by the simple acceptance of Lionel's death. The terrible wounds that Lionel had suffered only fortified Miles' courage and compelled him to look closer at his former student.

Miles had never seen a dead body before, not even his father's. That had been a conscious decision he'd made years earlier when his father had died. It was a decision he maintained at all funerals, and one that he had never regretted. But now, he imagined Lionel's parents grieving for this unfortunate boy. Examining the body *was* important – it was an act of duty and respect – an act of faith.

He began to scan Lionel's body, starting at the legs. The feet were missing, the legs mangled. The midsection was intact but bloated. He paused to look closely - clinically. There was a terrible, round wound in the chest. Gunshot? The hands and parts of both arms were missing. The neck was also damaged. The face was bloated but still human-looking and recognizable. Male. Young. The eyes were closed as if resting – the facial expression peaceful - a bit incongruous given the state of his body.

"It's Lionel," said Miles.

"You're sure?" asked the coroner.

"It's Lionel Ames."

The whole thing had taken only a few minutes. It felt much longer. He found Hopkins waiting outside in the hallway. On their way out of the morgue, Sergeant Booker stopped them at the front door.

"Along with the body, we recovered a wallet that belonged to Ames," said Booker. "We were pretty certain the body was his. Still, it helps to have a positive I.D." Booker looked over at Hopkins and placed a hand on his shoulder. "You Ok, Pro-fessor? You don't look so good."

"Seeing that boy was a shock," said Hopkins, "It made me sick."

"That's a pretty common reaction, Doc."

Booker held out some papers on a clipboard. "Sign right there," he said, pointing at the bottom of the page. "Then you can get out of here."

Both men signed and handed the clipboard back to the Sergeant.

"We still have to request his dental records - just to be sure," said Booker. "Can't afford any mistakes with something like this."

"Certainly not, Sergeant," said Hopkins.

"Getting his dental records may take a while since Ames was a South African."

Booker pushed open the front door for them as they were leaving. "I guess the coroner told you that this is a murder investigation now?"

"I thought his death was an accident?" said Hopkins. "The coroner said the alligators ate him."

"It's murder all right. Ames had a shotgun wound in his chest. He was dead long before the alligators got hold of him. The police chief called in the GBI, of course, and the FBI since he was murdered on Federal property."

"Oh, God," said Hopkins.

"Something wrong?" asked Booker.

"We don't need the publicity - isn't there a way we could avoid this getting out in the press?"

"I'm afraid we're way beyond that now. A news crew came up from Jacksonville yesterday, asking questions about the body we pulled out of the swamp. Some national reporters are coming in today for an interview with the coroner." Booker turned to Miles. "There is one thing you can help us with."

"Anything, Sergeant," said Miles.

"The police chief wants to have a face-to-face interview with Susan Swail about those emails we discussed earlier. We need Dr. Swail to come down to answer some questions. The sooner, the better. Especially now, in light of these circumstances."

Miles had forgotten about the emails.

Hopkins piped up when Miles didn't respond immediately, "We can do that, Officer. Miles will call Professor Swail and make the arrangements for her to fly down. Right away. Right, Miles?"

"I'll call her today," he agreed.

When they were outside, Hopkins asked, "What's this business about Swail's emails?"

There was no way to avoid telling Hopkins now.

"Susan corresponded with Lionel at some point. Personal correspondence, I think. I don't know much more than that," said Miles.

"This doesn't sound good, Miles." Hopkins was shaking his head as they walked along. "We need to find out how she's involved in all this. Go ahead and give her a call right away. I'll need to talk to Fitz."

"I'll call her tonight. First, I'm going to notify Lionel's parents that he's dead."

Doris was on the sofa watching TV when Miles returned home that evening. She had the channel tuned to CNN and they were covering the Lionel Ames murder story in the Okefenokee. Miles watched the screen for a few seconds, just long enough to recognize a wide shot of the coroner's office. He turned away and walked over and kissed his mother's forehead.

THE ELVIS BIRD

"Poor, poor boy," she said. "I feel sorry for his momma and daddy," she continued. "I wish there were something we could do for them, Benjamin."

"I talked with his parents on the phone this afternoon. I told them what little I know about the whole situation. I don't think it helped much."

"What did you tell them, Honey?"

Miles glanced at a small grouping of family photos on the end table before turning his attention back to Doris. "I told them their son was happy here, and that he was happy at Cornell."

"Was he happy, Benjamin?"

"I don't know, Mom. Maybe. I hope so."

"What else did you say to them?"

"I said he would be remembered. At least that much is true."

"Who would murder a young man like that, Benjamin?"

Miles left the question unanswered. On the TV, a reporter was interviewing the Charlton County coroner. The image changed to one of the public entrances to the Okefenokee Wildlife Refuge. There was an ambulance and several police cars parked near a canal. The reporter began questioning the tourists who had been on the Admiral's boat when Lionel's body was discovered.

Miles picked up the remote and lowered the volume.

"The Folkston police want to interview Susan," he said.

"Really?" Doris reached out for Miles' hand. "Now, that *is* interesting. I've been wanting to meet Susan."

"They want her to fly down to answer some questions."

"Then you should call her." A sly grin had returned to Doris' face.

"I believe the police think she had a romantic relationship with Lionel."

"Have you asked Susan about that?"

"No."

"Would you like me to dial the number for you, Honey?"

"No."

"Then why are you hesitant?"

"I'm afraid of the answer Susan might give me."

Doris gently squeezed his hand. "Well, Honey, the truth has to be easier to swallow than whatever it is you're imagining."

Miles reached for his cell phone.

"I'll give you some privacy," said Doris, getting off the sofa.

Susan answered on the third ring. In the background, Miles could hear the same audio for news story that was playing on Doris' TV.

"I can't believe Lionel is dead," said Susan.

"Are you alright?" Miles asked.

"I'm just so sad. He was a gifted student."

Miles saw his opportunity.

"How do you know he was gifted? You haven't taught any classes for us yet. How do you know him?"

She didn't answer.

"Susan?"

THE ELVIS BIRD

"I need to tell you something, Miles."

"I'm listening."

"Before Lionel applied to Cornell, he was a biology student at Stanford. He took a statistics course from me – he was my student and very bright. And he was crazy about birds. That's all he wanted to research for his class projects. When the semester was over, I advised him to consider applying to the Cornell ornithology program."

"I see."

"We looked into it together. That's when I discovered that your department needed a mathematician.

"Why would you apply at Cornell when you already had a job?"

"It wasn't a happy time for me at Stanford, Miles. Your job description fit me perfectly, so I applied. It seemed like a good excuse to get away for a while."

Miles interrupted her. "The police think you two were romantically involved – they've been going through all of Lionel's email."

"The police? Yes, of course, they *would* do that."

"So, what exactly was your involvement with Lionel?"

"We ate lunch together several times – to talk about his going to Cornell. He was excited and grateful. But he misinterpreted our relationship. And I was foolish – perhaps I stepped over a line with our relationship. Perhaps I got too close. He began emailing me, and it felt uncomfortable. I didn't answer his emails, but he kept sending them, so I finally confronted him. He took it reasonably well. Once I made our relationship clear, that was the end of it."

Miles decided not to ask about the line she had crossed. He didn't want to know.

"Now that he's dead, I feel responsible."

He could sense the regret in her voice, and in that moment, he decided to dismiss all of his doubts about her involvement.

"You're not responsible, Susan. You were just trying to help a student. Right?"

She didn't answer, so he continued, "The reason I'm calling is that the local police want to question you. They want you to fly down here – as soon as possible for an interview."

"An interrogation? The police want to talk to me?"

"They think you might be able to help with the case."

"They think I'm involved."

Miles took a seat on the sofa.

"I can go along with you to the interview. I know the police sergeant here personally."

"Is it really necessary that I come down there?"

"I don't think you can avoid it. We can make it a dual-purpose trip. I can show you what we do here in the field. It can be a working vacation. Do you have your laptop handy? We should make an airline reservation tonight."

"Yes."

They spent the next few minutes investigating flights.

"I'll need a hotel," she said after booking the flight.

THE ELVIS BIRD

"There are some nice hotels in Jacksonville, but that's a long commute each day."

"What about something closer to you?"

"There's the Cornell campsite, but you'd have to rough it there."

"I'm a city girl, Miles. I'm not camping out with a bunch of bird watchers. Isn't there a city nearby?"

"A hotel in Folkston?"

Miles pictured the two local motor hotels. Were they even still open?

"I don't think that would be a good idea."

Suddenly, Doris snatched the phone out of Miles' hand.

"Susan? This is Doris. Benjamin's mother. I couldn't help but overhear you two kids talking about accommodations in Folkston. Now, I won't have you living with those bird people out in the swamp, and the local hotels aren't suitable for special friends. What? ... no, Jacksonville is much too far away. The only solution is for you to stay here with me, Darling. I have plenty of room. Besides, Benjamin is driving me crazy, and I could use a woman's company. ... You'll be doing me a favor."

Miles frowned at his mother but was simultaneously intrigued to know how Susan would respond to Doris' bold offer of hospitality. He mouthed silently, "What did she say?"

Doris motioned him away with a wave of the hand and plowed ahead, "Really ... It would be no trouble ... I have an extra bedroom, and we girls could get acquainted ...

When is your flight? ... Tomorrow ...Benjamin can pick you up at the Jacksonville airport ... Two o'clock ...Perfect! ... All right, bye now, Sweetie."

Doris squinted at the phone, gave it a tap with her thumb, and handed it back to her son.

"I like her, Benjamin! She's got spirit!"

18. Understanding the Problem

Both birds work most assiduously at this excavation, one waiting outside to encourage the other, whilst it is engaged in digging, and when the latter is fatigued, taking its place.
-James Audubon, The Birds of America

Miles was running late as he stepped into the terminal, and weaved between the arriving passengers in the busy airport. He stopped to check the overhead Arrivals/Departures board (the plane was on time) before heading to baggage claim. He found the correct baggage carousel easily enough, but Susan was nowhere to be seen in the busy terminal. As he waited among a group of arriving passengers, a young father retrieved a bag from the moving conveyor and watched while his two children took turns jumping on and off the carousel. Susan sidled up to Miles unnoticed in the growing crowd.

"Where's your mommy, Benjamin?" she asked, sticking the needle in.

Miles had only to turn his head to look into her eyes.

"Don't call me Benjamin. And she's more like a force of nature than a mother," he observed, trying to appear unruffled.

"So, she didn't come along to chaperone?"

"Not a chance," he said.

"But she sounded so sweet on the phone."

"She's that, too," he conceded. Susan lifted the computer bag off her shoulder and leaned it against the edge of the moving ramp while they waited for her luggage to arrive.

"Something about you is different," said Miles, giving Susan the once-over. He took a step backward. "It's your hair." She was wearing trim, black pants, and a white top that fell to mid-hip. A single-strand, silver necklace hung around her neck.

"Sabrina," said Miles, "You look like Sabrina." He wagged a finger at her for emphasis.

"You are a movie buff."

"It's the hair. You cut it."

"Do you like it?" she asked, lightly patting the top of her head. Before Miles could respond, she pointed out a small valise that was moving away on the conveyor.

"There goes my other bag."

An hour later, they were driving north on US Highway 1. They had left the gated neighborhoods and fountained ponds of the suburbs behind and were traveling among the pine forests of South Georgia. The hardwood forests that had once defined the region a century earlier had disappeared —supplanted now by a monoculture cash crop of limb-deficient Loblolly pines.

Shortly after leaving the airport, Susan had gone silent. The monotony of the landscape wasn't helping. Miles stole a glance at his companion and she met his gaze.

THE ELVIS BIRD

"Sorry, Birdman. I'm just worried."

Miles understood. "Tell the police what you know. That should be easy enough."

"I've never been interviewed by the police."

"Just speak the truth. Only good things can come from that."

She seemed to be giving that idea some thought.

"What can I tell them? I don't know why anyone would want to kill poor Lionel."

"Perhaps you could start by telling me something about Lionel? I'd like to know more about him."

She shifted positions in the seat, putting her back against the door.

"There isn't much to say," she said. "He was a student at Stanford on a golf scholarship. I didn't usually get athletes in my classes – they tended to avoid math. Whenever I did get one, they usually kept a low profile. But Lionel was different. He was a talkative kid. Bright and handsome. Girls found him attractive."

"Shoulda been me," said Miles.

"You wanted to be a lady killer?"

Miles made a face. "No. I wanted to play golf in college."

"So, they have golf courses out here in the bottomlands?"

"Yes, ma'am, and we've learned to wear shoes, too. At least while we're playing golf."

"You grew up here, right?"

"We moved to Folkston when my dad joined the FBI. How about you?"

"California girl."

"Let me guess ... L.A.?"

She made a face.

"San Francisco, then."

She nodded. "Pacific Heights."

"Oh, ...a girl of privilege. No wonder you didn't want to rough it at the camp."

"You've been to San Francisco, have you?"

"I get around."

"What spirited you away from the sticks?"

"San Francisco is a major migration route. For birds and people. I finished a Ph.D. at UC Davis. What about you? How did you get into the math biz?"

"My dad was a mathematician at Stanford. Ever heard of Swail's Theorem? No? When I was a child, my dad and I liked to solve puzzles together. We never stopped doing that, and the puzzles became harder as the years passed."

"I'm no good with puzzles."

"What are you good at, Birdman?"

Miles gave it some thought.

"Observing," he said finally. "I'm a good observer."

He looked across the seat to emphasize the point.

"Observing is important, Miles. The first step in problem-solving. George Polya called that *Understanding the Problem* –Looking closely at what's in front of you and figuring out how the things you are observing relate to each other."

"Does that apply to us?"

Susan smiled but didn't answer, and they rode along in silence for another mile. When Miles stole another look, she was staring.

"So, who is George Polya?" he asked quickly.

"A famous Stanford mathematician – and a friend of my father. He wrote a book called *How to Solve It*."

"Never heard of it."

"You should order a copy. It was written for a lay audience. Even a humble ornithologist like you should be able to read it."

The needle again.

"It might help you solve your gunshot mystery, Birdman. I use his methods on every problem I tackle."

The idea of first understanding the problem got Miles thinking about the recording. What exactly had he overheard? He glanced at his passenger again. "When you're done with the police interview, I want you to examine all the machines in camp as soon as possible."

"Ok."

"Make a copy of all the audio material that was recorded in the Okefenokee. I'm looking for a complete copy of the gunshot recording, but any of that material might be helpful."

"Do you have access to the machines?"

"Yes."

Miles applied the brakes as they approached a crossroad up ahead. The area was populated with an odd collection of billboards and dilapidated buildings – the abandoned remains of a tourist trap. A garish billboard still dominated the dilapidated main building: WORLD'S LARGEST SERPENTARIUM, and in smaller letters underneath, LIVE ALLIGATOR WRESTLING. Susan looked at it curiously as they drove past.

"What was that?"

"The last remnants of old Florida. The rest of it died years ago."

"What killed it?"

"Walt Disney."

Susan insisted on being taken directly to the police station when they arrived in Folkston.

"We could drop off your bags first. You could meet my mom," Miles suggested when they were on the edge of town.

"I want to get this out of the way," said Susan. "It's all I can think about. Until I get past this interview, I'm not ready to meet Doris."

Miles parked the Lexus directly in front of the old police station, and they walked in together. The waiting room was cramped, with only a few cheap folding chairs against the wall and a video camera mounted in the corner of the room to keep an eye on the patrons. Opposite the front door and across the room, a short hall led into the police station proper. There was a plate-glass window along one wall with a round opening through which you could talk to an officer – if you waited long enough for one to appear. A sign, taped to the window, said *Ring the Bell and Take a Seat*. Evidently, the Folkston Police Department maintained order in Charlton County with an eye toward economy. With only a police chief and a part-time officer on the staff, you might have to wait a while.

Miles rang the bell. A few minutes passed by and Sergeant Booker appeared at the front window.

"We've been expecting you," he said to Susan. "Just a sec."

There was a loud buzz and a metal door popped open. Booker appeared in the doorway and held it open for Susan to walk through. "Step this way, Dr. Swail."

The Sergeant moved aside long enough for Susan to enter. He said to Miles, "I can call you when we're done, Pro-fessor, or you can just wait out here. Might take a while."

Miles looked around the empty room.

"I'll stay."

Miles entertained himself by reading one of the few magazines in the room - an old issue of AARP. The July/August issue featured a front-page photo of a smiling Kevin Kostner. New baby, New Movie, New Home. There was another article called *How To Have Great Sex After Thirty Years*

—an advice feature. Talk about cellulite. Talk about wrinkles. Ignoring changes in your body won't make them go away. Dress up like Tarzan. Or a nurse. No one else will know. Guess what? Many older couples don't like penetration. Luckily, it's not the only way to have fun. Do the dishes naked…

Miles lowered the magazine and imagined Doris washing dishes in the sink. He tossed the magazine on the floor, resolving never, ever to join AARP.

The interview took a couple of hours, and when Susan walked out with Booker she was visibly shaken.

"We'll call you if we need you, Pro-fessor Swail," said the sergeant. "I've got Miss Doris' cell if we need to reach you."

Outside the police station, Miles put his arm around Susan and helped her into the car. They sat holding hands until she felt like talking.

"They didn't believe me. They didn't believe anything I said."

"Who didn't believe you?"

"There was an FBI agent that asked most of the questions – the bad cop. And there was a GBI agent as well – the good cop. They kept asking me the same questions about Lionel. I told them everything that I've told you. But they just kept going over the same points – again and again. They wouldn't accept my answers."

"You're not really a suspect, are you?"

"I think I am a suspect. Yes, definitely. They said that when they found Lionel, he was wearing some of my jewelry."

"What kind of jewelry?"

"A gold necklace. They had it in a plastic evidence bag, and they showed it to me. The thing is ... it was *my* necklace. I don't know how Lionel got hold of it."

"Why would Lionel have your necklace?"

"I have no idea. I didn't know what to say to them. I think I should have hired a lawyer for this meeting."

She put her head on Miles' shoulder. "Just get me away from here. Please. I can't meet your mother like this."

"Just a second." Miles got out of the car and shut the door to make a call. The conversation was brief.

"I know where we can go," said Miles as he crawled back into the car.

Outside of town, the Lexus turned off the old state highway and into the graveled lot of Okefenokee Outfitters, where it skidded to a halt in a cloud of dust. They found the Admiral counting his money at the cash register in the back of the store. Perry Fielder removed his glasses and looked up from his work as they walked up to the counter. His expression was equal parts puzzlement and impishness.

"Madam, is this man bothering you?" The Admiral spoke slowly like a man chewing salt-water taffy. He turned to Miles. "You've been holding out on the old Admiral, you dog."

"You can cut the cornpone act," said Miles, "we just need a boat for a couple of hours."

The Admiral looked at Miles as if he'd just discovered a foul odor in the room. His attention quickly refocused on Susan. "Darlin', you remind me of the actress in that Billy Wilder film. Now what was the name of that movie? You know—the one with Humphrey Bogart and William Holden—two brothers fighting over the same beautiful woman." As he talked, he rubbed his thumb and forefinger together as if he was trying to squeeze the answer out of thin air.

"Sabrina?" asked Susan.

"Bingo!" said the Admiral. He pointed at her with a make-believe finger pistol.

"Well, that makes two Sabrina references in one day," said Susan. She looked from one man to the other. "I believe you boys are pulling my leg."

"Would we do that?" asked the Admiral.

Miles stepped in. "Susan, this is Perry Fielder. My oldest politically-incorrect friend. Most folks around here call him *The Admiral*. He's the best birder in Georgia, *and* the biggest liar, so don't believe a word he says."

The Admiral looked hurt and put his hand on his chest. "Done to death by slanderous tongue was the Hero that here lies."

"He also fancies himself a great actor."

THE ELVIS BIRD

The Admiral feigned surprise. "Beware, my lord, of jealousy; It is the green-ey'd monster, which doth mock the meat it feeds on."

"Good to meet you, Admiral," said Susan, offering her hand.

The Admiral leaned over the counter, took her hand, and kissed it.

Miles sneered, "I see you've memorized another line of Shakespeare since we last talked."

The Admiral cocked his head and looked into Susan's eyes. "Just a little local color, madam. Something to keep the natives entertained and the tourists spending money. I may look like a simple tour guide, but I'm really in show business. This humble shop is my stage."

"I was hoping you could take us on a tour of the swamp," said Miles. "We'd like to see the Okefenokee in the evening light. It's been a rough day."

"What's the problem?"

"Police interview," said Susan.

Miles stepped in. "The body that you found in the Okefenokee was identified as a former student of Susan's."

"Bad business, that," said the Admiral. "Dealing with our local constabulary is never any fun, is it, Miles?" He gave Miles a sideways glance. "But the good Lord always provides in our time of need." The Admiral reached under the counter and brought out three glasses and a half-empty bottle of Jack Daniels.

"I myself am an eternal optimist." He began to fill the glasses. "I like to think of every glass as half full. And then I proceed to fill them." When he finished pouring, he pushed Susan's drink closer to her. "Amen?"

Susan looked down at the glass. "Miles said that it was you who found Lionel in the swamp. Do you mind telling me more about that?"

"Perhaps we shouldn't speak of it, Dr. Swail. Especially since you've had a tough time of it today."

"Call me Susan. I need to know what you witnessed. I think it might help."

He gave Susan a long thoughtful look.

"All right, if you think it will help." He pushed her glass forward. "Have some courage first."

She raised the glass to her lips, turned it up, and put it down.

"Now, that's the spirit," he said, slightly surprised. He poured her another. "They say the truth makes us free, but in my experience, a little whiskey helps grease the skids."

The Admiral reached out and took her hand in his and pulled her closer until they were eye-to-eye. "This is the whole truth and nothing but the truth. It was at once horrible and holy, Darlin', wrapped up in a single moment - that boy floating beside my boat in the Okefenokee. I'll never forget it. But *you* shouldn't give much thought to the horror. The unpleasant parts of this life are transitory. Only what's good and true remains. That's my belief. Choose a pleasant memory when you think of that boy." He squeezed her hand and let it go.

Susan looked at him as if she wanted to ask another question but thought better of it. Instead, she took the glass, raised it to her lips, and tossed it back. "Thank you for finding Lionel and for pulling him out of the swamp. I'm glad it was you who found him, Admiral." She tossed back the rest of the whiskey.

"The Lord works in mysterious ways," he said.

When everyone had finished their whiskey, the Admiral began to tidy up. "We're losing the light," he said, "The Elvis tour leaves in ten minutes, and we only have room for two patrons. Follow me, children. I need to lock up."

###

As the sun was setting, the three friends stood in the skiff's bow —Miles in the middle with his arms around the other two — admiring the watery spectacle. The mirrored waterway of the Grand Prairie reflected the brilliant light of the setting sun and formed a golden, double image. For as far as you could see and even beyond, fields of water lilies extended away from the boat. For a few pleasant moments, the Okefenokee was silent and peaceful.

19. Sweet Arrangement

I observed that in two instances, when the Woodpeckers saw me thus at the foot of the tree in which they were digging their nest, they abandoned it forever.

-James Audubon, The Birds of America

It was mid-morning and Miles awoke with a start. He rarely slept late, but he and Susan had returned home late in the evening from the Admiral's tour. The night before, Doris had kept a simple meal ready for them on the stove, and after a late dinner, the three of them talked on the porch until after midnight. The women had hit it off famously.

Miles sensed that he was the last person to get out of bed, so after a quick shower, he slipped into jeans and hurried into the kitchen still barefoot and shirtless. Doris and Susan had already finished their breakfast and were chatting at the kitchen table.

"He's not much to look at in the morning, is he?" commented Doris as Miles walked into the room. "He was never an early-riser. More of a night-owl."

Miles stopped behind her chair and kissed the top of her head. "Good morning, ladies. Have your fun, Mom, but I need a clean shirt - I've run out of clothes."

THE ELVIS BIRD

"Top of the dryer," said Doris.

Miles ducked into the small laundry room that adjoined the kitchen and returned wearing a red Cornell tee shirt.

"Breakfast is on the stove, Honey, and there are biscuits in the oven. I need to get dressed —I have plans," said Doris, getting up from the table and leaving the room.

Miles walked over to the stove and opened the oven door. "Bless you," he said looking in. He gingerly removed two hot biscuits from the pan, tossed them on a plate, and carried them over to the table.

"Where is she going?" asked Miles.

"Beats me. Should she be driving?"

"No. I'd better offer to do it."

Miles poured sugar cane syrup from a large tin container onto the plate and dipped a biscuit into the dark, brown liquid before taking a bite.

"She seems fine," said Susan.

"My brother, George, is ready to put her in a nursing home." He took another bite. "He's afraid she'll have a stroke while living here by herself."

"What do you think?"

"I don't know. I don't want her to die here all alone."

"She seems pretty happy, Miles. Have you asked her how she feels about moving to a nursing home?"

"Not yet – but I can guess. George wants me to drive her down to Jacksonville to visit a home that's located on the beach - some fancy place with graduated levels of care. She won't like that."

Doris walked back into the kitchen. "What won't I like?" She had changed her dress and shoes, and a pocketbook hung on her arm.

"Nothing, Mom."

"Good. I like nothing. I'm going to the grocery store. We can talk about the thing I won't like later. Any requests from you two?"

"The doctor doesn't want you driving," said Miles, "I should do it." He started to get up from the table, but Doris put a hand on his shoulder and pushed him back into the chair.

"Nonsense," she said, "I'm expecting you for dinner at six o'clock sharp. Don't be late. I have a special event planned for both of you tonight, so don't make any plans for the evening. Have fun."

"You shouldn't be driving," said Miles.

"Too late!" said Doris. She held up a set of keys and shook them over his head as she walked out of the room.

###

The morning air was chilly, and the sky was cloudless as Miles drove along the old county road toward the Cornell camp. He had put the top down on the Lexus and was enjoying the breeze in his face and the smell of the Georgia lowland. Susan seemed rested after a night's sleep.

THE ELVIS BIRD

"I'll tell Hoppy you're going out with me," said Miles after he had parked the car in the camp. "You can borrow his computer and examine it for the missing recordings."

"He'll have to loan it to me. I'll need it overnight," she said.

"I see."

They discovered Hopkins sitting impatiently at a table in the main tent.

"You're late," he said irritably when Miles and Susan walked in. "Don't bother sitting down, Miles - you're coming out with me." He handed Miles a clipboard and started to get up. "Make yourself useful. We're replacing batteries in the ARUs today. If you move your ass, we might have time for some old-school birding this afternoon."

Susan, was standing off to the side, pouring a cup of coffee. "Let's bring her along," suggested Miles, confidentially.

"You'd like that, wouldn't you?" said Hopkins. He gave Susan a long look. "Can't really blame you. I'd much prefer looking at her all day rather than your sorry mug, but I have other plans for your girlfriend –she's going out with Bert. He needs an extra hand this morning."

Minutes later, the four of them set off in two skiffs in opposite directions. Miles watched from the stern as Bert eased his skiff down the dark riverway. When the boats were some distance apart, Miles waved goodbye, but he failed to catch Susan's attention. Bert's skiff disappeared around a curve in the river.

He walked forward and joined Hopkins at the wheel.

"Sweet arrangement, Miles," said Hopkins. He removed the aviator sunglasses that were perched on top of his hat and pushed them up snuggly on his nose.

"How's that?" asked Miles.

Hopkins smirked. "You and Susan, sharing a pillow."

"It's not what you think, Hoppy."

"I'm happy for you, buddy. That woman is easy to look at."

Miles ignored the remark and took a seat in the bow while Hopkins set a course for Blackjack Island. It was a remote site on the swamp's southern edge. The team had placed a few ARUs there the week earlier. Blackjack had once been home to Ivory-bills back in the nineteen-twenties.

The route to get to there was serpentine and would carry them through a series of prairies and narrow waterways. The trip took most of the morning. Along the way, Hopkins made a wrong turn that forced them to backtrack, so the two men had plenty of time to talk.

When it was apparent that they had taken a second wrong turn, Hopkins was fuming, "Damn it all. You can stand up, turn around in the boat, and get lost out here."

It was almost noon before they arrived and located the first ARU. Hopkins spotted the gray and white tube strapped to a tree on a peat battery.

"Time to earn your pay, Miles."

"You're not paying me."

THE ELVIS BIRD

"Then you can earn my respect - like a real ornithologist - out you go," said Hopkins. "Careful where you step."

Peat batteries are large masses of decaying plant material that accumulate over time on the swamp floor. The water's acidic nature encourages the formation of methane and nitrogen gases, which become trapped under the peat, causing the battery to rise and fall. Locals call these islands *blow-ups*. Occasionally, a battery becomes stable enough to support shrubs and small trees, but often they remain small, floating islands that drift and shift position in the wind. In a summer drought, forest fires often reclaim these islands and return the peat to ash in a complex life cycle that has been repeated for centuries.

Miles held on to the gunwale and tentatively placed one foot over the side. He stepped onto a solid-looking mass of mud, grass, and plants, but his leg quickly sank up to his knee.

"Hold up!" Hopkins shouted as he watched Miles struggle as he straddled the gunwale. "Let's move further down."

Hopkins eased the skiff forward.

"Once more," said Hopkins after shutting off the engine.

Miles tested the surface with his toe this time. It appeared stable, and he crawled out of the boat and managed to stand up straight on the battery.

"You'll need the ladder," said Hopkins, handing it over the side. Miles drug it along as he made his way over to the

ARU. With each step he took, the ground shook like Jello. It was similar to walking on a trampoline. Miles changed the batteries and made it back to the boat without incident.

"Only four more to go," announced Hopkins. "But before we do, watching you work has made me hungry. Let's eat."

Hopkins drew back a canvas cover over the wheel for some shade. He had packed two sack lunches, and he handed one to Miles. The two men sat down out of the hot sun.

Hopkins pulled an apple out of his bag and took a bite.

"Something's bothering me," said Hopkins, gesturing with the apple between bites.

"Nothing bothers you."

"I have feelings."

"So, what are you feeling, Buddy?"

"I wasn't prepared for what we saw at the morgue – that kid's body," said Hopkins. "It bothered me. Still does. I can't get it out of my head."

"What happened to him?"

"I don't know. He was reckless. I caught him several times taking a skiff out into the swamp by himself. I had to threaten to send him home to get him to stop. It's damned foolish, going out in this swamp without a partner."

"But you do it all the time."

"It doesn't matter about me." There was a certain sadness in Hopkins' expression that made Miles uneasy.

"Going out alone wouldn't get him murdered."

THE ELVIS BIRD

"I don't want to say bad things about the dead, but Lionel couldn't keep his dick in his pants. I mean, he was a good kid – he worked hard during the week, but on the weekends, he wouldn't stay out of the local bars. He was always chasing the local tail."

"The kid liked to party?"

"I didn't think much about it until a couple of locals came by the camp to complain. They were ready to whip his ass – or worse. I sent him home for his own protection."

"When was that?"

"A few days before the rest of the students left camp."

"Who came by to complain?"

"I don't remember his name. He was a tall guy in a big leather hat. Had his son with him. He insisted Lionel stay away from his granddaughter or else there would be trouble."

"Was his name Luther Preston?"

"Who is that?"

"An old-timer here. He gave me directions the night we got lost in the swamp. Tall. Wiry. Has a face like a hawk."

"Could be. That sounds about right."

###

Doris was waiting impatiently on the front porch steps when Miles and Susan returned from the camp that evening. She stood up as soon as the car turned into the driveway, and she walked up to the car as they were parking.

A BENJAMIN MILES MYSTERY

"You're late," she said, as they were getting out. "I was about to come looking for you. It's after six."

Doris herded them into the kitchen and began serving dinner. Susan assisted by filling three metal tumblers with ice and then pouring the tea. Miles removed the dinner plates from the cabinet. Doris began spooning the dinner onto the dishes directly from the stove, and handed each of them a full plate.

When they were seated, Doris took their hands and bowed her head:

> *Bless the meat,*
> *Damn the skin,*
> *Open your mouth,*
> *And poke it in.*
> *Amen.*

"Really, Mom?" said Miles after opening his eyes.

Doris shrugged. "We leave in five minutes."

No one said a word during the meal.

"Where are we going?" asked Miles after cleaning his plate. He was still chewing.

"The VFW. I need your help tonight, Benjamin. I can't let Mildred Terry beat me again. I've been trying to win for the last six months."

"Beat Mildred Terry at what?"

"Bingo, of course. It's Bingo night."

THE ELVIS BIRD

Miles remembered he had left Hopkin's computer on the back seat of his car. He had gotten Bert Williams to remove it from one of the university trailers that afternoon. He had planned for Susan to look it over that evening. Bert could return it in the morning before Hopkins discovered it was missing.

"I can't take you to Bingo tonight, Mom," said Miles. "We have work to do."

But Doris had an ace in the hole. "The other day you asked me what I knew about Luther Preston."

"I think he might be involved in Lionel's murder."

"Well then, if you come with me tonight to Bingo, you can question him yourself – he runs the game."

Doris picked up the car keys and began to shake them in Miles' face.

20. B-I-N-G-O

... strangers were very apt to pay a quarter of a dollar for two or three heads of this Woodpecker. I have seen entire belts of Indian chiefs closely ornamented with the tufts and bills of this species, and have observed that a great value is frequently put upon them.
-James Audubon, The Birds of America

The VFW Hall was a long, wooden building with a central entrance. A large, commercial kitchen occupied one end of the hall, and the other end contained a small stage. In between, there were four rows of folding tables, arranged lengthwise like dominoes to accommodate the large crowd.

Miles spotted the building as they were passing the Folkston Country Club. It sat back from the highway on the edge of a pecan grove. Despite Doris' exhortations, they arrived late, and the paved parking lot in front of the building was already full. The overflow (mostly pickup trucks sporting University of Georgia and NASCAR decals) had spilled into the grove, where they were parked in rows under the pecan trees. Traffic was still arriving for the event, and Miles followed a line of trucks into the grove.

Someone had tacked up a string of multi-colored Christmas lights around the hall's double entrance doors, and they glowed cheerfully in the twilight. People were streaming in.

"There's a spot!" said Doris pointing out a narrow parking space at the end of a row of trucks. Miles eased the car into the opening beside a mud-covered Dodge Ram. There was a fishing rod in the truck's gun rack.

"Don't you think the colored lights make the place look festive?" said Doris as they approached the building.

"They do add a note of fun," said Susan. She was walking arm-in-arm with Doris as they approached the building.

A short line of people had formed outside the entrance waiting for tickets. Strains of a Willie Nelson tune drifted out of the front doors. The place was packed, and Miles could see that most of the seats inside were already occupied.

"We're late," said Doris impatiently, "I hope we don't miss the first game." In spite of Doris' concerns, the line moved steadily, and soon they had worked their way up to the entrance.

"Five dollars a head," said the girl taking the money. She was sitting at a card table and looked festive in jeans, boots, and a red silk blouse.

"Have we missed anything?" Doris asked the girl.

"No ma'am. The first game starts in ten minutes."

"Great. Pay the girl, Benjamin," said Doris over her shoulder. "Merlene, this is our new friend, Susan." She patted Susan's arm and turned to look at Miles. "And this is my son, Benjamin. He's an ornithologist."

"A what?" asked the girl.

Doris leaned over the table and spoke confidentially as if she were discussing a medical condition. "He likes birds."

Miles fished a twenty from his wallet and held it out. The girl stuffed the bill into a cigar box that was overflowing with cash, and handed him back a five.

"Thanks, Merlene," said Doris. She brushed past the table with Susan in tow and stopped just inside the doorway. An identically-dressed girl sat at a second table covered with multi-colored Bingo merchandise – specialty items that Miles didn't recognize. She, too, had a cigar box full of money.

Doris reached for Miles' sleeve and tugged it to get his attention. "I play three cards on each game, Honey. You and Susan should do that, too. There are ten games in all, so you'll need to buy thirty cards for each of us. Ninety cards will maximize our chances of winning."

"What does a card cost?" asked Miles suspiciously.

"Just a dollar."

"Ninety bucks!" said Miles. "For Bingo?"

"It's for charity," said Doris, "Besides, it's lots of fun!"

Miles looked at Doris' smiling face and reached for his wallet. "Now, I understand why you brought me along." He pulled out five twenties and started to count them out into the outstretched hand of the second girl. Something about her seemed familiar. "You look like …"

"They're twins," said Doris, "This is Pearlene."

THE ELVIS BIRD

"Will there be anything else?" asked Pearlene.

Miles, looking down at the merchandise spread across the table.

"You'll need chips or daubers," said Doris. "I'm a dauber, but Mildred Terry's a chipper. What do you want to be?"

Clueless, Miles shrugged.

"Why don't you be a dauber," suggested Doris, "It'll be cheaper."

"Good idea," said Miles, still holding onto his wallet. "I like cheaper."

"Give us two EZ-Daubers, Pearlene," said Doris, "The big red ones."

"Don't you need one, Doris?" asked Susan. Miles gave her a look.

She raised a shiny hand bag at eye level. "I came prepared."

Pearlene selected two large markers and placed them in front of Miles.

"Ten dollars," she said.

"Can't we just share one?" asked Miles, reaching into his wallet.

"You won't have time for that," said Doris. She grabbed the ten from Miles' wallet and tossed it on the table. "I'll get our seats." She turned and headed off into the crowded hall.

Miles took Susan's hand and tried to catch up. He spotted Doris halfway down a middle aisle - she had stopped to survey the room. A short, older woman sitting near the front of the hall was waving at her furiously.

"Whoohoo!" shouted Mildred, "Come sit with me." She indicated three empty chairs across the table.

Miles scanned the hall for Luther Preston as he pushed down the aisle, but in the crowd, Miles didn't see him anywhere. Was the whole evening going to be a waste of time? They soon caught up with Doris who had taken a seat directly across from her friend.

Mildred was wearing black glasses and a card dealer's cap over her short, white hair. Her ill-chosen frames ended in points and dwarfed her diminutive face. Her floral-print dress was clean and neatly pressed, but slightly faded, and her demeanor seemed to be two parts childlike ebullience and one part devilment.

Doris positioned three Bingo cards on the table. A red dauber was hanging from a black lanyard around her neck. Susan and Miles took their seats on her left and right.

After a hurried exchange in which Miss Mildred remarked that *She wouldn't have recognized Miles because he had grown so much*, and *He really should visit his mother more often*, Doris introduced Susan as *Miles' special friend from San Francisco*. Susan accepted the description gracefully and seemed amused at Miles' discomfort.

After the introductions, Mildred reached across the table and took Susan's hand. "So, dear, San Francisco must be a beautiful city." She smiled and looked earnestly into Susan's

THE ELVIS BIRD

eyes. "Have you met Tony Bennett? I think he's just wonderful."

"No, Miss Mildred, I haven't had the pleasure. But he *certainly* is a wonderful singer."

The lively George Strait number that was playing on overhead speakers stopped abruptly. The crowd quieted and turned their attention to a tall man who had stepped onto the stage. Even inside the stuffy, packed hall, Luther Preston was still wearing his leather hat. He took a seat facing the crowd at a table that was draped in a white cloth and framed by American flags on each end. The arrangement reminded Miles of a patriotic Holy Communion, but instead of a cross, candles, and a chalice, there was a round, metal spinner filled with Bingo balls, an electronic switchboard permanently attached to the wall, and an old-style silver microphone. Preston flipped a switch at the base of the microphone and began tapping it with his finger.

"Testing, one, two, three," he said, leaning over to speak into the mic. His voice echoed loudly through the room.

He tapped the mic again, tested the switchboard by flipping a couple of switches, and gave the cage a turn. When he was satisfied with the setup, he looked out at the crowd and flashed a thumbs up.

"Welcome, everybody." There was a nasal quality in Preston's voice which sounded slightly exaggerated to Miles. "I'll be calling the numbers tonight for all you good people. Time to get started with some straight-up Bingo. Hold onto your knickers, Ladies, the first game's worth fifty dollars for the winning card."

The comment was met with scattered laughter, brief applause, and few hoots.

Luther waved a stack of Bingo cards over his head, and leaned into the microphone again. "Don't forget to buy a card for the thousand-dollar jackpot game at the end of the evening – only one to a customer. You can only buy one of them right here from me."

He adjusted the volume on the microphone to tamp down the feedback before continuing. "We'll be selling these jackpot cards all night long. Five bucks a card. Where else can you have so much fun for a five-spot? Goes to a good cause, too."

"Gimme one," someone shouted. A line of people quickly formed at the table, and Luther patiently took their money. When the line was empty, he gave the cage a spin, "Ready, folks?" he asked. The crowd cheered. "Here we go!" He pressed a lever on the side of the spinner and a ball rolled out into a metal cup.

"Turn the screw! N – 62," he announced as he flipped a switch on the board. The sign began to flash the number. Luther casually tossed the ball into a box beside his chair.

Mildred eyed her cards closely and shouted, "Mama's *hot* tonight!" She covered up a couple of squares with blue chips and began waving both arms over her head.

"Uh-huh! Uh-huh! Uh-huh!"

A man on the next row shouted, "You go, girl!"

THE ELVIS BIRD

Doris frowned after scanning her three cards. She leaned against Susan and whispered, "She *always* matches the first ball."

"Danny LaRue! O-52," announced Luther. The board behind him began to flash the second number.

Mildred smiled and placed another chip on a card. "Treat me sweet, Luther! Treat me sweet, darling!" She stood up and threw Luther a kiss.

"Damn and damn again!" said Doris, looking at her empty cards.

Susan whispered to Doris, "Is she always like this?"

"She likes to rub it in."

"Either way up! O-69," called Luther. The crowd chuckled.

Mildred's fist shot up in the air. "That's it! That's what I'm talking about, Luther!" She fished out two more blue chips from a cloth bag. "Come to Mama!"

"Mildred's at it again," yelled a woman at the next table. Everyone enjoyed the spectacle except Doris, who whispered to Miles, "Now, do you see why I want to win this thing so badly?"

After a few more frenzied minutes, someone at the back of the hall yelled, "Bingo!" and the crowd groaned. Doris tore her cards into tiny pieces and tossed them into the air. She frowned and shook her head as they floated to the floor.

An older man at the back of the hall began waving a card over his head. He shouted out, "Here's the winner! I gotta winner." He hurried up to the front to claim his prize.

Luther took his card, and the man stepped away from the table to await the decision.

Mildred removed a plastic stick from her purse and waved it over her cards. The blue metal chips leaped up like fleas onto the magnetic wand.

"He's right, folks!" announced Luther. "Vernon Jenkins wins the first game of the evening. Way to go, Vernon." Everyone began to applaud as Vernon walked away waving his fifty-dollar bill at the crowd.

In the meanwhile, A short, bald man brought out a second metal cage and an empty box. He placed them in front of Luther and removed the original cage and the box of balls beside Luther's chair. In this way, the cages were swapped out after each game, and the event moved along briskly.

Doris' mood shifted after setting out three new cards on the table. She bumped shoulders with Susan conspiratorially. "Isn't this a hoot! We'll do better this time."

"Your luck is sure to change," said Susan, hopefully.

Luther spoke into the microphone, "Time for the Four Corners game, folks. First person to cover all four corners on a single card wins fifty dollars. Here we go."

He spun the cage and pressed the lever.

"Time for fun. N - 41."

Mildred looked down at her cards and yelled, "Ring my chimes, Luther! Keep ringing 'em, darling!" She positioned another chip on a card.

THE ELVIS BIRD

After playing a handful of games, no one in their group had won a prize. Luther stood up and stretched before announcing a twenty-minute break. The overhead music began to play again, and the crowd headed for the exits, anxious to get some relief from the heat.

Susan commented to Miles. "They must raise a lot of money off this event."

Miles surveyed the exiting crowd and estimated the take. "Seven or eight thousand - easy."

By the end of the evening, the floor was covered with discarded Bingo cards. There was another break, and Doris remembered they each needed a Bingo card for the final jackpot game. She turned to Miles. "This is our last chance to win some real money. Be a good boy and buy each of us a jackpot card, Benjamin."

Miles surveyed the front of the hall. The line of people buying cards from Luther had dwindled.

"I'll be right back," said Miles. He eased through the narrow aisle making his way up to Luther's table. The old man recognized him immediately.

"I see you made it out of the swamp, Professor. How's your buddy doing?" The nasal quality of the old man's voice wasn't as pronounced while speaking one on one.

"You were right – his injury wasn't serious. Thanks for the help."

"Glad to oblige."

"Three cards for the jackpot game," said Miles. He handed Luther a twenty. The old man tossed the bill it into a cardboard box filled with cash, before counting out three bingo cards, and handing Miles a five.

"Your group's been snake-bit tonight, just like your partner."

"How's that?"

"You haven't won anything."

"Perhaps this game will change our luck."

"Maybe … " said Luther with a wry smile.

"I'm curious about something," said Miles. "Did you ever meet Lionel Ames? The student who died in the Okefenokee."

Preston didn't seem surprised by the question.

"I met him, alright. Didn't like him."

"Why was that?"

"He was running around on my granddaughter. She thought he was something special. Talked about him all the time. Then I discovered he was cattin' around with lots of other local girls – a real rooster, that boy. I had a talk with him and told him it would be healthier if he left my granddaughter alone."

He pulled out a handkerchief, removed his hat, and wiped the sweat off his forehead.

"Healthier?" asked Miles.

"We respect women around here. I suggested he might want to go back home – the sooner, the better."

"But he didn't leave."

"Evidently not."

THE ELVIS BIRD

"Was it you who came out to the Cornell camp to talk with Lionel?"

"My son and I paid him a visit."

"Do the police know about this?"

"I didn't kill that boy if that's what you're driving at."

"I didn't say that," said Miles.

"But that's what you were thinking."

"I'm just trying to find out what happened to Lionel."

"Then you're talking to the wrong person, Professor."

He put his hat back on and pointed at a line of people that had formed behind Miles. "Now, if you don't mind, I need to sell some Bingo cards."

The music began to play again as the crowd wandered in. Miles rejoined the women, and when the hall was filled, Luther announced, "Last game, folks. There's a one-thousand-dollar prize for the winner. As always, this is a *Blackout* game. You know what that means: You need to cover every square on your card to win. No exceptions. And don't forget – the winner can collect the prize money from me, right after the game."

The short man who had swapped out the cages all evening reappeared in the back of the hall. He was balancing a large cage filled with golden balls over his head. The crowd began to chant *Blackout, Blackout, Blackout* as he made his way to the front and placed the cage ceremoniously on the table. He turned and mugged to the crowd, and gave the cage a spin before leaving.

A BENJAMIN MILES MYSTERY

Luther watched the cage spin several revolutions and then pressed the lever on the side.

"Valentine's day! B – 14". The board flashed the number.

Mildred, who had decided to stand up through the entire game, put a chip down on her card, licked her index finger, and touched it to her butt.

"Sssss!" she said shaking her fanny to the delight of the crowd.

"Sit down and act your age," said Doris.

The game lasted fifteen minutes, and the crowd alternately cheered or booed as Luther announced each ball. By the end of the game, dozens of people, including Doris and Mildred, had filled their cards except for one number, and were eagerly waiting for it to be called. They all shouted out their special numbers each time Luther spun the cage.

"Doctor's orders! B-9," called Luther, finally.

Mildred raised her hands and yelled, "Bingo!" and started to jump up and down. Four opening twangs of a Gibson guitar rang out against a series of piano triplets, and a young Elvis began to croon *Money Honey* on the overhead speakers. Mildred hurried to the stage to claim her prize.

Luther quickly looked over Mildred's card and announced that she had won. He flashed a stack of one-hundred-dollar bills at the crowd and they began to cheer and whistle. Mildred stood there wide-eyed with her hand extended. As Luther dealt each bill into her open palm, the crowd counted along. When he counted the last bill, Mildred began to dance around, waving the cash in time to the music.

THE ELVIS BIRD

"Damn it!" said Doris. She threw the last Bingo card high into the air and watched as it spiraled to the floor and landed on top of all the others.

###

On the trip home, Doris was the first to mention the game. "How does she do it? She wins every other month. She'll be talking about this for weeks."

"Are you disappointed?" asked Susan.

Doris was sitting in the back seat, and remained silent, so Susan turned around to face her.

"No, I suppose not. She's too proud to admit it, but Mildred needs that money. Her husband died last year, and she's facing some large medical bills. I just wish she wouldn't lord it over me every time she wins."

"How often do you two play Bingo?" asked Susan.

"Every Wednesday night."

"And how many times has Mildred won?"

"Four times in the past six months – all four were jackpots."

Susan turned to Miles. "That doesn't make sense – mathematically."

"Why is that?" asked Miles.

"There must have been two hundred people in that room tonight, so the chances of winning are pretty small. The probability of winning the jackpot four times in six months is ridiculously small."

"Can you prove that?"

"Any mathematician would know that something's fishy."

"Are you suggesting it's a fixed game?"

"Polya would tell us to look at the problem in front of us and figure out how the parts are related."

As they drove along, Miles began to think about their night on the town. What exactly he had he seen? And what parts were important? Was there a common, unseen thread that connected everything? Did Luther rig the game?

21. The Memphis Fireball

For the first brood there are generally six eggs. They are deposited on a few chips at the bottom of the hole, and are of a pure white colour.

-James Audubon, The Birds of America

Doris had made a full breakfast and was adding another helping of eggs to Miles' plate. She patted his shoulder with her hand and touched his head, repositioning a wayward strand of hair off his brow—a simple gesture that made him feel like a kid. He watched as she returned the frying pan to the stove.

"Don't forget that your brother is coming for a visit this afternoon," she said, "He called this morning to remind you. He said you would probably forget."

Miles had, indeed, forgotten.

"But I'm scheduled to work with Hoppy in the afternoon."

"Can you change it? George is driving up here just to see you. He wants to know if I need to be shipped off to an old folks' home."

"He's worried about you, Mom."

"He's worried I'll keep on living in this house."

Miles didn't like the direction the conversation had taken. "I'll call Hoppy and cancel."

"Don't cancel, Miles." Susan had appeared in the doorway. "I can take your spot on the skiff this afternoon. And while I'm at the camp, I can return Hopkins's computer. I copied all the files after we returned from the Bingo game last night."

"Did you find the gunshot recording?" asked Miles.

"I did. Lots of others, too. At some point, Hopkins must have used his personal computer to transfer the audio files back to Cornell."

"Great!" said Miles. "While you're in camp, Bert can loan you one of the graduate student machines. You can start on those."

Susan removed a plate from the cabinet and helped herself to the grits and eggs that Doris had prepared. Miles considered how easily Susan had become part of the household routine. She and Doris seemed like old friends now, with a mutual sense of admiration. How did that happen, and why was he so happy about it? Susan had walked into his office with a similar effect. He had resisted until now. No more.

"Why are you staring at me, Miles?" asked Susan.

"I was thinking about ... Hoppy's computer."

Doris was standing at the sink drying a dish and seemed to sense Miles' discomfort. "Speaking of computers," said Doris, "I'd like you to teach me how to use one while you're here, Susan."

THE ELVIS BIRD

"What?" said Miles, turning around to look at her. "You've always hated technology."

"Mildred Terry uses one at the public library to get her email. I'd like to try that."

"I don't believe it," said Miles.

Susan pinched Miles gently on his arm and made a face.

"Good for you, Doris, we can start this evening," she said, "We can practice on my computer."

Doris folded the dish towel and laid it on the counter.

"I want to start Googling. Mildred raves about that."

She handed Miles a casserole dish. "Put this on the top shelf. I'm still tired from last night. I'm going to take a nap."

When she had left, Miles said, "What's going on with her?"

"Be happy that she has an active mind."

"She's up to something."

Susan leaned closer to Miles and whispered, "So how about you, Dr. Audubon? Would you like me to check your hard drive?"

Miles embraced her and they kissed.

"It shouldn't take very long," she said slyly after pulling away.

"Why is that?"

"You only have a thumb drive."

###

A BENJAMIN MILES MYSTERY

It was noon when George pulled into the parking lot across the street from the Okefenokee Restaurant. The two brothers had arranged to meet for lunch. Miles was sitting in a booth by the window when his older brother eased past the restaurant in a shiny Mercedes E-Class. He watched with interest as George drove over to the far side of the lot, away from the other cars, and parked straddling a line, taking up two spaces. His brother got out of the car to look things over. Satisfied with what he saw, he clicked the remote twice and the car lights flashed.

It had been a couple of years since Miles had seen his older brother, and by the looks of it, George was keeping the weight off his tall frame. He appeared fit and handsome as he stepped across the street. The two men hugged like bears when George finally appeared at the booth.

"Nice wheels," said Miles.

George's face lit up. "Came in just last week," he said, "Ordered it up custom from Germany. What are you driving these days, Benny-boy?"

"A bicycle."

"Well, if you're that damn poor, professor, how about I buy you some lunch?"

"You already have. I ordered a couple of barbecues for us and told the waitress to give you the check. That ok?"

"Don't I always buy your meals?"

A waitress appeared suddenly with two waters, put them on the table, and hurried off.

"How's Charlene?" asked Miles.

THE ELVIS BIRD

George raised his eyebrows. "Don't ask. I bought her a computer last year, and now she spends all her time on the internet. She hasn't looked up from that laptop in six months. Google. Twitter. Facebook. Instagram. Tic Toc. Skype. Second Life. You name it. I have no idea what half that stuff is, Benny boy."

George looked anxiously out the window as a car drove into the parking lot. "I'd be happy just to have a *first life*. In fact, I'd love to have my old life back – now that would be perfect. I have to send that woman an email just to get her attention in bed."

"Don't look to me for sympathy, brother," said Miles.

"Aren't you over that divorce?"

"I'm working on it."

"Got any fish nibbling at the bait?"

"I haven't been fishing, George."

A smile came over George's face. "You gotta cast the rod, Benny, or your hook'll get rusty. Anyway, Mom said you brought a woman down from Cornell."

"That's true – a colleague."

"Colleagues usually stay in hotels."

"Mom needed some company."

"Ha! That's a good one, Benny-boy. I gotta remember that one. This colleague gotta name?"

"Susan Swail"

"Am I gonna get to meet her?"

"Come to dinner."

A BENJAMIN MILES MYSTERY

Miles began to wonder what Susan would think of George. It wasn't hard to guess. Most women liked him instantly. George had some inner magnetism that seemed to attract women. He was a good-looking man who enjoyed talking and listening to women - a real charmer - and underneath all the bluster, a sweetheart.

George propped his arm on top of the booth and surveyed the restaurant, "I haven't been in this place in years. I see they still have the same damn sign outside. Doesn't anything ever change in this town?"

"Folkston wasn't a bad place to grow up," offered Miles.

"If you were an alligator."

"We had some good times here."

"The only good thing that ever happened here was Elvis playing the city auditorium, and that was over in Waycross, before we were born."

Miles knew what was coming. He had heard the story many times before. Still, he liked hearing his brother tell it. He liked seeing the faraway look in George's eyes as he imagined a twenty-one-year-old Elvis strutting out on stage so many years ago.

"I can't believe Elvis was on the bill with the Louvin Brothers and Maybelle Carter. They billed him as *The Memphis Fireball*," said George. "Tight black pants, a lime-green shirt, and black rhinestone cufflinks. The first song the band played was *Long Tall Sally*. The week before that, he had been on the Ed Sullivan Show. Can you imagine that?

THE ELVIS BIRD

New York one week and Waycross, Georgia the next. What must the King have thought about that?"

"He wasn't the King at that point, George."

"Elvis was always the King. People say he drove into town with a pink Cadillac full of good-looking women."

"Is that why you've always owned nice cars, brother?"

George glanced at his car across the parking lot. "Having a nice car doesn't hurt. You could learn a lesson about that. I'll take you for a ride when we're done."

Velvia, the waitress who had served Miles the last time he was in the restaurant, walked over and rested a tray of food on the table.

"Who's this you've got with you, Miles?" She looked at George like a kid admiring an extra dessert.

"This is my brother, George."

She took a step back to look George over. "I haven't met *you* before, George. I wouldn't forget a thing like that. You must be Benjamin's *older* brother."

"Guilty! I got all the looks in the family, and Benny here, he got all the brains," he said, pulling out a familiar line.

"Well, you didn't get short-changed on that deal, George, no, Sir-ree." Velvia chuckled and began to off-load their dishes onto the table. When she had finished, she tucked the empty tray under her arm. "Anything else you boys need?"

"Nothing on the menu," said George.

Velvia smiled at that old chestnut, and after taking one last glance at George, headed back to the kitchen.

"Do you flirt with every woman you meet?" asked Miles.

"Just the ones who like it. I am politically correct."

"How do you get away with it?"

"Everyone wants to feel desired, Benny-boy. Didn't they teach you that life-lesson at Cornell? No? Then you need to enroll in the University of George and learn from the master: Women like attention – we all do. If I can provide some woman a little happiness on an otherwise dull day, what's the harm in that? You ought to try it sometime."

"You're the expert, brother."

George picked up his sandwich and said, "I really shouldn't be eating this." He took a bite. As he was chewing, he mumbled, "Cholesterol."

"A little barbecue never hurt anyone," Miles suggested.

Between bites, George changed the subject. "Did you ever find that bird you were searching for? That Ivory-billed Woodpecker?"

"We thought we did –two weeks ago. Now, I think the influx of tourists may have frightened it away."

George put his sandwich down and reached for a napkin. "The old-timers used to talk about seeing Ivory-bills all over this swamp. But that was in the thirties and forties. You know what I think, Benny?"

"What's that, bro?"

"I never saw an Ivory-billed Woodpecker the whole time you and I were growing up around here, and we practically lived in that swamp when we were kids. I think that bird got out while the gettin' was good. Just like you and I did."

"Maybe so. Lately, I've wished that I hadn't come back."

THE ELVIS BIRD

"Why is that?"

"We lost a graduate student on this expedition."

George was about to take another bite but lowered his sandwich. "I read about that in the Jacksonville Times. What happened?"

"Someone shot him and left him for dead out in the Okefenokee."

"Do the police have any leads?"

"I don't know. Can you tell me anything about Luther Preston?

"You think he's involved?"

Miles shrugged.

"You stay out of it, little brother. Leave it to the police. Dad would tell you the same thing if he were here. Luther Preston is one bad apple."

Velvia reappeared at the table with two menus.

"How 'bout dessert, boys?" she asked.

George jumped in, "How's the peach pie?"

"Real good," she said. "We use fresh peaches."

"In that case, Velvia, bring us two slices. Three if you'd like to join us." Velvia giggled and walked back to the kitchen.

George wiped his mouth with a napkin and tossed it on the table. He leaned back in the booth and straightened his posture. "Look, Benny, we need to talk."

"I thought that was what we were doing."

"We need to talk about Momma."

Miles was dreading this conversation.

"Why don't you go first?" said Miles.

"Ok. She's gettin' older and starting to have some health issues. Charlene and I think she ought to sell her house and move closer to us in Jacksonville. I mean, you're way up in New York, and you can't be flying down here every time she needs some help."

"I know that, George."

"You flew down this time, but if she gets sick again, I'm probably the one that'll have to jump in."

"I know that, too."

"Charlene found this place on the beach especially designed for older folks. It's real nice with three levels of care. Momma can start out on her own if she wants to – completely independent. She can even have a room with a beach view."

George removed a slickly printed brochure from his coat pocket and offered it to Miles. "Check it out."

Miles opened the brochure and read the front copy. He flipped it over. There were photographs of older couples in active poses. Swimming. Tennis. Golf.

"Looks expensive," said Miles, putting the brochure back on George's side of the table.

"It is. But money's not the problem. I can afford it, and I'm happy to pay for it."

Miles nodded, lowered his voice, and said confidentially, "Mom thinks you want to move her out of Folkston so that you can sell her house."

"Sell her house?" he asked incredulously. "It's not worth anything, Benny. Who wants to move way out here in the sticks?"

"She doesn't want to move out, you must know that."

"That's why I'm asking for your help. Show her the brochure," he said, sliding it back to Miles' side of the table. "Drive her over to Jacksonville and get her to take a look at the place. She won't listen to me. We gotta do something soon."

Standing in the parking lot after the meal, George looked over his Mercedes like a proud father admiring a newborn. Miles circled the huge automobile, admiring its sleek lines while George enumerated its hidden features.

"Wanna try her out, Benny?" asked George, shaking the car keys in the air.

"Sure!" said Miles. He snatched the keys from George's hand and got in behind the wheel.

"I'll ride shotgun," said George.

"Where should we go?" asked Miles. He buckled his seat belt and started the car. The engine noise was barely audible inside the cabin.

"Why don't we head up to Waycross? You can really open it up on the open road. Let's see what she can do. The Germans built this car for the Autobahn, you know."

A BENJAMIN MILES MYSTERY

Miles backed out of the space and came to a full stop at the parking lot entrance. He looked both ways before easing the sedan onto Main Street. When he stepped on the gas, the sudden acceleration tossed his head back against the headrest, hinting at the engine's harnessed power.

"Let's drive by the Waycross auditorium and take a look at the old place," said George dreamily. "I haven't been up there in years." He was staring at the road ahead as if it led directly to some distant past.

Outside of town, Miles pressed down on the accelerator as they crossed the city limits. The speedometer eased up to eighty. It felt like forty.

"You know Elvis left that building years ago," said Miles.

George leaned forward and pressed a button on the CD player. The selector moved silently, and soon Elvis began to croon the lyrics to *Be-Bop-A-Lula*. George began to mouth the words and snap his fingers in time to the music.

He paused long enough to say, "Elvis may have left the building, Benny, but just like that bird of yours, he still ain't dead."

22. Anonymous Tip

The young are seen creeping out of the hole about a fortnight before they venture to fly to any other tree. The second brood makes its appearance about the 15th of August.
-James Audubon, The Birds of America

"After we sit outside for a while, we can all have dessert," said Doris. "I made some peach puffs. We can just leave the dishes for later."

With that maternal imprimatur, George, Miles, and Susan followed Doris guiltlessly from the kitchen table to the front porch. George and Doris were the first outside and claimed the old wooden rockers. Miles and Susan took the swing. Doris had prepared an early dinner so that George would have time to drive back to Jacksonville. The sun was just beginning to dip below the horizon. The ancient oaks in the front yard were turning gold in the diffuse light, creating a short-lived tableau as the day was coming to an end.

"I've never met any of Benny's *colleagues* before," said George. He winked knowingly at Miles. "This is a first, Susan. When I lived here, the only girl Benny ever brought home to Mama wore braces and pigtails."

A BENJAMIN MILES MYSTERY

"Don't believe a word he says," said Miles, propping his arm on the swing behind Susan, "By the time I was interested in girls, George was long gone. He's much older than me."

Undeterred, George plowed ahead, "Benny told me all about you on our drive up to Waycross this afternoon. He had lots of nice things to say."

"He did?" asked Susan, giving Miles an appraising look.

"Would you like me to give you a *for-instance*?"

"Sho nuff, George," said Susan with a smile.

"Well, for one thing, he told me you were from San Francisco."

"Born and raised."

"In that case, I just have to ask - have you ever meet Tony Bennett?" George struggled to keep a straight face.

"I believe you've been talking to Miss Mildred, George," said Susan.

"Come to think of it, Benny may have mentioned that you ran into her at the Bingo game last night."

"What else did Benny tell you?" She gave Miles a sideways glance.

"He said you were the best-looking mathematician he's ever met."

Miles raised his hand. "Now, I didn't say that, George."

"Well, you were thinking it, weren't you, brother?"

Miles nodded.

"Anything else?" asked Susan.

George rubbed his chin with one hand. "I believe he said that you're really good with numbers and computers. *Mathematical wizard* was the term he used."

"You wouldn't pull a girl's leg, now would you, George?"

"No, ma'am. Benny said you used cold mathematical logic to figure out that our local Bingo parlor was as crooked as the Suwannee River."

"There *is* something odd about that bingo game. The probabilities don't make any sense. I suspect Luther Preston's involved somehow."

George stopped rocking and leaned forward. "You can be sure that if Luther Preston is involved, something about that game is shady. That whole family's been on the wrong side of the law for as long as I can remember."

Doris disagreed. "Your dad would have arrested him years ago if he was a crook, Georgie. Nothing ever got by your father. I never heard him say a bad word about Luther."

"That whole family made their money running moonshine between here and Jacksonville," George insisted. "That's well-documented history. It's a whole generation of crooks."

"Ancient history," insisted Doris. "When your dad was still alive, he didn't put up with any shenanigans in his hometown."

"He's been gone a long time, Mom."

That idea seemed to derail Doris momentarily. "Sometimes, it feels like that part of my life happened to someone else - someone I don't remember." She paused.

"Then again, some days, it wouldn't surprise me to see your dad walk right through that door and ask for his supper. It would be so natural if he did that, so easy. We would pick up right where we left off."

"Doris, you're going to make me cry," said Susan.

"I'm ok with it now, honey. It was a long time ago. I wouldn't change anything about my life. When you get older, the harder parts of life – like dying or losing someone – don't seem as painful as when you're young and foolish and in love. You start to take a longer view of things."

Doris' comment seemed to resolve all concerns for the moment, and everyone sat enjoying the evening, their thoughts interrupted only by the chattering of tree frogs in the distance. After a pause in the conversation, Doris announced, "I think it's time we sampled those peach puffs."

Miles's phone began to chirp as the group headed back to the kitchen. He glanced down at the display: Sergeant Booker. Miles waved for Susan to go ahead and waited to take the call on the porch.

"Glad I caught you, Pro-fessor," said Booker, "I wanted you to hear this from me before you saw it on the news. We've made an arrest in the Lionel Ames case – just this afternoon."

Miles walked to the end of the porch. "Who was it?"

"We arrested Luther Preston. If all goes as planned, he'll be formally charged with murdering Lionel Ames tomorrow afternoon."

THE ELVIS BIRD

"Why did you arrest him?" Miles wanted to hear the reasons, even though he thought he already knew what they were.

"I can't give you any of the details at this point. I can tell you that we received an anonymous tip which led to some hard, physical evidence tying Preston with Ames."

"What sort of evidence?"

"I'm not at liberty to say. The GBI has been working with us since the coroner determined that Ames was murdered. The evidence is com-pelling. We even collected some DNA, but that will take a few months to analyze. We still have to convince the DA that there's enough evidence to prosecute him. We'll be meetin' with her in the morning. That recording you gave me will help with that. I just thought you'd want to know about the arrest as soon as possible."

"Thanks, Sergeant. Thanks for calling me."

"There is somethin' else."

"What's that?"

"We ruled out your colleague, Susan Swail. The evidence involves her, so we had to check things out. The interview she gave turned out to be pretty helpful."

Miles turned and looked inside the house through the front porch window. He could see the group chatting around the kitchen table.

"Exactly how is Susan involved?"

Booker hesitated. "I can't tell you that. I've already said more than I should have."

"Well …I appreciate your call. I'll let Susan know what has happened."

"If anything changes, I'll get back to you."

So, Hopkins was right. Luther took retribution against poor Lionel after all. Miles rejoined the others and relayed the details of his conversation with Booker, but he omitted the part about Susan's involvement.

They all moved into the living room to have dessert and to watch the story breaking on a Jacksonville news channel. The segment featured an interview with the Folkston police chief, followed by images of Luther Preston being loaded into the back of a police cruiser. An officer pushed Luther's head down as he got into the car, and tossed Luther's leather hat into the back seat before closing the cruiser door. Doris returned to the kitchen to make coffee. George had a second peach puff before heading back to Jacksonville.

After Miles had gone to bed, Doris tapped lightly on his bedroom door. She opened it slowly to see if he was still awake. He was. She entered his room and sat next to him on the bed before taking his hand.

"I need to ask you something, Benjamin."

"What's that, Mom?"

"I want to know why Georgie really came here today." The dimly lit room couldn't mask the concern on her face. "He wants to send me to a nursing home, doesn't he?"

Miles met her gaze. "He's worried about you."

"He just wants to get rid of me."

THE ELVIS BIRD

"He thinks it's what you need." Her look of concern slowly changed to disappointment.

Miles adjusted his position in bed. "George brought me a brochure. I left it on the dresser for you. Why don't you take a look at it? It looks like a nice place. We could ride over to Jacksonville one afternoon next week. George invited us to come for dinner."

She seemed to be weighing the options. "I want you to know that I'm not ready for that yet. Maybe someday, but not now." She got up to leave.

"Will you at least look at the brochure?"

Doris walked over to the dresser, picked up the brochure, and examined it in the hallway light.

"I don't play golf or tennis, Benny. And I don't have my husband, like the women in those pictures. As long as I live here, your dad is still alive for me. Do you understand?"

Miles nodded.

She returned the brochure to the dresser and walked out, closing the door behind her. Miles felt awful. Why did he ever agree to show her the brochure? What had started as concern for her health now felt like a betrayal. He had difficulty falling asleep and dozed fitfully through the night.

23. Bingo Scam

The young are at first of the colour of the female, only that they want the crest, which, however, grows rapidly, and towards autumn, particularly in birds of the first breed, is nearly equal to that of the mother.

-James Audubon, The Birds of America

The next morning, Miles discovered Doris standing at the kitchen counter when he wandered in from his bedroom, still shirtless. She was laying out a single bowl and spoon beside a box of cereal.

"Oh, good, you're up," she said when she saw him come in. "You'll have to fix your own breakfast today, honey. Susan and I are driving to Jacksonville —we're going shopping."

"You and Susan?"

"Girls' day off. Fend for yourself."

"What are you shopping for, Mom?"

"Can't tell you, sweetie. It's a secret. We're taking your rental car. My old clunker might not make it." She walked over to the door and added, "Come show me how to use that satellite thingy in your car."

"The GPS?"

THE ELVIS BIRD

"That's it." she said, as she headed out.

Miles called to her, "Why all the mystery?"

No response.

###

A heatwave had moved into Georgia, and by mid-morning, vapor was rising from the dark waters of the Okefenokee, adding to the oppressive humidity. The birds and beasts of the swamp were hiding from the heat. Even the clouds seemed fixed in place. Everyone in Fortson said it felt like a sauna. The dogs of the town had taken refuge under the generous front porches of the homes along Main Street, and the children played electronic games indoors, free of parental admonitions.

Hopkins and Miles had taken a skiff into the central part of the swamp for the morning. They anchored their boat to a large peat battery, tying it off on a tree limb. A chorus of frogs was complaining about the disturbance that Miles was making as he moved around the floating island.

"I've changed my mind about you, buddy," yelled Hopkins – he was lying in the shade of the tarpaulin on the deck of the boat, hidden from view.

"How's that?" Miles yelled back.

"I'm glad you came down here, after all."

The battery was huge and had become permanently anchored in the swamp bed by the roots of the vegetation it supported. Miles made his way across it like a man walking on a waterbed. He negotiated his way to an ARU that was lashed to a pond cypress.

"What would I do without you?" continued Hopkins. He raised his head off the deck to gauge Miles' reaction. "After all, you've become quite adept at changing batteries."

Miles raised his arm over his head, middle finger extended. Hopkins smiled and lay back down.

"Don't forget to copy the data off that drive," reminded Hopkins. Miles sighed and retrieved a flash drive from his pocket and inserted it into a slot on the ARU. He pressed a button and waited as a light on the device flashed on and off. The process took several minutes – much slower than the other ARUs. When the light finally turned off, he put the flash drive into his pocket. It was then he heard the metallic snap of a gun barrel from behind. Miles wheeled around and stared at the boat. Hopkins was nowhere to be seen.

"Hoppy?" shouted Miles.

There was no response.

"Hoppy!" Panic seized him suddenly, racing into his being on a single breath. He hurriedly scanned the boat, then the swamp, then the boat again. His hands and feet were frozen and useless.

Hopkins finally raised his head. "What are you yelling about? I'm trying to sleep."

Miles exhaled and took a breath.

"Jesus," whispered Miles. He stared at Hopkins and waited for his heartbeat to moderate.

"What's wrong with you?" asked Hopkins.

THE ELVIS BIRD

"Nothing," said Miles, shaking his head. He began to retrace his steps. After reaching the boat, he grabbed the gunwale, and in a continuous motion, tossed his leg over the side and rolled in. He sat up and looked at the skiff anew, searching for a gun. A sudden breeze shifted the boat against the battery. It jarred a loose metal push-pole lying on deck. It rolled against an equipment locker with a clatter.

"Jesus," he whispered again.

Lionel's death had made him jumpy. A single noise had implanted a doubt. Did the police have the wrong man?

Hopkins, who was now standing behind the wheel, walked over and untied the boat from the overhead branch. He hoisted the loose pole off the deck, secured it against the gunwale with a rope, and pushed the skiff away from the battery.

"Are you just going to stand there?" he asked. He handed the pole to Miles and walked back to the wheel. Minutes later, they were back in an open channel. The boat picked up speed as it moved into deeper water. Miles rejoined Hopkins at the helm, and the two men began to talk loudly over the engine noise.

"Where's your girlfriend today?" asked Hopkins.

Miles didn't want to admit that she was in Jacksonville with his mother. "She's been working on an algorithm for detecting double-knocks," said Miles.

Hopkins continued to gaze at the waterway ahead. "If she has something useful, I want to see it. Fitzsimmons will pull the plug on this expedition if we don't find something soon. He asks for a progress report every day now. And he calls me every night."

It was a bad sign that Fitzsimmons was involved in the expedition on a daily basis. Running the Cornell bird lab was a full-time job for anyone. Things were worse than Miles had imagined.

Hopkins slowed the boat to a crawl as the waterway suddenly narrowed.

"The administration is on his ass. The university president doesn't like the negative publicity this project has generated. He wants proof that the bird exists. If Swail has something, we need it now."

"I get the picture, Hoppy. I'll tell Susan to speed it up."

The skiff moved into a channel filled with submerged tree stumps. They were artifacts left behind by failed logging operations. Miles stepped forward to look for obstacles, and Hopkins slowed the boat to a crawl. It took several minutes to navigate the narrow raceway. When it was clear ahead, Miles rejoined Hopkins at the wheel. Miles decided to prod Hopkins for information.

"There's something bothering me, Hoppy."

"Et tu, brother? Everybody wants something from me these days."

"The police called me last night," said Miles. "They received an anonymous tip that led to Luther's arrest."

"Is that so? Good for them."

THE ELVIS BIRD

"I think they got their information from you. You knew that Luther had threatened Lionel. You argued with him about it."

Hopkins took a step closer to Miles, still holding onto the wheel.

"I told the police exactly what I told you. Preston and his son came out to the camp one evening to complain about Lionel. He wanted Lionel to stay away from his granddaughter, and frankly, I couldn't blame him. Hell, I agreed with him. Lionel wanted to nail everything in Folkston wearing a skirt."

"What else did you tell the police?"

"I told them Preston and his son looked like tough characters – which they are. And I told them that I sent Lionel home for his own good."

The boat was approaching Floyd's Island, and Hopkins turned the skiff sharply into a small riverway, heading back to the Cornell campsite.

"Luther Preston killed Lionel," stated Hopkins, "You know that, right? It's the simplest explanation."

Miles hesitated. "Why would Luther kill Lionel after talking with you?"

"Lionel was an impudent kid. Full of himself. Maybe he just pushed the old man too far and paid the price."

"Could someone else have held a grudge against Lionel?" Miles asked.

"Are you kidding? All the girls wanted to screw him, and all the guys wanted to be like him. I even think Swail took a turn before we hired her. Why else would she follow him to Cornell?"

"Leave her out of this," said Miles, raising his voice.

Hopkins held up both hands.

"I see I touched a nerve. Have things progressed that far?"

"Nothing happened between Susan and Lionel," said Miles.

Hopkins continued to press. "If nothing happened, why did the police call her in for an interview?"

"She was trying to help the kid."

"You're telling me she left a cushy position at Stanford to come here to work with birds? She has no background in ornithology. Did you even ask about her relationship with Ames before you gave your heart away, buddy?"

Miles didn't want to think about it. He turned and walked back to the stern of the boat to get away from Hopkins. Neither man mentioned Lionel or Susan again that day.

###

That evening after returning home, Miles waited impatiently on Doris' front porch for the two women to return from Jacksonville. Most of the townsfolk had gone to bed hours earlier. Miles could hear the Florida orange train in the distance as it rumbled through the Folkston funnel —a chokepoint for all trains traveling to and from Florida. It was heading north to Waycross and points beyond. The rumbling of the trains carried for miles in the warm night air. The only other competing noises were the nearby tree frogs and crickets.

Miles nodded off while sitting in the rocking chair. He was awakened by the noise of the Lexus and the flash of the headlights as it turned into the front yard. Doris was driving, and she tapped the horn twice after parking near the porch. The two women got out of the car, giggling like childhood friends as they collected their packages from the back seat.

"Benjamin," said Doris, "Your GPS is a hoot!"

"You're late," said Miles. He walked down the steps and greeted Susan. She handed him two packages.

"Your mom programmed the GPS like a champ. She found us a great Italian place on the way home."

"You gotta get me one of those," said Doris, looking directly at Miles.

Miles realized she was serious. "Why would you need a GPS around here, Mom? You never go further than Folkston for groceries. There are only two main roads in the whole town. Besides, you've lived here for fifty years."

"It's like having a friend come along to tell you where to turn, Sweetie. You know - *You are approaching your exit. Prepare to turn right in one hundred yards.* If you miss the turn, the darn thing figures that out, too. I'll set it up to speak in Italian." said Doris. "*La signora, si prepara per girare a destra in cento yarde.*' I'd like that. Wouldn't that be something? Mildred Terry will be green with envy."

Miles stared at his mother in amazement, "You speak Italian?"

Doris tapped Miles' chest with her finger. "You're not the only one who's been to college, Pro-fessor."

"I had no idea," said Miles, dumbfounded.

"Why would I speak Italian around you? You wouldn't understand a word I said."

"True, but I still don't understand why you want a GPS."

"Honey, when you live alone, you need to hear the sound of another human being occasionally – even if it's just a disembodied voice coming out of an electronic thing-a-ma-jig. I turn on CNN just to hear another voice in the room."

"I get it. I'll buy you a GPS. Why are you so late getting home? You two left early this morning."

Susan sidled up to Miles and put her arm around his waist. "Your mother wanted some Italian food. We had a lovely three-course meal and a dessert at a small place downtown."

"Don't forget the wine," reminded Doris.

"Yes, we had a nice bottle of wine, as well," said Susan.

"And the dessert wine. Don't forget that," said Doris.

"Are you two tipsy?" asked Miles.

"I'm not," said Doris.

"Your mother and I had an excellent meal and some wonderful conversation. We took our time. You should try it sometime. You could learn a thing or two from your mother."

"What's that supposed to mean?"

THE ELVIS BIRD

Susan began to recite Yates she walked up the steps:

Wine comes in at the mouth
And love comes in at the eye;
That's all we shall know for truth
Before we grow old and die.
I lift the glass to my mouth,
I look at you, and sigh.

At the top of the steps, she turned and threw Miles an air kiss.

"You are tipsy!" he said indignantly.

"Perhaps. But I won't be tomorrow. You, however, will still be a stick-in-the-mud." She began to giggle. "Your mother thinks so, too."

"She does not!"

Doris took Miles' arm.

"We decided that you are a bit of a wet rag, sweetie," said Doris. "You're very clever, Benjamin, you always have been. And sweet. But the only thing that attracts your attention in this world is birds. Just open your eyes, Honey. That's all we're saying."

Miles wrinkled his brow. "I always knew that George was your favorite."

Doris pulled him closer.

"Your brother George knows how to have fun," she said, patting his back.

Miles pushed her back to arm's length.

"Both of you have had way too much wine. That's what I think," he said.

"In vino veritas, Benjamin," said Doris, "Now come see what I bought." She opened the door and Miles followed her into the house. They all moved to the kitchen, and Doris placed her shopping bag on the floor. She reached into it and removed a black presentation box, which she placed proudly on the table.

"A MacBook?" said Miles.

"The salesman said it would do everything I need. I also bought a wireless internet card, so it's ready to go. Crank it up, Benjamin. I want to try it out."

Miles removed the computer, opened the cover, and pressed the start button. The machine began to whir and the screen filled with icons.

"Now, pull up the browser," said Doris. "You know what a browser is, don't you?"

"I know what a browser is, Mom."

Miles reached for the mouse and clicked on an icon. Instantly, the Google browser appeared on the screen.

"What should we search for?" asked Doris.

Susan jumped in before Miles could respond, "Try *Bingo scam*."

24. G-52

The males have then a slight line of red on the head, and do not attain their richness of plumage until spring, or their full size until the second year.

-James Audubon, The Birds of America

"This must be a new scam. I can't find a description of it anywhere," said Susan, turning away from Doris' laptop. The three of them were still sitting at the kitchen table after spending a half-hour searching the internet.

"How did you discover that Luther rigged the Bingo game?" asked Miles. His ego was still smarting from Susan calling him a *stick-in-the-mud*.

"It came to me in the restaurant tonight while Doris and I were waiting to be seated," said Susan. "The hostess took our names and gave us a ticket. We had to wait until she called our number. It was as simple as that."

"I'm not following you," said Miles.

"Remember what Polya advised?" said Susan.

"Who's Polya?" asked Doris between sips of coffee. She had brewed a pot of coffee and was finishing the first cup. The caffeine never seemed to affect her sleep and she would drink coffee at any hour.

"He's a mathematician, Mom. I'll explain it later." He turned to Susan, "Polya said we need to look closely at the facts."

"And what else did he advise?"

"That we should examine how the facts relate to each other."

"So –what are the facts we witnessed at the Bingo game?"

"That funny little man working with Luther brought in a new set of balls after every game. Did the scam have something to do with the balls?" asked Miles.

"No. The balls were perfect spheres."

"Luther would spin the cage, select a ball, and then call out the number. He placed the used balls in a box and flipped a switch to light up the board."

"That's right," said Susan.

"Did Luther deliberately miscall the numbers so that Mildred Terry could win?"

"No." Susan shook her head. "Too obvious – and dangerous. Luther called every ball correctly, and in the same order that the ball was selected during the game."

Doris had her own theory, "I'll bet he rigged the cage."

"I considered that, but the cages were fine," said Susan. "I looked one over after the game."

Miles had another idea. "The grand prize game was *Blackout*. You had to cover every square to win."

"Bingo!" said Susan. "That's an important fact."

THE ELVIS BIRD

Susan waited patiently, but Miles and Doris were stymied. How could a blackout game figure into a Bingo scam?

"Those are all the relevant facts I can remember," said Miles. "I give up. Just tell us. How did Luther rig the game?"

"When I learned that Mildred had won four times over the last few months, I knew that something was fishy. The odds of that are infinitesimal. I began to think back over the entire evening. I decided to do some research, and I learned that Bingo cards are sold in stacks of six thousand."

Doris had gotten up from the table and was refilling her cup.

"That's a lot of Bingo games," Susan observed. "Every card in a single stack has to be different —otherwise, you might have multiple, simultaneous winners."

"That makes sense," said Miles.

"There were about two hundred people at the Bingo game the other night, and almost every person bought a card for the grand prize game. It was Luther who sold all of those cards, right? No one else."

"That's right," said Miles.

"Now suppose the grand prize game cards were rearranged in a stack so that the first two hundred cards on top, the ones that would be sold to the regular folks, all contained the same number, say G-52. They could even contain several common numbers. It would take a while to sort the cards out that way, but anyone could put together an arrangement like that."

"Why would you do that?" asked Doris.

"I'm coming to that. The person arranging the cards could also place a single card on the bottom of the stack that didn't contain the number G-52. And when Mildred Terry came up to buy her grand prize card, they could make sure they sold her the card on the bottom of the stack."

"I still don't get it, Susan," said Doris.

"Keep talking," said Miles. "I think I see where this is going."

"The number G-52 acts like the number the waitress gave me at the restaurant tonight that prevented us from getting a seat. With the Bingo game, until G-52 gets called, nobody holding one of the first two hundred cards is going to win the game."

"I see that," said Miles, the light finally dawning. "But I still don't see the whole picture."

"Well, suppose you sell the cards in this prearranged state, every Wednesday night for several months."

Susan waited for it to sink in before continuing. "One night —maybe even on several of those nights —the number G-52 will be called toward the end of the game. And until Luther calls G-52, there's only one person in the room who has a chance to win – the person with the bottom card."

"Mildred Terry." Doris and Miles spoke in unison.

Doris looked puzzled "But arranging the cards in this way doesn't guarantee she's going to win."

"You're right. That's the beauty of this scam. It doesn't have to guarantee a win. In fact, Luther didn't want her to

THE ELVIS BIRD

win every time. That would be too obvious to everyone. He simply wanted to increase Mildred's chance of winning significantly every time she played. Over a year, she would win more often than anyone else. That's why she's won four times in the last few months."

"That's brilliant!" said Miles, amazed at Susan's guesswork and analysis. "I would never have figured that out."

"I'd say Luther Preston is the brilliant one."

Miles closed the computer. "It's perfectly obvious now. And there's no way to detect it. When the game is over, the balls, the cage, and even the cards all look perfectly normal – they are perfectly normal. Luther could play the game and call the balls normally, knowing that no one was going to pick up two hundred cards off the floor for comparison."

"Oh, no!" said Doris.

"What's wrong?" asked Susan.

"Is my best friend a cheat?"

Susan reached across the table and took Doris' arm. "This is all speculation, Doris. We don't know if any of this is true. And even if it is true, we don't know that Miss Mildred was involved."

25. Italian Men

No sooner, however, are the grapes of our forests ripe than they are eaten by the Ivory-billed Woodpecker with great avidity. I have seen this bird hang by its claws to the vines, in the position so often assumed by a Titmouse, and, reaching downwards, help itself to a bunch of grapes with much apparent pleasure.
-James Audubon, The Birds of America

The skiff was rounding the last bend in the river before returning to camp, when Miles spotted Susan standing on the dock. He had worked in the swamp all morning servicing ARUs for Hopkins, and he was weary of crawling in and out of the boat. Susan waved to them as the boat drew nearer.

Hopkins, who was behind the wheel, eased the skiff alongside the landing and shut off the engine. Miles jumped out and began to tie off the boat to a piling. Through the space between the boards of the dock, he could see an adult alligator sleeping in the mud. It was a common sight in the river that ran past the camp. The gator remained motionless even when Hopkins jumped noisily onto the dock.

Susan walked over to Miles and took his arm when he was done. "Take me to lunch, Birdman. I've made a breakthrough on the algorithm. I want to celebrate."

Hopkins stopped unloading his equipment and joined them when he overheard the conversation. "What's this about? A breakthrough I hope?"

"We have a database again," said Susan. "I've pieced together the data that was stored on the computers here in the camp. Fortunately, most of the local data that was collected here was transferred to Ithaca from a single machine."

"Which machine was that?"

"Yours."

"I didn't ask you to do that. You looked at my machine behind my back?"

"I needed the data and you needed your database, right? I didn't think you would mind."

Hopkins expression suggested he did. "Tell me about the breakthrough."

"I modified the old search algorithm. Now, I can control the searches in a way that makes them more accurate and efficient. I've been testing it on the gunshot recording."

Hopkins erupted, "I'm busting my ass to make recordings of birds, and you're still chasing down a gunshot? Leave the detective work to the police."

"Calm down," said Miles, putting a hand on his shoulder.

"I had to run tests against real data," argued Susan. "I'll be able to use the same technique to search for your bird."

"This is my job is at stake," said Hopkins. "I don't have time for nonsense. The police have already arrested the murderer." Hopkins turned his ire toward Miles. "Did you know she was wasting time on this gunshot recording?"

Miles stood his ground. "The work she's doing will help the search."

"When? This project is almost finished. When is it going to help?"

"It's ready now," said Susan, "I've already written the code. It's just a matter of changing the target sounds."

"I want to see what you've done. Show it to me now."

"Let me get it." Susan dashed off to retrieve her laptop.

The two men walked the short distance to the community tent. Miles took a seat at an empty table. Hopkins paced around the tent until Susan returned with her laptop. Soon the three of them were staring at the sonogram of the double knock of a Campephilus woodpecker.

While the audio recording played quietly, the screen image appeared hypnotic – a fiery band of reds, yellows, and purples, morphing as they drifted across a black background. Many of the pixels represented sounds beyond the range of the human ear.

Susan began to argue her case, "Up until now, we've focused our attention on only two sounds – the bird's kent call and its double-knock. The approach has been to filter out all other ambient noise and concentrate on those two things alone. We compare a known double-knock or kent call from the database against the recordings we've made in the swamp. The algorithms identify candidate noises in the database, and we revisit the places where those recordings were made."

"So, what's different?" asked Hopkins, impatiently.

"Conversations, even between birds, are two-way streets. It dawned on me that by removing the ambient noises around the target, we miss half of every conversation. I decided to use wider samples to capture both sides of a conversation. I decided the birds might be responding to stimuli that humans can't hear. The idea is to include those noises in the target recording. In that way, we might get a much richer target."

"This seems like a long shot to me," said Hopkins.

"Our only confirmed recordings of Ivory-bills are the ones that Tanner made in 1937," said Susan. "But we have a few recordings of other birds in the Campephilus family made right here in the Okefenokee. If I try sampling around those, I might capture a complete conversation instead of a one-sided interaction. If it's successful, we'll have a target that is specific to this reserve. We can use that target to search the entire database. At least the identifications will be different from the identifications we're getting with the old algorithms."

Hopkins looked at Miles, skeptically, "What do you think?"

"The current algorithms aren't working," said Miles, "What do we have to lose?"

Hopkins remained dubious. "Why are you using the gunshot audio? There aren't any birds on that recording. It seems like a waste of time."

"I needed to test the algorithm. I've been searching for human voices similar to the ones on the gunshot recording. I sampled the voices to see if there were any other ambient sounds them that we could match."

"Did it work?"

"I need more samples."

"So, it *was* a waste of time."

"No. It was just a way to test my theory, Hoppy – that's all. I don't need to use it again."

"All right," said Hopkins, finally conceding. "Why don't you come out with me this afternoon? We can record some Campephilus samples that are specific to the Okefenokee for your new algorithm. The swamp has a good many Pileated Woodpeckers. We can try different locations and recording distances. You can use those results to search the database."

Susan turned to Miles. "Looks like you're off the hook for lunch, Birdman."

Miles remembered his last outing with Hopkins and suddenly felt uneasy. Susan had little practical experience in the swamp. "I'll come along with you," said Miles.

Hopkins pushed away from the table. "No you won't. You stay here and review the data we collected this morning. Then make a work schedule for the rest of the week," said Hopkins. He looked back at Susan. "Meet me at the skiff in thirty minutes."

"I can make the schedule tonight," suggested Miles.

"Do it now. I'll give Susan a ride home when we're finished." He walked off without waiting for Miles to protest.

Susan started to leave and Miles reached out and took her arm. "I was wondering," said Miles.

"And what are you wondering about, Birdman?" She sat down beside him.

"Would you come to dinner with me tonight?"

"What about Doris?"

"I wasn't going to invite Doris. It would be … like a date."

"Oh, like a date?"

"Yes, like a date."

"And where would we go on this thing … like a date?"

Miles hadn't anticipated resistance.

"Look, I'm just trying to be spontaneous for once, like my brother. We can just punch something into the GPS and see where it takes us. Is it a date or not?"

"So, now, it's a date, is it?"

"Lionel's death interrupted us. I'd like to start over again, make a fresh start."

Susan hesitated, "Can you make the GPS speak in Italian?"

"Certemente," said Miles with a southern lilt.

"Well, I could never resist Italian men."

26. Sinking Spell

- The strength of this Woodpecker is such, that I have seen it detach pieces of bark seven or eight inches in length at a single blow of its powerful bill, and by beginning at the top branch of a dead tree, tear off the bark, to an extent of twenty or thirty feet, in the course of a few hours, ...

-James Audubon, The Birds of America

Miles grew worried when Susan didn't return on time from the reserve that evening. He called her cell phone repeatedly, but each unanswered call only increased his concern and impatience. Where was Hopkins? He and Doris had been waiting on the porch swing since sundown. It was eight o'clock now.

As a young woman, Doris had spent many nights worrying whether her own husband would return safely from some dangerous FBI business. All that waiting had turned her into a hard-boiled pragmatist. At some point, she had simply dismissed worrying as a useless indulgence.

"She's a smart woman, Benjamin. She can take care of herself," offered Doris, cheerily.

He laid his phone on the swing and took a sip of tea. Doris reached over and patted his knee. The two of them kicked their feet rhythmically as the swing moved back and forth.

"The way she figured out Luther's Bingo scam was amazing."

Miles heard an approaching car, stopped the swing with his foot, and waited expectantly. The car passed the house without slowing down. Miles pushed the swing with his foot to get it moving again.

"Your dad would have been impressed."

"You think so?"

She patted his knee again, got out of the swing, and picked up their empty glasses. The sound of another vehicle on the highway made her pause. This one seemed promising - it was slowing down. A white university van appeared at the end of the driveway and turned into the yard. The van's lights briefly illuminated the porch. It pulled into the yard, and stopped near the porch.

Susan got out and began to apologize.

"It's all my fault," she said.

Hopkins opened the driver's door and leaned out while holding onto the steering wheel with one hand. He kept one foot inside the van.

"We had a little accident," he said, "Nothing serious. More like an initiation. She fell into the river as we were docking." Hopkins sounded nonchalant. "She can tell you all about it. I'll see both of you in the morning. Don't be late." Hopkins shut the door before Miles could ask questions. He backed the van out of the yard and drove away.

Susan stepped into the porch light, and Miles could see that her hair was still wet and her clothes were soaked.

"Look at you," said Miles.

"I was so clumsy. I need a shower."

Doris opened the screen door and guided Susan inside. "I can handle this," she said, waving Miles off. She turned back to Susan. "Let's get you dry, honey."

Miles sat down at the top of the steps, relieved. The women's voices were barely audible inside the house, but he could hear cabinets being opened and closed. Someone turned on the shower. Eventually, Doris opened the screen door and poked her head outside.

"She's almost ready for your date."

Miles looked puzzled. Under the strain of the evening, he had forgotten their dinner plans.

Miles turned northward onto the Waycross highway and pressed hard on the accelerator. They were making a late start, but Susan insisted there was still time for the short trip and a quick meal.

"You're not weaseling out of this," she said.

"Tell me exactly what happened," said Miles.

Susan leaned back in the seat. "We had a good day in the swamp. Hoppy found several Pileated woodpeckers. We made some good recordings – double-knocks and kenting. It was time-consuming, and we were late returning to camp.

THE ELVIS BIRD

We also made a wrong turn on the way back to camp, but Hopkins wouldn't admit it."

"Tell me about falling into the water."

"That was my fault. Hoppy pulled the skiff alongside the dock. I jumped off too soon, and the boat lurched forward. I lost my balance and fell in."

"Why did the boat lurch?" asked Miles.

"Hoppy was still maneuvering it up to the dock. I should have waited."

"There are large alligators under that pier," said Miles.

"I know – I saw one up close. I yelled for help, but Hoppy couldn't hear me over the engine noise. Bert Williams saw me fall in, and ran over and pulled me out."

"Alligators think everything in the water is dinner."

"Let's not think about that. Where are we going on our date?"

By the time they reached Waycross, the only restaurant still open was a barbecue joint out on the highway. The concrete block building was painted enamel white, and there were two picture windows on either side of the entrance. A neon sign of a stylized pig wearing a chef's hat filled one of the windows. Susan glanced at it as they walked in. The pig was naked except for a smile and the hat.

"Ignore the self-referential irony of the sign," said Miles.

The waitress behind the counter, an older woman with a tired expression, said, "Sorry, we're closed, folks."

"Could we get a take-out?" asked Miles. "We drove all the way from Folkston to get a meal."

The waitress gave it some thought before reaching for a pad and a pencil.

"Two sandwiches, two teas," said Miles, "Lots of pickles."

The waitress scribbled the order onto a pad. "You're number eighty-seven." She handed him a ticket and walked away. Miles looked around the restaurant. They were the only customers in the place.

The waitress returned after a few minutes with a tray and two paper bags. "Here you go, honey," she said. She took Miles' money, handed him two cups, and pushed the tray across the counter.

They ate the sandwiches in the car.

"Good choice," said Susan, out of the blue. "Where's my dessert?"

Miles, looked back at the restaurant. "They put a closed sign on the door as we were leaving."

"That's not what I had in mind. Come closer, Birdman."

"What?"

"You heard me. Move over here, Miles," she said, grabbing his collar and pulling him across the seat. She proceeded to give him a long, slow kiss.

"Not bad for an ornithologist," she said when they were done.

Miles pulled her back for a second kiss.

###

THE ELVIS BIRD

Susan fell asleep on the way home. Miles was about to turn into Doris' driveway, when he spotted the flashing lights of a police car parked in the front yard. The eerie, blue light of the cruiser filled the yard hypnotically and filled his heart with dread. Did Doris have another attack?

Miles parked, and dashed out of the car. He found his mother lying on the settee in the front room, her head supported by a sofa cushion. Sergeant Booker was sitting beside her in a rocking chair. The big man was sitting on the chair edge, looking at Doris with a concerned expression.

"What happened?" Miles asked earnestly. Doris opened her eyes, reached out her arms to him, and smiled.

"I'm fine," she said.

Miles gave her a hug as Susan appeared in the front doorway.

"Miss Doris phoned me about an hour ago," said Booker. "I found her on the floor beside the phone. She wouldn't let me call an ambulance."

"I had another sinking spell," Doris explained. "Suddenly, I felt dizzy, so I lay down on the floor. I crawled over to the phone and called Pete. But I'm much better now."

"We really should call an ambulance," said Booker. He was looking directly at Miles. "Let's get her checked out properly."

"No," said Doris. "No doctors. I know what's wrong with me. I'm old, and that's all there is to it. Can you two fix *old*?"

The two men glanced at each other, stymied.

"I didn't think so."

Miles took a seat on the settee. "Tell me exactly what happened."

"It was just like the first time. My vision got blurry, and I began to feel dizzy and weak – this time, I just gave in to it and lay down. I didn't want you to come home and find me passed out on the floor, so I called Sergeant Booker."

Miles looked gratefully at Booker. "Thank you for coming, Sergeant."

"Glad to do it, Pro-fessor," said Booker. He stood up to leave. At the door, Booker turned back to look at the patient, "Miss Doris, I can have the ambulance here in a few minutes if you just say the word."

"I'm better off in my own bed tonight, Pete. Thank you for coming, though. These two can take it from here."

There was a mirror near the door, and Booker used it to adjust his hat. "Night, folks," he said as he was leaving.

Susan returned from the kitchen with a glass of water for Doris. "You need to stay hydrated," she said.

Doris looked sheepishly at the two of them, saying, "I'm sorry I spoiled your evening."

The three of them chatted for the next hour while Doris lay peacefully on the settee. Miles and Susan were watchful and observant, and avoided mentioning Doris' condition again. They talked about many things that evening: Miles' father and his career in the FBI; growing up in Folkston; George's love of cars and Elvis. They laughed about

THE ELVIS BIRD

Mildred's excitement over winning the Bingo game and they recalled their old family vacations in Miami. Susan described what it was like to grow up in San Francisco. The conversation was strangely therapeutic and the evening passed by without further incident. Somehow, while revisiting all of those memories, they came to a tacit agreement that Doris was fine for the moment, and that the danger had passed.

27. Counterfeiter

This species generally moves in pairs, after the young have left their parents.
-James Audubon, The Birds of America

Sergeant Booker returned the next morning, banging loudly on the front door before Miles had finished his breakfast.

"How is Miss Doris this morning?" Booker asked when Miles opened the door. The officer was smiling broadly and seemed cheerily unaware of how hard he had been knocking. Miles looked him over. The big guy was all spit and polish - shoes, belt, and badge. He filled up a doorway impressively.

"She's fine, Sergeant. Did you drive out here just to check on her?"

"Actually, I'm here about something else, Pro-fessor Miles. I didn't want to mention it last night - Miss Doris being sick and all."

"Come in, Sergeant, and sit down." Miles pointed him to a chair in the corner of the room and took a seat on the sofa. "What's this about?"

Booker adjusted the position of the chair slightly before sitting down.

THE ELVIS BIRD

"You already know that we arrested Luther Preston for the murder of Lionel Ames. Now, the district attorney is pressing us for more evidence. Our problem is that Luther is refusing to talk to anyone - even to his lawyer."

"Why would he do that?" asked Miles.

"Who knows? He's a hard-headed old coot. Some of these old guys like Luther, are pretty distrustful of everyone."

"What does this have to do with me?"

"Luther's been asking for you, Pro-fessor Miles."

"Really?"

"He wants to talk with you. He says he won't talk with anyone *but* you."

"I hardly know the man," said Miles.

"We don't understand it either," said Booker. "Do you know of any reason Luther Preston would want to meet with you?"

Miles shook his head slowly.

"Are you involved, or have you ever been involved with Luther Preston?" Booker's voice suddenly sounded official, and Miles wondered where this was going.

"I don't have any connections to Luther Preston."

Booker straightened himself up in the chair. "Good, that's good."

There was an awkward pause as he chose his words.

"This whole situation is highly unusual, but the captain would like you to come down and have a talk with Luther," said Booker.

A BENJAMIN MILES MYSTERY

"Why?"

"The captain thinks he'll tell you something that will help us develop some evidence against him."

"You want my help convicting him?"

"All you have to do listen to what he has to say. If there's anything useful, you can tell us. That's all. We just want to know the truth."

Miles settled back on the sofa. What good could come from talking with Luther? The old man needed a lawyer, not an ornithologist. Miles wondered if he needed a lawyer as well?

"I'm sorry, Sergeant. But I have no connections with Luther Preston. I don't see how my talking with Mr. Preston could help anyone. You'll have to develop your own evidence."

Booker was prepared for Miles' resistance and played his hidden ace. "Luther wanted you to know that he has information that would interest you. He said it was something important."

"What would that be?" asked Miles, completely puzzled by this new angle.

The sergeant removed a notepad from his front pocket, opened it, and began to read the dictation he had taken. "If you want to find that bird, you should pay me a visit." He closed the notepad and put it back in his pocket. "That's it, word for word."

THE ELVIS BIRD

Miles was stunned but didn't want to take the bait. What possible connection could Luther have with Ivory-billed Woodpeckers? The old man must be working an angle.

"What do you think Luther meant by that, Pro-fessor? Is he talking about this Elvis bird that's been in all the papers?"

"He's bluffing, Sergeant. He doesn't know anything of interest to me."

"So, you won't come to the jail and talk with him?" asked Booker.

Miles hesitated as George's words came to mind - *a whole generation of crooks*. Was it possible that Luther had killed Lionel over a bird? If Luther had information about Ivory-bills, Miles wanted it.

"What do you think Pro-fessor?"

Miles' thoughts were racing. Talking with Luther would be pointless. How could he be sure of anything the old man said? It was Susan who seemed to understand how Luther's mind worked.

"I'll talk to Luther under one condition," said Miles.

"What's that?"

"My colleague, Dr. Swail, gets to come along."

Booker's smile faded. "I don't know about that Pro-fessor. The captain didn't mention anyone else meeting with Luther. He won't like that idea one bit."

"Better check with your captain, then. That's my only offer."

Two hours later, after the captain had agreed, Miles and Susan drove downtown and parked in front of the old jail.

Miles left the air conditioner running while they sat in the car.

"Have you ever been inside a jail cell?" asked Susan.

"As a matter of fact, I have. Twenty years ago, I was arrested for counterfeiting and they put me in this very jail." Miles raised his eyebrows and waited for a response.

"I don't believe it. You would have been a teenager. What did you counterfeit?"

"Ten-dollar bills."

Susan looked at him skeptically, but Miles' expression remained serious.

"You are a much more complicated man than you appear at first glance," she said.

"Is that a compliment?"

"I'll tell you later. Just give me the details. I want to know everything."

Miles twisted in the car seat so he could face Susan directly and began to tell the story.

"It was all the Admiral's idea," he said.

"So, you're blaming your buddy?"

"Yep. The Admiral had a bright idea. We were in high school, and he worked in the principals' office every afternoon. He thought it would be fun to print up some ten-dollar bills on the copier. He said we could pass them around to everyone and act like big shots."

"So, you Xeroxed ten-dollar bills?"

"Front and back. Cut them out with scissors and taped them together."

THE ELVIS BIRD

"Black and white?" asked Susan.

"Yep," Miles added.

"That wouldn't fool anyone."

"We weren't trying to fool anyone. It was all a big joke. We made fifty or sixty bills and passed them out to all our friends."

"So, how did you get arrested?"

"Some kid tried to spend one of the phony bills at the local drug store. The pharmacist wasn't amused. He called the cops, and the cops called the FBI who, by the way, investigate all cases of counterfeiting, no matter what the circumstances."

"No!"

"Oh, yes. It gets worse. Since the crime occurred in my dad's district, it was his case. When he figured out that I was involved, he decided to teach us a lesson. He sent two of his toughest agents up from Jacksonville to arrest us. They pulled us out of school and locked us in a cell. They proceeded to give us the full treatment - handcuffs, lie detector, polygraph, even a fake lawyer. I've never wanted to see the inside of another jail."

"Well, I do. I love crime shows. I'm going to ask Sergeant Booker to show me around." Susan put a pencil in her mouth and pretended it was a cigar. "Ok, Big Louie, let's get out and crack this joint."

Miles followed her into the jail. Booker met them in the waiting room and led them into an interview room. The room was empty except for a table and chairs.

"We rarely keep prisoners at this jail anymore. It isn't secure," explained Booker, "The county jail is overflowing, so we have to make do. Have a seat. I'll be right back."

He returned in a few minutes with Luther in tow. The old man was still in street clothes. Luther was surprised to see Susan sitting at the table with Miles. Booker made the introductions.

"Why is she here?" Luther asked. "I only want to talk with the professor. She can't stay."

"We're a team, Luther," Miles interjected. "You'll have to talk to both of us. Otherwise, we both leave."

Luther was unhappy with that idea, but he relented and took a seat in the chair next to Miles.

"Glad that's settled," said Booker. "If you need anything, I'll be right outside. Just holler when you're ready to go." He closed the door with a loud snap on his way out.

"I need your help, professor."

Luther wasn't one to waste time.

"You need a lawyer," said Miles.

"I hate lawyers."

"Then what do you expect *me* to do?" asked Miles.

Luther angled his chair so that he could look at Miles directly.

"You can prove that I'm innocent. Prove that I didn't murder that boy – that student of yours."

"Lionel Ames."

"Yes, that's right, Lionel Ames," agreed Luther. "I didn't murder him. I would never do that."

THE ELVIS BIRD

Miles took a long, hard look at Luther. He seemed older now.

"Mr. Preston, I hardly know you. But, my colleague, Jim Hopkins, says you were angry with Lionel. He says you came out to our camp and made an official complaint against him. You threatened him. The police have evidence that connects you to Lionel. Were you angry enough to kill him?"

"I was angry enough to try to run him off. I wanted him away from my granddaughter. That boy only wanted to chase women, and I had no use for him. I can't lie; I wanted to be rid of him."

"Were you angry enough to murder him?" Miles repeated.

"I didn't kill that boy."

"He had a name," Miles insisted.

Luther took a few seconds to recover.

"I didn't kill Lionel Ames."

"The police think you did."

"That's not possible. I warned him to stay away from my granddaughter. That's all I did. Please believe me."

"I can't believe a word you say."

"Why not?"

"Because you're a cheat."

"What are you talking about?"

"We know that you fix Bingo games," said Miles, "And that you've done that for years."

Luther's eyes darted between Susan and Miles.

"That's a lie."

"I don't think so. My colleague doesn't think so."

Luther eyed Susan with suspicion. "What does she have to do with it?"

"She figured out how your scam works."

Susan jumped in, "I know that you pre-arrange your Bingo decks, Mr. Preston."

"What difference would it make if I did? It's just a random collection of sheets."

"I'm a mathematician, Luther," said Susan. "That's my job. I know how to compute odds. I know you place the losing cards on top of the deck, and the winner goes on the bottom."

Luther quickly pivoted.

"That doesn't make me a murderer."

"It makes you a cheat and a liar," said Miles.

"Your daddy didn't think so," he said defiantly. "He understood."

The mention of his dad threw Miles off balance. "My dad would have tossed you under the jail."

"You're wrong about that, Professor. Your daddy knew all about the Bingo scam and he looked the other way."

"You're a damn liar!" said Miles, standing up from the table.

"Hold on, now. Sit down. Don't get me wrong. I liked your daddy. He was a stand-up guy. But he also knew when to look the other way when things were gray - when it might help somebody."

"What is that supposed to mean?" Miles demanded.

THE ELVIS BIRD

"This county is a mighty poor place, Professor. Back in the twenties, Northern industrialists tried to cut down and carry off every hardwood in the Okefenokee. And they damn near did it. All they left us was a treeless swamp. Then the federal government come in and took that, too. There are lots of people here that could use a hand up. If a few down-on-their-luck old ladies happen to get a winning Bingo card once in a while ... well, your daddy knew that wasn't such a bad thing."

"Like Mildred Terry?" asked Miles.

Luther nodded. "Miss Mildred doesn't have anyone to look after her. She's been pretty sick this year and has lots of hospital bills. I don't see the harm in pushing a little luck her way, do you?"

Susan turned to Miles. "I think he's telling the truth." She reached across the table and placed her hand on Luther's arm. "That was a very clever idea you had, Luther – arranging Bingo cards like that."

Luther smiled. "It come to me one night."

"Even if you are telling the truth, I don't see how I can help you," said Miles.

"Maybe you can't, Professor. But I can help *you* find that hoo-doo bird. You're looking for Ivory-billed Woodpeckers, right?"

Miles had a sinking feeling that Luther had cooked up another scam.

"When you folks came here, I didn't really want you to find that bird."

Miles continued to stare at the old man.

"The way I see it, finding that bird would just mean more tourists and strangers coming around, taking the place over, changing it. It's already overcrowded – boats everywhere, tour groups, directional signs even – in a swamp. It ain't right. You know that ain't right."

"So, where's the bird, Luther?"

"I don't think that bird wants to be found. It just wants a place to live, free and undisturbed. Like me. I don't think that bird wants to be studied and gawked at."

"What have you done with the Ivory-bill, Luther?"

The old man looked down in his lap and seemed to be debating how much to reveal.

"I relocated it," he finally said.

"Luther, no," said Susan. She sat back in her chair.

"The bird's in a safe place for the moment. It has food and water, and nobody can find it. I put it in a special place."

"Where is it, Luther?" Miles sounded desperate.

"I'll tell you, but you gotta do something for me."

"Tell me where it is!" demanded Miles.

"First, you've got to get me out of this jail. I'm not going to trial for something I didn't do. You get me out of this jail, and I'll take you straight to that bird."

"You don't have bail. I can't do that!"

"You're gonna have to find a way doc, or that bird will die. It'll starve."

"What are you saying?"

THE ELVIS BIRD

"That bird has about a week, maybe two, before it needs more food and water. Get me out of here so we can set it free."

"That bird is one of the last of its kind," said Miles calmly. "If it dies, the whole species may die with it."

"Just get me out of jail, Professor, and everything will be fine."

###

After the interview, Booker debriefed Miles and Susan in the tiny waiting room just off the jail entrance.

"He didn't have much to say," Miles assured Booker. "Just a plea for help. Nothing of interest."

Susan, who was standing behind Booker, raised her eyebrows at Miles.

"We didn't expect he would say much in this first interview," said Booker. "Luther wouldn't trust his own mother to fix dinner. Can you to come back and talk with him again tomorrow? Gain his confidence?"

"Sure, Sergeant, we can come back - tomorrow."

"That's good. That's real good. After he sits in jail awhile, things will begin to look different to him."

Outside in the car, Susan asked, "What are we going to do?"

Miles reached for his sunglasses, adjusted them in the mirror, and turned to face her. "Little Louie ... I have a plan."

28. No Cigar

When taken by the hand, which is rather a hazardous undertaking, they strike with great violence, and inflict very severe wounds with their bill as well as claws, which are extremely sharp and strong. On such occasions, this bird utters a mournful and very piteous cry.

-James Audubon, The Birds of America

Doris cut two wedges of apple pie and placed the slices on the table in front of Susan and Miles. She cut a third sliver for herself.

"Everything looks better over dessert," she said, joining them at the table. Pie was Doris' answer to life's most important problems. Pie and coffee.

"Benjamin, do you really think that Luther has that bird penned up somewhere?"

"I don't know, but I have to find out. Perhaps Luther followed Hoppy to the tree where the bird was nesting. It would be a simple matter to put a trap over the hole in the middle of the night and wait for the bird to leave the nest the next morning. That could explain why it disappeared."

"Why would he kidnap a bird?" asked Susan.

"Because he's a crazy old man," said Miles. "And he wanted an insurance policy. I think he knew the police would make him the prime suspect. After all, he threatened Lionel publicly and even made a formal complaint against him."

"How long can an Ivory-bill survive penned up in a swamp?" asked Doris. The coffee maker had finished percolating and she had gotten up to retrieve the pot.

"Luther said a week or two, but I think we only have a few days to find it. Anything could happen to a caged bird in that swamp. We've got to do something now."

Doris began to circle the table refilling their coffee cups. "Perhaps he was bluffing, Honey."

Miles was about to take a bite of the pie, but lowered his fork. "Do you think Dad knew about Luther's bingo scam?"

"Your Dad didn't tell me everything about his work. He was always a little secretive." She gave Miles a sweet smile and turned to Susan. "I think it's a mistake for couples to reveal everything, don't you?"

Susan gave Miles a quick glance. "Not to worry, Doris."

"A marriage needs plenty of space for the truth," said Doris, continuing her thought, "but it also needs some room for mystery and the unknown, don't you think, Benjamin?"

Miles wasn't paying attention. "If Dad knew about the bingo scam, would he have looked the other way as Luther claimed?"

"It sounds like something he might do," said Doris. "He could be tough with criminals, hard even, but your father was a kind-hearted man to people in need. He always thought the federal government was heavy-handed in the way it kicked people out of the Okefenokee to create the reserve - taking their land for cents on the dollar. If he thought that a bingo scam could help a few old ladies, he might have decided to overlook it."

"Then we have to assume that Luther has an Ivory-billed Woodpecker caged up somewhere," said Miles, "and we don't have much time to find it."

"What are you planning, Benjamin?" asked Doris.

"I'm going to break Luther out of that jail."

Susan looked aghast. "You're not serious."

"I am serious. And I'm going to need both of you to help me with this."

Doris was about to take a sip of coffee but paused and lowered her cup. "How exciting!" she said, "Tell us more."

That evening, Miles peeked out of the front door and found Susan sitting in the swing. She had pulled a chair up as a desk for her laptop. Spotting him, she beckoned him forward with her finger.

"How long have you been out here?" he asked as he joined her.

"A couple of hours."

"How's it going?"

"My latest algorithm isn't working." she said, "I thought my new technique was helping, but it isn't. I *have* to make this work, Miles. I don't want you involved in breaking Luther out of jail."

THE ELVIS BIRD

"I'll be fine," said Miles.

"No, you won't. It's illegal. They'll put you in jail. Again!"

"Just explain your algorithm to me," said Miles sympathetically. "It may help to talk about it."

She closed the laptop and sat back in the swing. "I took samples of the gunshot recording. Not just the human voices, but of larger, random time intervals around each incident. I thought that by doing that, I might pick up on other noises that we can't hear – noises beyond human perception."

"Good idea," said Miles. "What else?"

"I matched those samples against our reconstructed database. That's the part that takes lots of computer time. The idea is to identify other similar events in the database."

"It sounds reasonable."

"But whenever I run a search using these samples, I either get no matches at all, or the algorithm identifies hundreds. None of the selected samples contain human voices."

"That is odd," said Miles.

"I'm at a dead-end," said Susan.

"So what would Polya do?"

"Well … he would ask more questions, of course – always have another question in mind, otherwise, the jig is up."

"More data might help as well," said Miles. "I believe I may have some data that you haven't searched. Wait here."

He went into the house and returned with a small, red, electronic stick.

"Voila!" He held out a flash drive.

"What's on it?" asked Susan.

"Some recordings that Hoppy and I collected off the ARUs recently. Try your algorithm on this."

Susan pushed the stick into the port and typed several commands. The machine began to whir. After a short delay, line after line of data began to scroll past, filling the screen.

Susan frowned and shook her head. "See how much it's writing? The software doesn't discriminate between events. It's identifying everything on the thumb drive as a potential match and making a record of it. There are so many matches that the whole thing is worthless. I need to fine-tune the algorithm so that it identifies only the best possible matches in the database."

They both stared at the screen as data continued to fly past. Susan finally typed a command and interrupted the program.

"Sorry, Birdman. Nice try, but no cigar."

It was then that Doris decided to join them on the porch. She sounded gleeful. "Isn't this jail caper exciting?" she said.

"Frankly, it terrifies me," said Susan.

Doris took her hand. "Don't worry, Sweetie, if we get caught, I'll tell Pete Booker it was all my idea."

THE ELVIS BIRD

"You don't have to be involved at all, Susan," said Miles. "Just say the word, and you're out. In any case, I devised a plan in which you won't be blamed."

"We're talking about breaking an accused murderer out of jail. Are you seriously considering this?"

"I can't take a chance that the bird will die," said Miles.

He could see by her expression that Susan was upset and didn't want to discuss it further. He didn't mention the topic again. Doris finished her coffee and decided to go to bed early. Miles silently reviewed the details of his jailbreak plan, while Susan continued to speculate out loud about the search algorithm and why it wasn't working.

A storm front had moved up from the gulf, bringing a layer of clouds that covered the moon and the stars. The darkness which surrounded the house seemed to weigh on Miles' shoulders, and was only occasionally relieved by the lights of a passing car.

29. Miss Delaney

The female is always the most clamorous and the least shy. Their mutual attachment is, I believe, continued through life.
                            -James Audubon, The Birds of America

Perry Fielder's house sat on a rolling, sandy bluff that overlooked a bend in the St. Marys River. The water flowed dark black there, and Live Oaks lined the river banks. The majestic trees dipped their branches into the water's edge as if to take a drink. The locals called the river *Styx* because of its color, and the shadowy passages created by the overhanging canopy. The river followed a serpentine path from the base of Georgia through Florida before escaping into the Gulf of Mexico. The bluff itself was the geological remnant of a barrier island system that once marked the ocean's shore. The Okefenokee and the St. Marys River were left behind when the sea retreated even further south during the Mesozoic era.

Perry Fielder was standing on the dock of his house when the blue Lexus pulled into the driveway and Susan and Miles got out of the car. The Admiral was dressed in khaki shorts, a designer tee shirt, and pristine McHugh boots. He wore a faded baseball cap atop his thick, wavy hair, and there

THE ELVIS BIRD

was a highball glass in one hand. He raised it in greeting as Susan and Miles walked up the driveway.

The Admiral was delighted to see Susan again and made a production of taking her hand and kissing it. Perhaps it was his friend's athletic good looks that jarred Miles into speaking up. "Cut the crap, Admiral. We came here because we need your help."

Perry raised his hand to his chest and feigned indignance. "I'm going to ignore that remark." He turned his attention back to Susan, swirling the liquor around in the highball glass invitingly, like a hypnotist manipulating a watch on a chain. "How about a little snort, darlin'? My old friend has temporarily forgotten his manners."

"I'm in," said Susan, starting up the steps to the house. The Admiral followed along and Miles trailed behind them.

Once inside, Susan noticed a collection of geologic maps spread across the kitchen table. She picked up one of the charts and examined the legend. Miles stood off to the side while the Admiral poured the drinks.

"Are you planning a trip?" asked Susan.

The Admiral dropped an ice cube into a glass and looked back over his shoulder. "I'm always going somewhere. That's my job and my avocation."

He finished up at the bar and handed out the whiskey. Susan noticed his well-worn hat was adorned with the letters *C-A-L* in yellow script.

"Where did a southern boy like *you* get a hat like *that*, Admiral?" said Susan, looking it over.

The Admiral touched the brim. "This old thing?" He was about to offer an explanation when Miles intervened.

"I neglected to tell you that the Admiral was a pretty fair student before he turned to a life of defrauding the public. He won a full scholarship to the University of California. Majored in biology, didn't you ol' boy?"

"I *am* a proud graduate of that fine institution." The Admiral smiled, raised his glass again, and took a swallow. "That scholarship was my ticket out of Georgia. Back then, I wanted to get as far away from Folkston as possible."

He reached for the bottle of Wild Turkey and topped up his glass. "I couldn't wait to leave this place – neither could Miles. We were best friends, and we both wanted to be ornithologists. Of course, I was much smarter than him, so I followed my nose west. My buddy here had to settle for the University of Georgia."

"So, why did you come back, Admiral?"

"I got my fill of birds – at least as objects of academic study. And I was homesick. After four years of looking at those barren, western foothills, I decided that California wasn't for me."

"We have lovely mountains in California," said Susan.

"And very few trees – at least where I was living. This old boy has the soul of a flatlander. Did you know that the Okefenokee is only a hundred feet *above* sea level? We live in a saucer. There was something about staring at those treeless hills that made me homesick for this old swamp."

"Poor, baby," said Susan.

THE ELVIS BIRD

"Say what you will, but those barren hillsides made me lonesome. I soon realized that I missed this place and wanted to come back and live here forever. It was quite a surprise when I figured that out. The old-timers used to say that once you take a drink of swamp water, you can't get it out of your blood. I guess, in my case, they were right."

"Why did *both* of you want to become ornithologists?" asked Susan.

Miles jumped in, "That was Miss Delaney's fault – she was our ninth-grade biology teacher."

"He's right," said the Admiral. "She was our *ornithological* muse."

"Tell me more," said Susan, intrigued.

The Admiral began a wistful explanation, "Miss Delaney was young, and smart, and beautiful with lots of curves in all the right places – everything a red-blooded, ninth-grade, American boy could desire in a female biology teacher."

"I'll drink to that," said Miles, "She was lovely." He reached for the bottle to refill his glass.

"And she loved birds," said the Admiral.

"She did love birds," agreed Miles. "So, we began bringing her bird eggs. It made Miss Delaney quite happy, as I recall. We found the easy ones at first: sparrows, blue jays, cardinals, wrens. You could find those just about anywhere."

Miles took another sip. "As time went by, it got to be more challenging," he continued, "We went after warblers, woodpeckers, thrashers … even gulls. Soon, we had to search farther, wider, and deeper into the swamp."

"Isn't collecting eggs a terrible idea?" asked Susan. "After all, you're killing a potential bird."

"It's awful," said Miles. "No one does it anymore. But at the time, we didn't know better. We finally drew the line at owls and hawks. It was just too dangerous."

The Admiral picked up the story. "We must have collected sixty different bird eggs over one summer, and we presented them to Miss Delaney in long wooden boxes filled with powdered detergent."

"This is beginning to sound like a morality tale," said Susan.

The Admiral gave a confirming nod.

"She broke our hearts when she eloped with the football coach and moved to Jacksonville – we never saw her again – or the eggs," said Miles.

"But we left the ninth grade much older and wiser, you have to admit that," said the Admiral. "And we devoted our lives to ornithology – at least Miles did."

Miles confided, "It sounds silly to say this now, but searching for those bird eggs got me hooked. I'm still searching. But now, I only search for the rarest birds – the ones that are disappearing." He turned up his glass and finished the last swallow of whiskey. "It's rewarding. How many people living today have seen an Ivory-billed Woodpecker? Probably fewer than the number of fingers on your hands."

THE ELVIS BIRD

"The most important thing I learned in Ornithology 101? *You can't fly on one wing.* Let's have another tipple," said the Admiral. "Hand me that bottle."

"You've already had a couple of wings," suggested Susan.

The Admiral ignored her and poured a swallow into everyone's glass. "I raise a toast to Miss Delaney – the first bird we failed to capture!"

They all touched glasses. The Admiral tossed back the liquor and placed his glass on the table. "A man should know his limit, and that's mine. I'm guessing you didn't come here to talk about the past. You said you need something. What is it?"

"The kind of help that might get you into trouble," said Miles.

"More trouble than counterfeiting ten-dollar bills?"

Susan sidled over and took the Admiral by the arm. "So, you *were* involved in the infamous counterfeiting scheme," said Susan, "I thought Miles was just pulling my leg."

"Just a few tens, darlin'. Nothing, really."

"Enough talk of that," said Miles. "We need your help."

"Just name it, buddy."

"For starters, I need a place where I can camp overnight in the swamp. A place where no one will find me. I'll also need a boat to take me there."

"You could pitch a tent on Billy's Island. It's a central location. It's well-known, but I know a secluded spot there where no one would find you. There's even a place to moor a small boat."

"That might work."

"When do you need it?"

"Tomorrow," said Miles.

"What's it for?"

"It's better that you don't know, Admiral."

"Tell me, anyway."

"Luther Preston claims to have captured an Ivory-billed Woodpecker and has it caged somewhere in the Okefenokee. He might be telling the truth. It would explain why we haven't found the bird that you identified."

"I thought Luther was in jail?"

"He is. He wants me to break him out. It's a trade – his freedom for an Ivory-billed Woodpecker."

"This is much more serious than counterfeiting, isn't it?"

"That's right," interjected Susan. "Tell him this plan is crazy, Admiral."

"Hold on, now, Susan. I've never known Miles to be rash. Finish your drink and let's think about this thing. It never hurts to make plans. You can always change your mind."

"Both of you are nuts," said Susan.

But the Admiral was warming up to the idea. "We can leave for Billy's Island in a few minutes and give it some more thought along the way. There's plenty of time for second guessing ourselves."

THE ELVIS BIRD

"Susan's not involved," said Miles. "Leave her out of this."

"Speak for yourself, Birdman."

"If we leave now, we can stop by the outpost, and put some supplies together," said the Admiral. "Then we can take my boat and set up a campsite before sunset." He glanced at his watch. "It will be dark before we get back."

They drove to the Admiral's outpost in separate cars. The Admiral packed two waterproof bags with supplies and began loading them onto a sleek-looking boat that was moored behind his building.

"What is this thing?" asked Miles, admiring the boat. He and Susan were standing on the dock.

"That's my new Tiburon. Eight-inch draft."

"Is it fast?"

"She'll do fifty – easy. Did we pack everything?" asked the Admiral. "How about a gun?"

Miles shook his head. "Don't won't one."

"I never go out in that swamp without one. You can have one of mine."

"Take his gun, Miles," said Susan.

But Miles refused.

"It's your funeral, buddy."

The Admiral was about to step off the dock. Instead, he patted his leg, and reached into his pants pocket. "Almost forgot." He removed a small electronic rod, slid it into Miles' front shirt pocket, and fastened the button.

"What was that?" said Miles.

"GPS. I make everybody take one. I've pulled way too many greenhorns out of that swamp. It's bad for business when the customers disappear."

"Good idea," said Miles.

"Yes, good idea," said Susan.

The Admiral gestured around the yard. "All my boats have them, too. I can find you if you just stay with the boat. Are we ready to go?"

Miles turned to Susan. "Why don't you take the car and go back to the house?"

"You're not getting rid of me that easily, Birdman." She jumped into the boat and took a seat.

As a final task, the Admiral tied a metal johnboat behind the Tiburon before setting off. The tiny tributary behind the Admiral's place proved to be a small finger of a larger stream leading deeper into the Okefenokee. The group reached the landing on Billy's Island in less than an hour. An alligator that was sleeping beneath the dock raised its head as the boat approached. After tying off, the Admiral jumped onto the dock. The gator crawled out of the mud, bellowed its disapproval, and swam away. Susan shuddered as it disappeared beneath the black water.

"We have just enough time to pitch the tent," said the Admiral.

"How large is this island?" Susan asked.

"One mile wide and about five miles long," said the Admiral. "It's in the middle of the reserve. We'll pitch the tent about half of a mile from here."

THE ELVIS BIRD

They had only walked a short distance when Susan spotted the shells of two roofless buildings in the distance. She also noticed some abandoned railroad ties along the trail.

"What was this place?" she asked.

The Admiral looked to see what had caught her attention.

"Do you want the short answer – or would you prefer my tourist pitch?"

"Lay on, Admiral," said Susan, "I have nothing but time."

The Admiral lowered his voice a bit and began to sound somewhat more southern and formal –spreading it on thick and adopting the tone he often took with tourists.

"In the nineteen-twenties, the Hebard Cypress Company of Waycross, Georgia, built a city for six hundred brave souls, smack dab in the middle of our lovely Okefenokee swamp. At the height of its success, there were fifty buildings here, including a general store, two boarding houses for the bachelors, a restaurant, a barbershop, a church, two schools, even a picture show – that was for *public* entertainment. Want me to continue?" They continued to walk along.

"I'm all ears," said Susan.

"There was an electric light plant, a waterworks, a juke joint, and even two moonshine stills – for *private* entertainment."

"You really shouldn't encourage him," said Miles, who trailed behind.

"People fell in love here, got married, made families, baptized their babies, and buried their dead - all on this little island in the middle of the swamp. They had hopes and dreams for this place. There was even a small railroad that would bring you out here to this very spot. The Jacksonville newspaper famously described it as a Garden of Eden. Now look it." He waved his arm in a circle and began to recite as they walked along:

> *My name is Ozymandias, king of kings;*
> *Look on my works, ye Mighty, and despair!*
> *Nothing beside remains. Round the decay*
> *Of that colossal wreck, boundless and bare*
> *The lone and level sands stretch far away.*

Susan clapped when he finished his oration.

"It's not exactly a desert here, but the desolation is the same," said the Admiral.

"Is it true about this being a Garden of Eden?"

"Every word," said the Admiral.

"What happened? Where did it all go wrong?"

"After a few successful years, the lumber business collapsed overnight when they realized that all the old hardwood had been removed. Everyone picked up and left. Equipment that wasn't carried off, was abandoned where it sat in the swamp. It's a sober reminder of man's feeble grip on the things of this world, madam."

"What do you charge for this tour, Admiral?"

"Twenty-four ninety-five. That includes a round-trip boat ride and a complimentary non-alcoholic beverage of your choice. Children under five are free."

"Cheap at twice the price."

"I hate to interrupt you two," said Miles, "But it will be dark soon."

They hiked a bit further before the Admiral declared that they had arrived. He had selected a secluded spot, and they pitched the tent near the water, in a place that was hidden by trees and shrubs. After storing the supplies, they retraced their steps and returned to the dock as the sun was setting. The Admiral untied the johnboat, moved it to a secluded slough, and showed Miles how to get it running.

"That's all we can do for now," said the Admiral. They hiked back to the boat. The sun had already dropped behind the trees by the time they arrived at the dock.

"Careful," said the Admiral, taking Susan's hand as she stepped into the boat. Miles crawled in unassisted and took a seat beside Susan in the stern. The return trip was aided by the light of a full moon. The Admiral seemed preoccupied and became uncharacteristically quiet on the return trip. Along the way, Miles put his arm around Susan and pulled her close and kissed her.

"I have a bad feeling about this, Miles," said Susan, as she pulled away from his embrace.

"Are my kisses that bad?" he asked.

"You know what I mean, Birdman."

She looked beautiful in the moonlight. Perhaps she was right. Was he about to commit a felony in order to save a bird? Time would tell.

30. Souvenir

A broad band of white runs down the neck and back, on either side, commencing narrow under the ear, and terminating with the scapulars. The five outer primaries black, the rest white towards the end, the secondaries wholly white, so that when the wings are closed, the posterior part of the back seems white, although it is in reality black.
    -James Audubon, The Birds of America

After returning to Okefenokee Outfitters, Susan helped the Admiral tie the Tiburon up at the dock. Miles left them working there and headed for the parking lot to make a call – Hopkins answered on the first ring.

"Why do you always call me so God-awful late?" asked Hopkins.

"We need to meet," said Miles.

"I'm busy."

"We need to meet *now*."

"I'm in no state to drive. You'll have to come here if you want to talk with me," said Hopkins.

"You shouldn't drink alone, Hoppy."

"Then get your ass over here. Bring Susan along. This place could use a cheerful face."

A BENJAMIN MILES MYSTERY

Miles could hear a slow blues number playing in the background. Hopkins continued, "Bring me good news, brother. Don't bother to come if it's bad."

Miles glanced across the yard at the dock. The Admiral had gone inside to turn the lights on. Susan was waiting for him on the front porch steps.

###

It was late in the evening when Miles and Susan arrived at the Cornell campsite. The place looked deserted in the moonlight, and most of the tents were dark. They found Hopkins sitting at a table under the main tent. A single Coleman lantern hung from a support in the corner and offered a meager, flickering light. *Smokestack Lightnin'*, the Howlin' Wolf version, was playing though a speaker near the coffee pot – streaming over Hopkin's phone. The drummer and bass player were quietly laying down a relentless beat.

"Wahooohhhhhhh!" howled Wolf. "Wahooohhhhhhh!"

Hopkins was nursing an open bottle of whiskey. He looked up from his glass when they walked over, but didn't offer to share.

Miles took the seat directly across from Hopkins, and Susan sat between the two men at the end of the table. "Turn that down," he said. "Let's talk. Something important has happened - something you should know about."

Hopkins, sipped his whiskey. "The Ivory-bills have disappeared, Miles – that's what I know. We didn't see one

THE ELVIS BIRD

today. We didn't see one yesterday, or the day before. We aren't going to see one tomorrow. Royally screwed – that's what we are."

"Wahoooooooohhhhhhhhh!" howled Wolf.

"Turn it down," said Miles.

Hopkins reached for his phone and complied.

"I know why we haven't been able to find an Ivory-bill," said Miles.

Hopkins stared at him and tried to focus. "Please tell me the bird's not dead. I couldn't take that."

Miles didn't like seeing his friend in this sorry state.

"Luther Preston says the bird is alive. He claims it's here in the reserve."

Hopkins held onto to the glass with both hands like it was a life preserver. "What's Preston got to do with it? That bastard is in jail where he belongs."

"I talked with him yesterday."

"In jail? How?"

"Luther wanted to see me. He wouldn't talk with anyone else, not even his lawyer. The police agreed to let me visit him."

"What did he tell you, buddy?" asked Hopkins. He kept his grip on the glass.

"He said he was innocent."

"Ha. That's a surprise."

"I think he *is* innocent, Hoppy."

Hopkins shook his head. "The police found hard evidence against him; didn't they tell you?"

"What are you talking about?" asked Miles.

Hopkins glanced at Susan and then back at Miles. "Perhaps we should talk about this at another time, Miles."

Susan stiffened. "You can say anything in front of me. I have no secrets. What evidence do the police have?"

"Ok. It's your neck, Susan. You weren't the only person the police interviewed. They questioned me as well. This morning. The police found a medallion when they searched Luther's truck. It matched a necklace that was found on Lionel when he was pulled out of the swamp."

Hopkins looked directly at Susan. "Your medallion, your necklace, your initials."

"I did lose a necklace with a medallion, but that was in Ithaca. How did Luther get my medallion?"

"He must have taken it off Lionel after he shot the boy in the swamp. Just a little souvenir. One thing is sure; the necklace ties Luther directly to Lionel."

Susan turned to Miles. "I told the police I was wearing the necklace on the night of the fire. When I woke up in the hospital, my necklace was missing. I never found it. I thought it was lost in the fire."

"Perhaps Lionel took it from you?" suggested Hopkins.

Susan seemed to be giving the idea some thought.

"But that would mean that Lionel came into the lab that evening – that he knocked me unconscious – that the fire wasn't an accident."

THE ELVIS BIRD

"There's something you should know about Lionel," said Hopkins. "It's information I gave the police when they interviewed me."

"What's that?" Susan asked.

"Lionel had a history of complaints from the women he dated. He made a habit of collecting souvenirs from each of his conquests – articles of clothing, jewelry. He even bragged about his trophies to other graduate students."

"Where did you hear that?"

"I hear lots of things on committees – especially disciplinary committees. Some students complained."

"You think he took my necklace? As a trophy? That's what you think?"

"I know this is upsetting," continued Hopkins, "but the police investigated Lionel very thoroughly. I'm afraid it's all true."

Miles tried to make sense of the news about Lionel. Did Susan have an affair with Lionel?

Susan seemed to sense Miles' discomfort and took him by the hand. "Lionel was never my lover, Miles." She continued, "I *wasn't* one of his conquests. There was nothing between us. No romance. Nothing improper. I took an interest in him when he was at Stanford, and I helped him get an assistantship at Cornell. That's all I ever did."

"Then why did you follow him to Cornell?" asked Hopkins.

Miles was thinking the same thing. But instead of admonishing Hopkins, he fell silent.

Susan shifted in her chair.

"No need to answer," said Hopkins. "Let's have a drink and put all this behind us." He reached for the bottle. "We may never know how Lionel came to have your necklace. We should just forget it and move on." Hopkins poured the whiskey sloppily into his glass.

Susan pulled her hands away from Miles. "Give me the car keys," she demanded.

"Let me drive you home."

"Just give me the keys, Miles!"

He handed over the keys, and she walked out of the tent. Miles followed her outside and watched as she got into the car and drove away. Hopkins joined him as the taillights of the car disappeared among the distant trees. Why did he hesitate to speak up?

"She'll get over it, Miles," said Hopkins. The two men walked back inside the tent, and Hopkins took a seat at the table.

"I need a glass," said Miles, looking around. He found one beside the coffee pot. Hopkins filled it up.

"Women are stronger than men," said Hopkins. "She'll recover. You and I have more important things to discuss at the moment – like Luther. You said he claims there's an Ivory-bill here in the reserve. Is that true?"

Miles suddenly felt exhausted. "Luther says he trapped one and has hidden it in the swamp."

"Really? *That* could be our salvation. If Luther has an Ivory-bill, we could give the finger to all those media bastards and all the other nay-sayers. We could make up for all the humiliation. But why would Luther Preston trap an Ivory-bill?"

"He wanted to make us leave the Okefenokee," said Miles. "He didn't want us to find Ivory-bills here. He hated the publicity, and the tourists, and all the other things that our discovery would bring. He offered to tell me where he was keeping the bird if I would get him out of jail."

"Whoa. You could go to jail for that, buddy. You don't even know that he has a bird."

"I'm convinced he does."

"Let me think about this," said Hopkins, wiping his brow with the back of his hand. "Can you really get him out of jail?"

"Maybe. There's only one officer. The place hasn't operated as a jail for years. They're keeping Luther there because the county jail is full. They won't be expecting anyone to help him escape."

Hopkins emptied the last of the whiskey into his glass. He threw the bottle at the trash can near the coffee pot. It struck the side of the can and rattled away.

"This is nuts, buddy. If you did get him out, what would you do with him? Where would you go?"

"There's a campsite on Billy's Island where we can stay overnight. When things settle down, Luther can take me to the bird. We can still have a successful expedition, but I need your help."

"Why?"

"I'll need you to take pictures and videos. We'll have to document everything about this bird. I want incontrovertible evidence that this Ivory-bill is still alive. We're not getting screwed again."

"We could both end up going to jail."

"I can't do this alone."

Hopkins placed his glass on the table. "What the hell? I'm probably screwed anyway. I'll do it."

"If something happens to me, make Luther take you to the bird. Beat it out of him if you have to. We can't let that bird die."

"He'll talk," said Hopkins, "One way or another. You can count on that."

Miles held up his glass and looked at the liquor through the lantern's light. It distorted everything in the tent. His thoughts returned to Susan, and suddenly his feelings became clarified: No matter what had happened, he trusted Susan.

Miles put the glass down. "I need to go home."

31. Archimedes' Lever

When wounded and brought to the ground, the Ivory-bill immediately makes for the nearest tree, and ascends it with great rapidity and perseverance, until it reaches the top branches, when it squats and hides, generally with great effect. Whilst ascending, it moves spirally round the tree, utters its loud pait, pait, pait, at almost every hop, but becomes silent the moment it reaches a place where it conceives itself secure.

-James Audubon, Birds of America

"Prepararsi a svoltare a sinistra in un centinaio di metri." The disembodied male voice gave directions as Doris drove along.

"I gotta get one of these," said Doris as she turned off Main Street and headed for the old jail. It was late afternoon, and the weather was muggy. There were only a few cars parked along the main street. Everyone in town was sheltering at home indoors.

"Why are you driving so slowly, Mom?" asked Miles. He was sitting in the back seat with Susan.

"We don't want to arouse suspicion, darling," she said earnestly.

A BENJAMIN MILES MYSTERY

"Avvicinando la vostra destinazione sulla destra di una cinquantina di metri." The voice was deep, sonorous, and only slightly electronic.

"How does he know that?" she said, shaking her head. She pulled the car carefully into a parking space in front of the jail and switched the engine off. Miles leaned forward and touched Doris on the shoulder.

"Are you sure you know what to do, Mom?" he asked.

"I'm fine, honey. I'll be back with the car in half an hour."

"Perfect," said Miles. "And do you remember where to go after that?"

"I've got it all programmed in here," Doris patted the dashboard. "Even if it doesn't work, I know how to find the Admiral's outpost. After all, I've lived here all my life, right?" She smiled sweetly.

Miles reached over the seat and pulled his mother close. He hugged her tight and kissed her.

"Make your daddy proud," she said.

Miles took Susan's hand, "Are you ready?"

"Ready, Big Louie," said Susan, bravely. "No copper's ever gonna take us in." She reached over and hugged Doris, as well. They left her sitting in the car and walked into the police station lobby. It was empty. The same worn magazines lay on a table in the corner. Miles walked up to the counter and peeked in the reception area window. The room was empty. He tapped on the glass. No answer. He looked inside again. The tiny office was filled with boxes and stacks of paper. Even the filing cabinets were stacked high with papers. A hand-held police radio lay balanced on a coffee cup on top of the desk. Miles pushed the call-button and heard a buzzer ring somewhere in the back of the building.

They waited. Finally, there was movement in the hallway. Sergeant Booker appeared at the window. He seemed surprised to see them. "Oh, hello, Pro-fessor – Miss Swail."

"We'd like to talk with Luther."

A concerned look came over Booker's face.

"The captain isn't here today. He went deep-sea fishin' down in the gulf.

"It's important that we see Luther today. He's expecting us," said Miles.

Booker gave the idea some thought and then waved them back. "I'm the only one here at the moment." He bent over the receptionist's chair and pressed a button that was under the counter. Miles heard an electronic bolt retract in the metal entrance door.

They walked into the empty hallway, and Miles noticed a camera mounted above a door at the end of the hall. The entrance door slammed shut behind them, and the bolt in the door reset loudly. Booker appeared at the end of the hallway.

"We gave most of our space to the county extension office a couple of years ago, so we don't have an interview room anymore. We kept a couple of holding cells to use as overflow from the county. You'll have to use the captain's office. I'll get Luther."

A BENJAMIN MILES MYSTERY

He pointed them to the first office off the hallway. "Have a seat in there. I'll be right back."

The captain's paneled office was about the size of the front reception area and had a single, barred window that looked out onto an alley. Miles checked the ceiling as they walked in. There were no cameras. Was the captain camera shy?

Five sturdy oak chairs were arranged in a semi-circle around the captain's desk. Miles grabbed one and pulled, and discovered that someone had bolted the chairs to the floor. The wall opposite the desk was covered with plaques, photographs, and framed resolutions. An American flag stood at attention in the corner. They each took a seat in the semi-circle. The door opened and Luther entered wearing a bright-red jumper. He was followed closely by Booker.

"Here he is," said Booker, shutting the door behind them. His placed his hand on Luther's shoulder and guided the old man into the room and sat him in the middle chair of the semi-circle.

"You've got thirty minutes, then it's back to his cell. Them's the rules," said Booker. He looked over at Miles. "You need me to stay?"

"Heavens no" thought Miles. "We'll be fine," he said.

Booker removed a pair of handcuffs from his belt and fixed one cuff to Luther's wrist and the other to the arm of the chair. When he was satisfied that the cuff was tight, he said, "I'll be down the hall if you need me." He walked out, shutting the door behind him.

THE ELVIS BIRD

Miles looked at the cuffs and his heart sank. He started to apologize. "I'm sorry, Luther. I thought if we got you out of your cell, without constraints, you might have a chance to escape. I didn't know Booker was going to handcuff you to a chair."

"That was your big plan?" asked Susan. "You were just going to get him out of the cell? And then what?"

"Well … I thought you could talk to Booker – maybe distract him for a few minutes while Luther escaped."

"I hope you never have to spring *me* out of jail," said Susan.

Luther stood up with his wrist still firmly attached to the arm of the chair. He began yanking on the handcuffs, but the chair wouldn't budge. By the look of the chair's arm, Luther wasn't the first prisoner to test the its strength. Frustrated, he tried kicking it. No luck. He desperately scanned the room. "Bring me that flag pole, Professor."

"Why?"

"You remember what Archimedes said, don't you, Doc? *Give me a place to stand, and I will move the earth.*"

"The Romans executed Archimedes," Miles pointed out, morosely. He retrieved the flag pole and handed it to Luther who shoved it under one side of the chair. Luther adjusted the pole's grain like a baseball player preparing to bat and looked at Miles, imploringly.

"Give me a hand."

Miles grabbed the flagpole and began to push. Luther got under it and lifted with his back and legs. The chair legs suddenly creaked, and after several more attempts, they began to pry one leg off the floor.

"It's working," said Susan. She grabbed the pole and tried to push along with the men.

There was a sudden pop, and two of the legs were off the floor.

No turning back thought Miles.

"Now the other side," said Luther. He wedged the pole under the other two legs, and they all pushed together. It was easier this time. There was another smaller pop, and suddenly, the chair broke free.

"Eureka!" said Susan. "Now what?"

"Careful," said Luther, handing the pole to Susan. "It's bad luck to let the flag touch the floor."

Susan stifled a comment.

The chair was still handcuffed to Luther's arm. "We don't have time to remove it," said Miles, looking over the handcuffs. "You'll have to carry the chair. There's a release button under the table in the room across the hall. It unlocks the entrance door. My mother is waiting for you in a car outside the jail."

Miles turned to Susan. "Find Booker. Keep him busy for a few minutes. Buy us some time."

"What about you, Professor?" asked Luther.

"I need you to punch me. Knock me out. It's the only way this can work. There are cameras monitoring the hallway and the front entrance. You'll have to let yourself out – otherwise, Booker will know we helped you escape."

THE ELVIS BIRD

"I get it," said Luther. "So, how do you want it, Doc?"

"On the chin, I guess," said Miles. He straightened himself up, closed his eyes, and grimaced.

"I'll do it on three, Professor," said Luther drawing back his free hand. "One, …"

"Wait a minute," said Susan. Luther relaxed, and Miles opened his eyes. "I don't want to be here to see this," she said.

She walked up to Miles and kissed him before turning to Luther. "Give me three minutes to find Booker. If I'm not back you'll know that the coast is clear."

She walked over, opened the door, and peeked out. "Good luck, boys." She slipped out of the room.

The two men stood silently watching the clock as the second hand circled the dial three times.

"OK, Professor, I guess it's time. Are you ready?"

Miles straightened up again and closed his eyes. "I'm ready."

"On the count of three," said Luther, "Brace yourself. *One*, …"

Miles never felt the punch that Luther landed on *Two*.

Miles could hear Sergeant Booker calling his name from a great distance. The Sergeant sounded concerned. He called out urgently, but Miles was too tired to respond. He just wanted to be left alone. After all, it was such a peaceful sleep, and he wanted it to continue, but the Sergeant's voice was very insistent.

"Pro-fessor! Are you Ok?"

Miles opened his eyes and wondered why he was lying on the floor, cradled in Booker's muscular arms. Susan had returned and was kneeling beside Booker; their heads were close together looming over him, looking him over. His chin began to ache.

"Pro-fessor! Are you ok?" repeated Booker.

Miles nodded.

"I think he's awake now, Miss Swail. Can you look after him?"

"Gladly," said Susan, taking Miles into her arms. She put her hand on his forehead and brushed the hair out of his eyes before kissing him several more times.

"Poor Baby!"

Booker reached for the two-way radio attached to his shirt. "Don't move around Pro-fessor, I'm calling the EMTs to have you checked out." A look of concern formed on Booker's face. "I better call the police chief, too," he said resignedly, "He's gonna be pissed!"

###

Doris was waiting in the car when Miles and Susan exited the police station arm-in-arm an hour later. She waved to them from the driver's seat. Susan helped Miles into the front seat.

THE ELVIS BIRD

"I was worried when the ambulance drove up. What was that about?"

"I'll tell you later, Mom," said Miles, rubbing his chin.

"You look a little shaky, Benjamin," said Doris. "Are you sure you're ok?"

"Luther punched me, that's all."

"Luther hit you, Sweetie?"

"It was part of the plan, Mom."

"Some plan," said Susan from the back seat.

Miles ignored her. "How *is* Luther?"

"He's fine It was so exciting, Honey. Everything went off without a hitch. Luther ran out of the police station and hopped into the back seat. Why was he handcuffed to a chair?"

"I'll tell you later. Let's get going."

Doris started the engine and continued her story. "I covered him up with the blanket, and I drove the get-away car straight over to the Admiral's place. Luther's there now. He's waiting on the boat."

Doris backed the car out of the parking spot and drove a couple of blocks before turning onto Main Street.

"Continua a metà di miglio sulla via principale."

"You can turn the GPS off, now," said Miles.

At the edge of town, Doris pulled onto the Okefenokee Highway. She eased off the accelerator when the speed hit twenty-five.

"Luther and I had an interesting conversation about your dad," said Doris.

"Really?" said Miles. He readjusted his position in the seat.

"Luther told me that he occasionally worked for your father. Your dad sometimes asked him for information."

"Did you know about that?" asked Miles.

"Your father never talked much about his work. He was pretty tight-lipped when it came to FBI matters."

"He probably didn't want to worry you, Mom."

"Perhaps not. Luther told me something else that was quite wonderful."

"What was that?"

"He said your dad once saved his life. He said he would always be grateful, and forever in his debt."

"Dad never mentioned saving anyone to me."

"Your father was a very private person."

A few miles south of the town, the landscape along the highway became low and boggy. Cypress and bay trees began to dominate the flora instead of pines. Doris slowed the car when she spotted the Admiral's outpost and turned off the highway. She parked the Lexus behind the main building near the dock where the Admiral maintained his small fleet. The Admiral was standing ready at the helm of one of the smaller cabin boats as they drove in. He waved them over.

Miles leaned across the seat and hugged his mother once again.

"Be safe, Benjamin, and take care," she said. "You're doing a good thing, son."

THE ELVIS BIRD

Susan reached into the front seat, placed her arms around Miles' neck, and hugged him tightly. Miles turned and kissed her before getting out of the car.

"I'll see both of you soon," he said.

He shut the car door and ran towards the dock. He paused at the dock's edge and glanced back at the car, and then jumped onto the boat deck before crawling into the cabin. The Admiral started the engine, and a gray cloud of smoke floated up from behind the stern. It drifted away on the breeze. The water behind the boat began to churn as the craft slowly backed up in the slough. When the boat had cleared the slip, it changed direction and edged forward down the winding stream before heading out.

Miles found Luther lying comfortably on a blanket in the bow. His arm was extended, still attached to the chair.

"You made it," said Luther, who held up a bolt cutter with his free hand. "Your friend had the tool, but he wouldn't help me."

Miles took the bolt cutter and proceeded to lop off the cuff.

"You done good, Doc," said Luther when Miles had finished.

"I committed a crime."

"It'll be worth it – for both of us. You'll see."

"So, you really did capture an Ivory-bill, and you have it trapped somewhere in this swamp? You didn't just con me."

"Guess you'll have to wait and see, won't you, Doc?"

Miles wanted to punch him. There was plenty of time for that. Instead, he leaned back against the hull. Could Luther be trusted? Doris and Susan seemed to think so. For the moment, he would have to trust Luther as well. It was too late to change the plans now.

The Admiral set the boat on a steady pace, and the engine adopted a soothing, monotonous rhythm that made Miles sleepy. As they drove along, he breathed in the earthy aromas of the swamp – familiar, comforting, childhood smells – the smells of an ancient cycle of life and death. For a few moments, he pondered the otherworldliness of the swamp, of its watery plains, and the animals and plants that were dependent on them.

He closed his eyes and thought of Susan, and felt the mysterious pull she had on him, and the hopefulness of new love. The boat continued to push deeper into the swamp, rocking him gently between consciousness and sleep, until he finally surrendered and was transported to a place only accessible in dreams.

32. Hoo-doo Bird

It seldom comes near the ground, but prefers at all times the tops of the tallest trees.
　　　　　　　　　-James Audubon, Birds of America

It was mid-afternoon when the Admiral's boat arrived at the landing on Billy's Island. The Admiral tied off on a wooden pile that swayed gently in the mud as the boat rocked against it. The boat was pushed by the gentle current of water that flows constantly through the Okefenokee.

Miles and Luther appeared on deck, shielding their eyes from the sun as they emerged from the boat's cramped bow.

"Hurry," said the Admiral.

The three men followed a path along the shoreline, with the Admiral in the lead. After walking a few hundred yards, the terrain changed as they passed dramatic stands of bay and cypress trees submerged in the brackish water. The path turned inland and then narrowed, before running out altogether amid a forest of pine trees and oaks. The dense canopy shaded the men from the afternoon sun and provided respite from the heat as they hurried along.

The campsite was less than a mile from the dock; the tent and the stack of supplies they had delivered the previous day were still sitting undisturbed when they arrived at the campsite. Miles spread a tarpaulin on the ground in front of the tent.

"Tell me what happened at the police station," said the Admiral. He was speaking to Miles, but Luther interrupted. "You boys didn't think to bring coffee, did you? I haven't had a decent cup since they arrested me."

"Let me get it," said the Admiral. He crawled inside the tent and began rummaging through the supplies. A hand appeared at the tent flap holding a coffee pot. Luther took it. Other items emerged: water jug, filter, cups, spoons. Finally, the Admiral appeared at the flap and tossed Luther a box of matches. "You'll have to make the fire yourself."

Luther clambered to his feet. "I'll find some wood – you boys can talk things over." He got his bearings and wandered off.

"Can you trust that guy?" said the Admiral when Luther was out of earshot.

"I don't know."

"Watch your back."

"I will."

"So, what happened at the police station?" said the Admiral, "How did you get him out?"

Miles related how Booker handcuffed Luther to a chair in the captain's office, and how Luther had used the flagpole to pry the chair off the floor.

"How did you get past the cops?" asked the Admiral.

THE ELVIS BIRD

"Booker was the only person at the station," said Miles. "Susan distracted him. After Luther cold-cocked me, he just walked out the front door."

"Pretty good punch, wouldn't you say, Professor?"

Luther was standing at the edge of the campsite with an armload of limbs and sticks. He dropped the load beside the tarp and started to make the fire.

"I don't know how you got away with it," said the Admiral.

"The best part is that I'm not in trouble with the law," said Miles.

"You're not in trouble until the cops figure it out," said Luther. He began to chuckle.

Miles hadn't considered that the cops might figure the scheme out later. Instead, he had focused on getting away with the escape. He had operated on the unexamined conclusion that finding the bird would make everything better.

Miles put his hand on Luther's shoulder. "I'm afraid we only made things worse for you."

The old man looked up from his work. "What's worse than murder? I just wanted a chance to clear my name. You gave me that."

"We'll all be in trouble soon enough," observed the Admiral. "Especially if the cops find us."

"You got time for coffee," stated Luther as a fact. "It won't take a minute."

Luther spooned some coffee into the pot of water and placed the pot directly on the blazing fire. The men all sat down and waited. When the pot started to boil, Luther pulled it out of the fire with a stick and poured three cups, carefully filtering each one through a strainer.

"That's awful," said the Admiral, after taking a sip. He tossed the rest on the ground. Miles found it barely drinkable, but Luther finished his and poured himself a second cup.

What would his dad would think of him now? Helping an accused murderer escape from jail? He hoped Susan's instincts about Luther were correct. He had already made his own decision – finding an Ivory-bill would be worth whatever trouble might result.

"There's one thing I don't understand, Luther," said the Admiral. "Why did you trap that bird in the first place?"

Luther shifted positions on the tarp. "I thought that Hoo-doo bird needed some help."

"So, you're a philanthropist. That's what you want us to believe?"

"People have lots of reasons for the things they do in this life. Pure motives rarely drive anyone. I'll admit I needed an ace up my sleeve – something I could hold over that bunch of scientists – something to make them leave town."

"That sounds more like it," said the Admiral. "The truth comes out."

Miles had grown impatient. "Where are you keeping the bird, Luther?"

THE ELVIS BIRD

"Like I told you at the jail, it's penned up out here in this swamp."

Miles stepped over to the old man.

"I've kept my end of the bargain. You're free. Tell us where you're keeping the bird."

Luther took a sip of coffee and seemed to relish the moment. "It's south of here," he said, nodding his head to indicate the direction, "On a small island."

"How far away is it?" asked Miles.

"Four miles, maybe less."

"I can take us there now, Miles," said the Admiral, "Just say the word."

Miles was tempted. He imagined being minutes away from a bird that had occupied his thoughts and dreams over so many years. But now he was harboring a fugitive – an accused murderer. And he was responsible.

"The police are after us, Admiral. I don't want you involved. Luther and I can take the johnboat out in the morning, before they come back to search again," said Miles, "Just go home. Tell Doris and Susan that we're safe and that everything is going to plan."

"I'll do it, buddy," said the Admiral. "But I don't like leaving you here with him." He stared openly at Luther.

"There *is* one last thing you can do," said Miles.

The Admiral got up and dusted off his pants. "Just name it."

"Have Susan contact Jim Hopkins at the Cornell campsite. Tell him we're on Billy's Island. Get him to bring his cameras and video equipment. Have him join us here in the morning. He needs to be here before sunrise. I'll be waiting for him on the dock."

"I'll do it, Miles."

The two men embraced and thumped each other heartily on the back with their fists. The Admiral pushed Miles away and walked out of camp without looking back. Minutes later, Miles heard the crank of an engine. It continued to purr as the Admiral's boat meandered away from the island and then faded away altogether.

Luther decided to keep the fire going and began to scout the area for more branches. Soon he had collected enough to last through the evening. The sun dipped behind the tree line, and darkness descended over the campsite. Luther crawled into the tent and reemerged with two bags of noodles and a jug of water. He set about preparing dinner, and when it was ready, they sat down on the tarp to eat.

"You surprised me, Doc." Luther had a bowl of noodles in one hand. He fished out a spoonful and blew on it.

"How's that?" said Miles, studying Luther's face.

"I didn't think you had the guts to spring me out of jail. You being a professor and all."

"No?" said Miles.

"Maybe you are your father's son, after all. You look just like him. Something about your eyes. In any case, I owe you one."

Miles reached over and pulled a branch from the stack of firewood and tossed it on the fire. "Just so we are clear:

THE ELVIS BIRD

If I didn't think you had trapped that bird, I would have left you in jail to rot."

Luther began to chuckle. "Ha! You are your father's son. I'll take you to the bird, Doc. You can count on that. Just for the record, I didn't murder Lionel. I'm sorry that boy died. No one deserves to die like that. I didn't want him around my granddaughter; that's true. I would have run him off if I could, but I didn't murder that boy."

"The police found a medallion in your truck that ties the two of you together."

"Someone is trying to frame me." He gestured with the spoon to make his point.

"Who would do that?" asked Miles.

"I wasn't the only person in Folkston who wanted that boy to leave town. He chased every skirt he saw. I don't know who killed him, but I intend to find out, or die trying."

The old man sounded sincere.

"I'm want to believe you, Luther."

"Your daddy would be proud of what you've done for me, Miles. Believe that."

Luther had always been a mysterious figure when Miles was growing up. He was someone who lived on the periphery of ordinary life in Folkston. Good folks speculated about him as they sat on their porches in the evening. Even now, Miles wasn't sure exactly how the old man made his living.

"How did you know my father?" Miles asked. He lay back and waited.

"Your father knew everybody in town, and everybody knew him. We crossed paths from time to time. My family's been living in this swamp for a long time. Part of the Stone family. Ever heard of Lydia Stone?"

Miles shook his head.

"People around here called her *Queen of the Okefenokee* — a self-made woman. She used to say that her daddy gave her a sow and a cow, and she turned them into a million dollars. She was a logger."

Miles had heard a few stories about the Queen. Old-timers often mentioned her name whenever they traded recollections about how things used to be before the swamp became a federal refuge.

"Didn't she marry a much younger man?" asked Miles.

The old man's face lit up. "That's right. Her first husband died when the Queen was sixty-three. She didn't have any kids, and she was worried she wouldn't have an heir to inherit all that wealth. So, she married one of her hired hands. A guy named Melton Crews. He was twenty-one years old at the time. She said she liked the way he plowed a field."

"I'll bet she did," said Miles.

"Melton was my granddaddy," said Luther proudly.

"So, the story wasn't an exaggeration."

"It's all true, and there's more to it. Melton got in trouble up in Atlanta for killing a man, and they put him in the state penitentiary. So, the Queen decided to go get Doll Baby out of jail. That's what she called him — Doll Baby. She got on a

THE ELVIS BIRD

train, rode up to the Capitol, and bribed the governor of Georgia with a ten-thousand-dollar check. She insisted on one condition: Doll Baby had to come home with her that same day."

"That took some nerve," said Miles.

"The governor took her check, and had the warden at the penitentiary release him. When she and Doll Baby got back to Folkston, she went straight to the bank and canceled the check."

Luther laughed out loud at his own story before continuing. "Ever since then, we've been a family of gamblers. Hell, people used to gamble right here on this island. Besides schools and churches and houses, they were sensible enough to put up a honky-tonk. It was *my* family did that. We ran it until everyone packed up and left."

The old man looked happy for the first time since breaking out of jail. "People need more than just a roof over their heads to get through this life. You gotta have some fun while you're still above ground and kicking."

Miles nodded.

"If a few people get skinned out of a little money in the process, well, that's ok. I think your dad felt the same way."

"Just what was your relationship with my dad?"

"He knew the world wasn't just black and white, like that bird you're chasing. He understood there are some grey areas where things aren't so clear cut."

"That doesn't explain how you knew him."

Luther looked Miles in the eye.

"He came to me for information. Who stole this? Why had that disappeared? Where might a missing car be found? That sort of thing. In exchange, he turned his head and overlooked a few things that involved my family."

Miles was about to say "Quid pro quo," but instead, he raised a finger to his lips. "Shhh!"

The fire continued to crackle as they waited.

"Did you hear that?"

"I didn't hear nothing."

Miles stood up and walked to the edge of the campsite.

"It's a boat," said Miles. "And it's getting closer."

"The police?"

"We need to find out," said Miles. "Let's go back to the dock."

"Did you bring a gun?" asked Luther.

"No."

Luther slowly shook his head.

Without the moon overhead, it was pitch dark outside the campsite. Miles searched the tent and found a flashlight among the supplies. Luther set about extinguishing the fire. The two men began to retrace their steps back to the dock. The flashlight's small circle of light illuminated their path back through the undergrowth. The sound of the boat grew louder with each step they took as they hurried back along the water's edge.

33. Change of Plans

Bill of an ivory-white, whence the common name of the bird. Iris bright yellow. Feet greyish-blue. The general colour of the plumage is black, with violet reflections, more glossy above.
                                        -James Audubon, Birds of America

The two men hid in a stand of pine trees and watched as the bowrider pulled up to the dock and the engine shut down. The boat's red and white running lights were left on. Miles could see movement at the wheel. A man jumped onto the dock and proceeded to tie off the boat.

"It's not the police," whispered Miles.

When the boat was secure, the man on the dock shouted out, "Miles!" The distinctive, deep voice of his colleague was easy to recognize.

"Over here, Hoppy." Miles stepped out of the trees and walked toward the dock. Luther followed along but stayed well behind in the darkness.

"You're supposed to show up *tomorrow*," said Miles. As he approached Hopkins, he aimed the flashlight at his colleague's chest. Hopkins extended his hand in greeting.

"I couldn't wait. The police came by the camp looking for you just hours ago. They're onto you. They know you're out here in the reserve. Your buddy told them everything.

"The Admiral? How do you know that?"

"Because he told me. They stopped by his place and questioned him. It's damned hard to lie to the police when they ask you a direct question. Your buddy couldn't do it. He called and asked me to warn you."

"Warn us about what?" asked Luther. He stepped out of the darkness and into the light.

Hopkins eyed him, suspiciously. "The police want to put your ass back in jail. We don't have much time before they'll be here," said Hopkins. "I left camp as soon as the Admiral told me where you were. I have the video equipment and the lights. We can photograph the bird before the police arrive. But we need to leave now."

Miles and Luther stepped onto the dock.

"Where are you keeping the bird, old man?" asked Hopkins.

Miles looked over the gunwale. Hopkins had stowed the photographic equipment neatly in the stern.

"Take us to the bird, Luther!" said Miles. He pointed the flashlight at Luther's head.

The old man shielded his eyes with one hand. "I'll take you," he said, turning his head away from the light, "Let's go."

Hopkins untied the boat from the piling and tossed the rope onto the deck. The three men got on board.

THE ELVIS BIRD

"Where are we heading?" asked Hopkins.

"South," said Luther, "toward Honey Island."

Hopkins used a pole to turn the boat around in the channel before taking the helm and starting the engine. He eased the boat along at first, but when the channel widened, he pushed the throttle forward with authority. The bow rose out of the water momentarily before the boat settled back and righted itself.

It was a short trip. Soon, they found themselves in a forest of cypress trees with trunks that rose up like pilings out of the black water. The trees were broad at the bottom and narrowed as they rose skyward. Their blackened canopies towered over the swamp below and Spanish moss hung down like curtains. As they eased forward, the boat's headlamps produced an eerie atmosphere that felt otherworldly in the moonless evening.

"Where do we put in, Luther?" asked Hopkins as they drew nearer to the island.

"Further down a-ways, there's a small opening off this main channel. It's hard to spot. You'll need to slow down."

Luther crawled up on top of the bow to watch for the opening. When they had traveled a few hundred yards, he raised his hand. Hopkins pulled back on the throttle, and the engine began to purr gently as the boat slowed to a crawl.

"There!" called Luther.

The slough's entrance was covered with overhanging limbs that reached out from both sides of the passage, making it difficult to spot. As the boat drew near the opening, Luther raised the branches for the boat to pass under. The boat creeped into the narrow rivulet.

"Not much farther now," said Luther.

Miles crawled up onto the bow beside Luther and aimed the flashlight into the darkness, trying to get a feel for the terrain. The thick overgrowth made it impossible to see more than a few feet ahead. The channel narrowed and became barely wider than the boat as the limbs began to impinge on the boat's progress.

"Whoa!" hollered Luther. He waved his arm over his head.

Hopkins shut off the engine.

"This is it," said Luther. The two men crawled down from the bow.

Someone had fashioned a landing area, and there was a primitive dock made of tree limbs that had been lashed together and driven into the mud. Beyond the landing was an opening. Miles could see a dark green net suspended in the air. The net formed a large four-sided box around the base of a giant oak tree.

The men stepped carefully onto the make-shift dock and approached the improvised cage as a group. Miles aimed the flashlight at the tree and strained to see what was inside the netting. He spotted some movement on the ground.

An Ivory-billed Woodpecker was sitting at the base of the tree. It began flapping its wings nervously in the light and shifted positions as the men approached the net.

"It's the Lord God bird," said Hopkins.

THE ELVIS BIRD

"It's Elvis, all right," said Miles.

The three men stared at it for several minutes. No one said a word.

Miles finally broke the silence. "I didn't believe you, Luther. I thought you had trapped a Pileated woodpecker, but the wings don't lie." There, plain as day, was the tell-tale white underwing and the black horizontal stripe. It was just like the image Miles had memorized from the old Tanner photographs. Seventy years had passed since those photographs had been taken. Seventy long years.

"I told you it was that Hoo-doo bird."

"The bird survived," said Miles, trying to believe it.

He got down on both knees to get a better look. There was the regal, red cap, and the long, ivory-colored bill. There was the lightning-shaped white stripe down the neck, and the eyes! The eyes were bright and piercing and angry, giving the bird a kind of crazed look. By some miracle, this bird had survived. Perhaps it was the last in a long slender thread of survivors. Miles hoped not.

"It's at least eighteen inches tall," said Hopkins.

"Get the cameras, Hoppy. We need a record of this."

Hopkins ran back to the boat.

Luther, who was standing directly behind Miles, spoke up, "It wasn't easy catching this bird, Doc. I nearly broke my neck climbing a tree on Billy's Island."

"Was there a second bird, Luther? This is important. Did it have a mate?" asked Miles.

Luther shook his head. "I only saw the one bird."

Hopkins returned with a large equipment bag and began to unzip it. He pulled out a camera with a row of lights mounted on top and began recording. The bird became agitated by the lights and began hopping from the ground to the tree and back. Hopkins tried photographing the bird from various angles. He moved around the cage alternately kneeling or standing to change angles.

At one point, Luther stepped into the frame.

"Get your ass out of the shot," said Hopkins, "You can't be here. I'm not giving the police the evidence they need to hang me."

The old man stepped away as Hopkins continued to photograph.

"That's enough video," said Hopkins, finally. He handed the camera to Miles and grabbed a digital camera from the bag to take some still shots. He rattled off several hundred images in just a few minutes.

When he had finished, Hopkins set the camera on the ground beside the cage. "That should be enough evidence for any skeptic," he declared. He fumbled to retrieve something from his shirt pocket, and finding it, held up a tiny transmitter for Luther to see. "Let's glue this to his back."

"I'm not getting in that cage with that bird," said Luther.

"I'll do it," said Miles.

Hopkins went back to the boat and returned with a net on the end of a pole.

"Open the cage," he said.

THE ELVIS BIRD

Within minutes, Miles had recaptured the Ivory-bill. The two men glued the GPS to its back while the Ivory-bill mournfully called out, "Pait! Pait! Pait!"

"I want to be the one who releases it," said Luther when the men were done.

"What's that?" asked Hopkins.

"I caught the thing. I should be the one to set it free."

"Have at it then," said Hopkins. He was kneeling on the ground, holding the bird with both hands.

"Let me see it first," said Miles.

Hopkins stood up and handed it over.

Miles held the bird out at arm's length and looked it in the eye. "I've dreamed about you, buddy." The Ivory-bill stared at him coldly. "Let's hope you have a mate."

The old man moved in closer, and Miles handed the bird over. Luther kneeled and then carefully released his grip. The bird advanced slowly on the ground, now aware that it was free. It leaped forward suddenly with several powerful strokes of its wings and disappeared in the night.

"Damn!" said Miles.

The three men began to laugh at the abrupt departure.

"Let's check the monitor," said Hopkins. They hurried back to the boat and huddled around a computer mounted near the wheel. The screen showed a topographic image of the Okefenokee. A tiny red square in the center of the screen denoted their position, and beside it, a white pixel inched northward.

"There," said Hopkins, pointing at the white dot.

"Where is it going?" asked Luther.

"North, back to the nest," said Hopkins. "We may as well follow it."

Hopkins cranked the engine and began to back the boat out of the rivulet. Miles and Luther remained in the stern to help navigate. After several minutes of maneuvering backward through the limbs, they broke free and backed into the main channel. But instead of heading north, Hopkins turned left. Miles immediately recognized the mistake.

"Wrong way, Hoppy!"

"Change of plans, Miles." The voice behind him sounded familiar.

Miles turned to see Fitzsimmons standing beside Hopkins at the wheel. He must have hidden away in the bow, thought Miles. The light of the boat's instrument panel reflected off the barrel of the shotgun that Fitzsimmons held draped across his arm.

"Who's that guy?" asked Luther, looking back.

Miles couldn't answer. The sight of the gun had made him nauseous. The lab director held the gun so casually. At the wheel, Hopkins shifted gears and the sound of the engine modulated slightly. The boat assumed a gentle pace. They were taking their time. Miles stared at the two men, unable to move, transfixed by the shotgun. The fact that Fitzsimmons wasn't pointing the gun at him directly made Miles feel even worse. Would his own death be recorded by a nearby ARU?

34. Common Denominator

They sometimes cling to the bark with their claws so firmly, as to remain cramped to the spot for several hours after death.
- James Audubon, Birds of America

The boat followed a southerly course and then turned west before approaching the western end of Honey Island. After traversing the tip, they headed east into the great expanse of the Okefenokee prairie. The moon had risen in the last hour, just above the trees, and glistened brightly on the shallow water, its reflection broken by the dense growth of golden-club and water lilies.

Miles thought briefly of escape. But where? And how? Outside the boat, he would be an easy target. Would he be able to move around at all? He stole a look at Luther, who was staring straight ahead. The old man had intuited what was happening and seemed stoically resigned to meeting death this evening. If the two of them worked together, they might overpower Fitzsimmons. But there was the gun. They would have to wait for the right opportunity.

Up ahead, the waterway narrowed considerably, and the boat reduced speed. The open plains gave way to mounds and forested areas. Over the next half-hour, they wound monotonously through watery trails, occasionally meeting a dead-end and having to back up. Miles lost all sense of direction. Soon, they were passing older batteries covered in sedge and shrubs. Some of the larger batteries supported small cypress trees. Without warning, Hopkins pulled back on the throttle, and the engine went silent. The boat continued moving forward until it came to a jarring halt in the muck.

Miles had no idea where they were.

Fitzsimmons roused himself and swung the shotgun toward the men sitting together on the deck in the stern.

He called out to Hopkins. "Why don't you help our friends get out of the boat?" He indicated the direction they should take with a flick of the gun barrel.

Luther moved unsteadily to the side of the skiff and Miles followed just behind him. His arms and legs felt so heavy. He was moving in slow motion. Hopkins gave them each a hand getting out of the boat, Luther first, and then Miles.

With the men standing on the battery, Fitzsimmons took up a position beside Hopkins. He rested the shotgun on the rail, aimed directly at the pair of men. "Now, step away from the boat, gentlemen." He waited for them to comply.

Miles took several steps backward. With each step, the ground trembled under his feet.

"That's far enough," said Fitzsimmons.

"You don't need to do this, Fitz," Miles pleaded.

"I think I do." Fitzsimmons raised the gun off the rail.

THE ELVIS BIRD

"Why, Fitz?"

"Don't you know?" Fitzsimmons looked disappointed. "It's your girlfriend Swail's fault. She's too smart for her own good. Or perhaps I should say too smart for *your* own good. You shouldn't have given her your flash drive –the one you made with Hopkins. That was unfortunate."

Miles was confused. How did his flash drive figure into this?

"Susan keeps me posted on her work. Didn't she tell you? No? It won't be long before she makes the connection between the recording of Lionel's death and the recordings on your flash drive."

"What are you talking about, Fitz?"

"It's the boat – it's Hopkins' skiff."

Miles suddenly understood.

"She's been wondering why were there were so many false-positive identifications when she compared the recording of Lionel's death with the recordings that you and Hopkins made in the swamp. She even called me to discuss it. That's when *I* figured it out. Hoppy's skiff is the common denominator. The engine on his skiff has a very distinctive sonogram. That boat is the only thing that was present at all of those events."

Miles took a step backward.

"Eventually, she'll put two and two together – mathematicians often do that. I can't take the chance that she'll figure it out."

Miles stepped backward again and felt his foot sink deeper into the mud. Hopkins was leaning forward on the gunwale, frozen.

"Were you part of this, Hoppy?" asked Miles.

Hopkins didn't say a word. Fitzsimmons answered for him. "Your buddy here didn't have the guts to kill Lionel. I did that. He just went along for the ride. Didn't you?" Fitzsimmons gave Hopkins a look of disdain.

"Fitz said we were just going to throw the fear of God into him, Miles. I swear I didn't know he was going to kill that boy."

"Why *did* you kill him, Fitz?" asked Miles.

Miles took another small step backward. Fitzsimmons watched closely and lowered the gun, letting it rest on the gunwale.

"I suppose you deserve to know that much, doesn't he, Professor Hopkins."

Hopkins lowered his head.

"Lionel came down here on a lark, Miles. He was never a serious student. And he should never have found that Ivory-bill. Not *him*. Not someone who was about to be kicked out of school."

Fitzsimmons absentmindedly rubbed the gun barrel with his free hand. Miles couldn't take his eyes off the gun.

"The little bastard tried to extort me. Can you imagine that? He called and threatened to publish his photograph of the Ivory-bill if the university didn't cough up some money *and* a degree. I wasn't about to let him steal the credit for our discovery."

Fitzsimmons adjusted his aim.

"I convinced your buddy Hopkins, here, to try to save what was left of his pathetic career by helping me get rid of this problem. I didn't count on Lionel sending the photograph to a reporter. But it's okay now. I have it under control."

Miles watched as Luther kneeled on the shaky battery to steady himself.

The director continued. "When you and Swail came to my office to talk about the recording and a possible murder, well, I had to try to get rid of the evidence. I decided the police wouldn't know what to make of that recording, but Swail might. It became clear to me that she would eventually figure it out."

"So, you started the fire at the lab."

"Yes. I found Swail working in the lab that night. I slipped in and hit her on the back of the head. Not to kill her. I just needed her out of the way. She fell out of the chair and onto the floor. Funny thing. She was wearing a gold necklace with a medallion. That's when I had the inspiration to take it and use it."

Miles tried to gauge his position on the battery. If he tried to run, Fitzsimmons would have a clear shot. "So, you planted the medallion on Luther."

"No. Your buddy Hopkins did that." said Fitzsimmons, "He had enough guts for that job, didn't you?"

Hopkins remained silent, and Fitzsimmons continued to talk. "I wanted to muddy the water a bit with the medallion – give the police something to think about."

Luther raised up and stepped toward the boat. "So, it was *you* who framed me!"

Fitzsimmons swung the gun in his direction, and Luther froze. "The police needed someone to blame for Lionel's murder. Why shouldn't it be you, Mr. Preston?"

"What about Susan?" asked Miles, "She still has the recordings." There was a note of desperation in his voice.

"It'll be hard to get rid of those, I'll admit. But I'm planning to fire Professor Swail for cause. The police recently informed me they have evidence of her inappropriate relationship with Lionel. There's the medallion, some email, letters between them. An affair. The university doesn't tolerate that sort of thing. Faculty really shouldn't screw around with their students, should they?"

"Susan will keep pursuing this. The truth will eventually come out," said Miles.

"You may be right, Miles. For all I know, Dr. Swail may have already connected Hopkins' boat to Lionel's murder. But there's nothing that connects me with the murder except Professor Hopkins here, and he's staying with you in the Okefenokee."

Hopkins spun around to face Fitzsimmons. "What do you mean, Fitz?"

THE ELVIS BIRD

The director swung, pressed the shotgun against Hopkin's chest, and fired. The blast drove him over the gunwale. Miles stumbled and fell backward.

Luther shouted, "I'll kill you!" The old man lumbered forward, and tried to crawl into the boat, but Fitzsimmons was ready. He aimed the gun and fired again. The shot struck Luther directly in the chest, and the old man fell backward into the mud.

Miles got to his feet and scrambled away from the boat. With each step, he sank deeper into the muck. Behind him, he heard the snap of the gun barrel, and he imagined Fitzsimmons chambering two shells. The gun barrel snapped again, and he braced for the inevitable. The blast and pain were simultaneous. The earth gave way under Miles' feet, and he fell forward.

The world was suddenly a mixture of fire, water, mud, and pain. There was a second blast, but it seemed to come from much further away. He was going to die in this place – submerged under the mire of a battery, choking and struggling, and unable to breathe.

35. Elvis Sighting

Excepting when digging a hole for the reception of their eggs, these birds seldom, if ever, attack living trees, for any other purpose than that of procuring food, in doing which they destroy the insects that would otherwise prove injurious to the trees.
        -James Audubon, Birds of America

Miles was floating. On air? On water? He wasn't sure, but when he turned his head, he felt the earth against his cheek – cool and soft and wet. He opened his hand and pressed down into the mud which oozed between his fingers. Still, there was the unmistakable sensation of untethered weightlessness. Floating. Too tired to open his eyes, he drifted away into semi-consciousness.

It was the knocking that brought him back to reality. The persistent knocking. He strained to see the disturbance and spotted it overhead. It was clinging to the trunk of a dead pine tree. The Ivory-bill's head was crowned by a brilliant, red top-hat, which ended in a point. It was perched upside down on the tree. The bird was searching for insects, and working its way down the trunk, getting closer to the ground.

It stopped hammering long enough to examine Miles. The bright yellow eyes stared at him with an intense, serious

THE ELVIS BIRD

gaze – taking him in – making a judgment before getting back to its work. The bill was vivid white and much different from the lifeless, skinned specimens arranged in neat rows in the cabinets back at Cornell. A second bird suddenly appeared in the tree, just above the first. Miles raised his hand in the air in an attempt to touch it.

Alerted by some distant noise, the birds darted away, flying off suddenly in a straight line. Miles tried to stand up, but he couldn't raise himself, and he lay back in the damp earth. His blood-stained shirt was a testament to the events of the previous night - the flash of the gun, the wound to his shoulder, his falling through the battery, and the struggle to swim out from under it.

The sound grew louder, and he soon recognized the familiar puttering of an approaching boat. Had Fitz come back to finish the job? The engine stopped abruptly, and Miles waited breathlessly.

"We're right on top of the transmitter," said the Admiral.
Miles raised his hand to catch his attention.
"He's got to be here somewhere," said the Admiral.
"There!" said Susan.

The Admiral pushed the skiff over to the battery with a pole, and Susan leaped over the side. She stumbled and then crawled over to Miles in the mud, first inspecting his wounds and then taking him in her arms.

"I saw Elvis," said Miles. He raised his arm and pointed at the cypress tree.

A BENJAMIN MILES MYSTERY

"You're safe now, Miles," said Susan. She took his hand and held it tightly against her face. "He's wounded," she called.

"I saw Elvis," repeated Miles.

"Quiet, you."

###

On the morning that Miles was released from the hospital, Susan appeared in his doorway and found him propped up in bed watching CNN. She closed the door to his room and locked it before walking over to his bedside.

"How's that wing of yours, Birdman?" she asked.

"It flaps. Let me show you," he said, holding out both arms.

The two embraced across the bedrail as the overhead TV played images of the Okefenokee. Susan leaned over and kissed him on the lips, and then as an afterthought, on his forehead.

Miles watched as she pulled a chair up beside the bed and sat down. He liked the way she crossed her legs. She found the remote and turned up the volume, and they watched a news segment on the recent events in the swamp. There were video images of the Cornell campsite and a skiff leaving the camp's dock. The scrolling banner read *Death in the Okefenokee*.

"What's the latest news?" she asked.

THE ELVIS BIRD

"They still haven't found Fitzsimmons," said Miles. "They located his boat near Blackjack Island this morning. He ran out of gas. Can you imagine? He must have panicked and gotten lost. The police are conducting aerial searches."

"Did they find Hoppy's video equipment?"

"They weren't in the boat. Fitz must have taken them."

"So, you don't have proof that the bird survived?"

Miles shook his head.

"Sergeant Booker came to the hospital while you were in surgery."

"What did he want?"

"What do you think?"

"Did he question you about Luther's escape?"

Susan looked amused. "He said he thought something was *sorta fishy* and that he needed to ask the *Pro-fessor* a few questions."

They watched TV for a few more minutes until Miles broke the silence. "I keep thinking about what happened. I can't believe Fitz was behind all this. Luther saved my life that night. If he hadn't rushed the boat, I wouldn't be here."

"Just be grateful, Miles."

He reached out for Susan's hand through the bedrail.

"Luther told me an interesting story while we were on Billy's island."

"I'm all ears."

"He said that years ago, a stranger walked into the swamp, but he never came out. Everyone thought the man had died there. No one knew how he met his fate.

Eventually, his body was found on Billy's Island. They gave the man a proper burial. They even erected a headstone and put the stranger's name on it."

"Where is this going?" asked Susan.

"The next spring, the stranger walked out of the swamp with a full-growth beard. They never discovered who they had buried on the island."

"Do you think Fitz is going to walk out of the Okefenokee someday?"

Miles shook his head. "Not a chance. The boat was found in the middle of that swamp. No one could walk out."

Susan lowered the bedrail and crawled in beside Miles.

"It's time for your medication, Birdman."

Miles raised his eyebrows, puzzled.

"It has to be administered orally, so pucker up." She kissed him with a passion that he felt in his belly – a kiss that loosened his brain.

"Ouch," he said, almost whimpering when she leaned against his arm. "Watch the shoulder."

Susan put a hand on his chest and pushed him back hard against the pillow. She leaned forward and then straddled him. "Shut up, and take your medicine like a man."

36. Certemente

I have frequently observed the male and female retire to rest for the night, into the same hole in which they had long before reared their young. This generally happens a short time after sunset.
-James Audubon, Birds of America

Miles was released from Mayo later that afternoon with orders to return in a month for a follow-up examination. Susan drove the Lexus back to Folkston while Miles dozed peacefully in the passenger seat. It was early evening when they returned home and found Doris' yard filled with cars. The lights in the front rooms of the house were all on, and people were standing in groups on the front porch. Miles had a fleeting thought that Doris was in trouble again; he held his breath and took a closer look before finally getting it right. It was a party with drinks, conversation, music, and lots of friends.

Susan parked at the end of the drive near the highway, and they walked up to the porch arm-in-arm. The Admiral was waiting for them at the top of the steps. "What took you so long, buddy? The party started an hour ago."

"I don't remember getting an invitation," said Miles.

"Hold up then." The Admiral raised his hand and turned to Sergeant Booker, who was sitting on the swing with Velvia. The waitress was leaning her head against his shoulder, using it like a pillow.

"What do you say, Sergeant?" asked the Admiral. "Should we let these two interlopers join us?"

"Come ahead," waved Booker, "But I'm keeping an eye on you two. No funny business Pro-fessor or I'll have to arrest you." Velvia giggled and patted Booker's arm.

Doris spotted the two arrivals through the living room window. She stepped onto the porch and gave them each a long embrace.

"Was this your idea?" asked Miles.

"Mildred helped me get the word out last week," said Doris. "Everyone wanted to celebrate the end of the expedition. I decided to throw a party and host it here."

"It's lovely," said Susan.

"I just wish Luther could be here," said Doris, "I'd like to thank him for saving your life, Benjamin." She patted his chest gingerly. Susan took her by the arm, and together they wandered into the house leaving Miles to fend for himself.

He turned around in a circle, slowly taking it all in. Everything seemed oddly different. The house. The people. Himself. Everywhere he looked, local folks mixed with colleagues in groups and pairs that spilled out into the yard.

He closed his eyes and offered a silent prayer of thanks that he had survived. Doris was right. If it weren't for Luther, he'd be dead. Doris and Susan would both be heartbroken. Miss Mildred would have many more bills. And Hoppy would still be alive. Much had changed. Perhaps himself most of all.

Someone inside turned up the volume on the CD player. The strains of a Little Richard tune drifted into the yard, giving the party a fifties feel. Miles peeked in the living room window. The room was filled with dancing couples. He spotted Miss Mildred dancing with Bert Williams as he twirled her gently in a circle. Mildred was shaking her hips shamelessly in time to the music. A small group gathered around, and began to clap, cheering her on while Bert looked on aghast.

Doris emerged from the kitchen holding a tray of hors d'oeuvres. She moved easily between the partiers, serving each guest, and trying to avoid the dancers. Miles stepped inside to give her a hand.

"Where did you get the music?" He yelled over the din.

"George brought all his CDs and Mildred supplied the player. Now look at her!" She pointed across the room. "She's dancing with every man she can corral."

"Are you jealous?"

"No!"

"Where's George?" asked Miles, scanning the room for his brother.

"Try the dining room. He insisted on being the DJ. He's been working on the setlist for days. At ten o'clock he's only playing Elvis."

Susan appeared holding a tray of champagne. Miles took a glass and guzzled it down.

"Grazie!" he said when it was empty. He placed the glass back on tray and wiped his mouth with the back of his hand.

Susan looked at him in disbelief.

"Liquid courage," he explained.

"Courage for what?"

"Vuoi ballare, signora?" asked Miles. He motioned grandly to the living room floor.

Susan looked at Doris for help. "What did he say?"

"He's asking you to dance, honey."

Doris took the tray. "I gave the boy a couple of Italian lessons in the hospital, and George showed him a few dance steps this afternoon."

Susan looked at Miles anew and took his hand.

They stepped to the center of the room and waited for the next song. He winced when she touched his shoulder.

"Scusi," she said.

"Certemente, madame."

The tune was a slow ballad and Susan slid her arm around his waist. They eased into the crowd, turning in small circles at first, and then working their way around the room. The song ended much too soon for Miles.

"Ancora?" he asked.

"Certemente."

Another song was about to start when George tapped Miles' shoulder and stole Susan's hand. "My turn Benny, you shouldn't overexert yourself. Besides, you've already used all the moves I taught you."

Miles stepped aside. "Perhaps you're right, Georgie. I'll just wait on the porch."

The music started again –a fast number this time. Miles paused at the front door to see George and Susan take the floor. Susan easily followed George's strong lead. In the middle of the dance George flashed Miles a smile and gave him a quick thumbs-up before spinning away in the crowd.

Miles' stepped outside to rest his aching shoulder. The party-goers had abandoned the porch for the dance. He sat down by himself in the swing. It was cooler now, and he closed his eyes for a moment. His rest was interrupted by the loud applause from inside. Curious, he peeked through the front window. George and Susan had become the center of attention. The crowd had moved against the walls to give them space, and they were doing a swing dance. They seemed perfectly paired. Every time George broke a move, Susan would respond with a move of her own – a kind of physical conversation that made Miles envious. When the chorus ended, his brother motioned the crowd to join in, and everyone began to dance.

Miles spotted Velvia as she pulled Sergeant Booker onto the floor. The big man lumbered clumsily into the crowd of dancers. It became apparent that Booker had no sense of rhythm, but it didn't seem to matter to Velvia, who was all smiles. Even Doris was dancing, and beside her, Miss Mildred had moved on to yet another partner. The song ended, and George joined Miles on the porch. They sat down together in the swing. George was winded and had worked up a sweat. He sat quietly catching his breath.

"Where is Charlene?" asked Miles, after a few minutes.

George began shaking his head, "I couldn't blast her out of the house with TNT."

"Too bad."

George's expression changed, and he placed his hand on Miles' thigh. "I don't want to spoil the evening for you, Benny, but we need to talk about Mom. I need leave soon. I told Charlene I wouldn't be late getting back."

Miles had hoped to avoid this conversation. Doris seemed so independent and at peace here at home. What effect would moving her to a nursing home have on her stubborn spirit?

"We should include Mom in this discussion," suggested Miles. "She may as well hear what we have to say, don't you think?"

George agreed. "I'll get her and meet you in the kitchen."

The party continued loudly as the three of them gathered around the kitchen table. George shut the kitchen door to dampen the noise. Doris started the discussion. "I'm not going," she said flatly.

"We haven't mentioned going anywhere, Mom," said George, obviously irritated.

THE ELVIS BIRD

Doris reached across the table and took his hand. "I know what this is about, Georgie, and I'm not going to an old folk's home."

"It isn't an old folk's home," said George, "It's a residential, graduated-care facility."

"Same thing," said Doris, "I'm not going to live in an old folk's home in Jacksonville."

"At least you can come look at it," said George.

"I've already looked at it. I didn't like it one bit."

"That was just a brochure," said Miles.

"No. I went there for a visit," said Doris.

"When was that?" asked Miles.

"When Susan and I went shopping in Jacksonville. They gave us a tour. That's a place where old folks go to die. I'm planning to live, and I'm not going there – not now."

Miles was puzzled. Why hadn't Susan mentioned their visit to the nursing home?

"Okay, Mom," said Miles, "You're not going. But you do have health problems that we need to consider. George and I worry about you living here by yourself. What will you do if suddenly you need our help? I'm in New York, and George is in Jacksonville."

"I'm way ahead of you," she said.

"What does that mean?" asked George.

"Wait here, both of you; I'll be right back."

Doris returned carrying her MacBook.

"Where did you get that?" asked George.

"Susan helped me buy it in Jacksonville. I've been practicing with it, and I've learned how to google." She looked at George. "Did you know that you can find information on almost anything on the internet?"

"Everyone knows that," said George.

"You just type in a word, and the browser pulls it up automatically. Do you know how to browse, Georgie?"

"I know how to use Google, Mom," said George. "What does all this have to do with your health problems?"

She opened the laptop and turned it on. "I want to show you something." She pushed the laptop across the table. "Try it. It's a browser. You browse with it. Just type *W-W-W-Dot-Doris-Miles-Dot-Org*."

George typed the URL, and a page loaded, then a pop-up dialog box appeared on the screen: "How Is Doris Doing?"

"What is this? It's asking for a password, Mom," said George.

"Type in *Bingo*," said Doris.

"What?"

"B-I-N-G-O. All caps."

George tapped out the letters with his finger. A video image appeared on the screen. The three of them were sitting together at the kitchen table.

"Hey, look, it's us!" said George. He turned around and spotted a camera mounted in the corner of the room.

"It's a webcam. I had it installed last week."

"I know what a webcam is, Mom," said George.

THE ELVIS BIRD

She pointed at a link on the screen. "Now click on that."

Two more images appeared. The first was of the living room filled with dancing couples. The second shot was of Doris' bedroom.

"Who is that?" asked Doris. She leaned forward for a closer look. A couple was standing in the doorway of the bedroom, locked in an embrace.

George squinted at the screen. "Ha! It's Sergeant Booker and Velvia! They better come up for air soon. Booker's gonna need CPR." He started to chuckle.

"Never mind that. I had three webcams installed in the house," said Doris. "You'll be able to see what I'm doing twenty-four seven."

"Twenty-four seven?"

"That means all day, Georgie."

"I know that, Mom."

"I also bought Mildred a computer," said Doris, proudly. "Now, we can monitor each other –morning or night. You won't have to worry about me. I'm on the web!"

"I don't believe this," said George.

"There's one more thing," said Doris. She pointed at an icon off to the side. "Click on that, Georgie."

He punched the mouse, and another image appeared. George leaned forward to get a better look. "Hey, that's my bedroom!" he said. "And there's Charlene – sound asleep. She's snoring! How are we getting this? I don't have a camera installed in my house."

"Charlene's computer has a built-in webcam. I'll be able to check on you anytime, Georgie. Isn't that great?"

George looked horrified.

As the evening wore on, the crowd drifted away in small groups, leaving only a handful of couples still partying. Susan had disappeared again, and Miles began to search the house for her. He stopped in the dining room. George, who was about to leave, had queued up the music for the rest of the evening – mostly slow romantic tunes to wind the evening down. He lowered the volume and waited for the first song to begin. A sequence of guitar triplets rang out, and Elvis started to croon *One Night with You*. It was rough and raw. Miles couldn't help but sing along.

"Bring it on, Pro-fessor," called Booker from the living room. He and Velvia were sitting on the sofa.

"Have you seen Susan?" asked Miles.

Velvia gestured like a hitchhiker catching a ride. "She's on the porch."

Miles looked out the front door. Susan and Doris were sitting together like old friends on the top porch step. They were chatting and leaning together, shoulder-to-shoulder. It was then that Miles realized the song's lyrics were all wrong. Elvis was mistaken. One night with Susan would never be enough.

Epilogue

So strongly indeed have these thoughts become ingrated in my mind, as I gradually obtained a more intimate acquaintance with the Ivory-billed Woodpecker, that whenever I have observed one of these birds flying from one tree to another, I have mentally exclaimed, "There goes a Vandyke!"

-James Audubon, Birds of America

One evening after the Cornell crew had packed up the camp and returned to Ithaca, Miles said goodnight to Doris and walked back to his bedroom for the evening. He sat down at his desk, and while he waited for his laptop to boot, he gazed out on the moonlit backyard where he had played as a child.

When the machine finished, he clicked on an icon of an Ivory-billed Woodpecker. A map of the Okefenokee appeared. He double-clicked the image and zoomed in until two tiny white dots appeared in the middle of the screen. He stared at them for a moment, before reaching out and touching each pixel with his fingertip, satisfied with himself.

Years before, as an adolescent, he had sat at the same desk reading Peterson's Field Guide, flipping slowly through the dog-eared pages of that book, and looking over the hand-painted images of birds that he dreamed of one day seeing in person.

Citations

Susan quotes Yates in Chapter 23 .
Yates, Willam Butler, "A Drinking Song.",The Green Helmet and Other Poems, MacMillan, 1910, p. 22.

The Admiral quotes Shelley in Chapter 29.
Shelley, Percy Bysshe, "Ozymandias.", Miscellaneous and Posthumous Poems of Percy Bysshe Shelley, W. Benbow, 1826, p. 100.

A day in the Okefenokee

Dr. David Woolbright finished math degrees at Davidson College, Emory University, and Auburn University, along with some post-graduate study in computer science at Clemson University. He enjoyed a long career teaching mathematics and computer science at Columbus State University. During his academic career, he also managed to train hundreds of corporate programmers for Fortune 500 companies. Several years ago, he was named an IBM Champion for Z.

As a young man, he studied creative writing at Davidson. Years later, much older and wiser, he studied creative writing at Merton College of Oxford University. These days, he enjoys the camaraderie of the group of writers at Elizabeth Starks' Book Writing World. He lives in Columbus, Georgia with his wife, Cathy. They have three children and three grandchildren.

Catch his fiction website at dewoolbright.com.

Made in the USA
Columbia, SC
09 August 2023